SHADE

We gratefully acknowledge the support of the Canada Council for the Arts and the Ontario Arts Council for our publishing program. We also acknowledge the financial support of the Government of Canada through the Canada Book Fund.

Cover design: Val Fullard

Shade is a work of fiction. All the characters and situations portrayed in this book are fictitious and any resemblance to persons living or dead is purely coincidental.

Library and Archives Canada Cataloguing in Publication

Herrera, Mia, 1989–, author
          Shade : a novel / by Mia Herrera.

(Inanna poetry and fiction series)
Issued in print and electronic formats.
ISBN 978-1-77133-289-7 (paperback).-- ISBN 978-1-77133-290-3 (epub). -- ISBN 978-1-77133-292-7 (pdf)

          I. Title. II. Series: Inanna poetry and fiction series

PS8615.E765S53 2016   C813'.6   C2016-900302-7
                                               C2016-900303-5

MIX
Paper from
responsible sources
FSC® C004071

Printed and bound in Canada
Inanna Publications and Education Inc.
210 Founders College, York University
4700 Keele Street, Toronto, Ontario M3J 1P3 Canada
Telephone: (416) 736-5356   Fax (416) 736-5765
Email: inanna.publications@inanna.ca Website: www.inanna.ca

SHADE
Mia Herrera

inanna poetry & fiction series

INANNA PUBLICATIONS AND EDUCATION INC.
TORONTO, CANADA

for Mama Nene

1.

WE HAVE DINNER AS PLANNED, even if Dad doesn't end up visiting. It's almost like every Monday dinner we have together, except that there are a couple more takeout containers on the table and Mom has changed out of her regular house-dress and into a crisp pair of slacks and blouse. As usual, Tom sits beside me at our round kitchen table, squeezing my hand in reassurance as the meal wears on and my patience grinds down. I draw comfort from his steadfast, deliberate manner and gentlemanly charm. He ruffles his hair – a well-worn habit – as he says, "It's too bad Mr. Manlapaz couldn't visit after all."

Mom looks up from her iPad. "I know, but the fish farm has been keeping him very busy. Did Benni tell you that he just acquired an island off the coast of Boracay?"

"Yes, she mentioned it." Polite as always, Tom doesn't point out that Mom has told him this at least four times tonight.

"Starting a business is very demanding. I'm sure you know how it can be, what with your dad's business and all," Mom says.

"Yes, as my father would say," Tom says, before dropping his voice an octave lower in imitation of his father's sonorous tone, "in those early days, when your mother and I arrived from China and were rolling pennies...." He laughs. "My father loves his Genesis story."

"Well, it's a good one," Mom says. "Your parents are far from rolling pennies now." She glances at the iPad again.

Tom smiles but doesn't reply. Knowing how awkward he feels when people mention his family's wealth, I pick up the conversation. "You have a Skype date with Dad soon, don't you?" I ask, looking at the iPad too. "We'll get out of your hair so you can chat with Dad. Thanks again for dinner, Mom." I push my spoon and fork to the side of my plate and move to stand, happy to end dinner early enough so Tom and I have some time alone away from Mom.

But Mom is faster, and before Tom or I can say anything, she shovels more *menudo* onto Tom's plate. She had picked up this traditional pork dish because it is Dad's favourite – even if it took her an hour's drive south to Scarborough and well out of her comfort zone that kept her mainly in our small town of Georgina, Ontario.

"Where are you going in such a rush?" she asks. "Dad will call when he calls." Then turning to me, she scolds, "Tom has hardly eaten. Let the man eat, Benni. You two got so skinny while you were away."

Tom, used to this treatment, picks up his fork and spoon and starts eating, giving my hand a squeeze as I feel my temperature rising.

"Mom, you need to stop pushing food onto people's plates. Tom's eaten plenty already," I say.

"But he got so skinny in Cuba," Mom says again, reaching over to squeeze one of Tom's broad shoulders. "You both did. You were away too long. Did they not feed you there?"

I feel a pang at the recollection of our trip away. It seems so long ago, though we just got back Friday night. It was so nice waking up to Tom each morning, relaxing on the beach, enjoying each other's company every day.

Mom takes my pause as confirmation of her suspicions. "I knew it. You starved, didn't you? You're so skinny and brown now. Benni, you almost look like an *Indio*." Mom clucks her tongue at the loss of my paper-white complexion. "Oh well, I'll take good care of you now. It'll be good. It was so quiet in the house without you." Mom's words linger as she shoots me a reproachful look across the table.

"Mom, we were gone for five days."

"Five days is too long," Mom says.

"Actually, two days too short," I say. Tom squeezes my hand again, but I persist. "Remember? Tom and I were supposed to have a seven-day vacation, but we came back early to see Dad."

Tom coughs. "Yes, I was excited to see Mr. Manlapaz, but no matter. I'll get a chance to ask him all my questions later." He smiles, and I flush. It's not the first time Tom's referenced these questions he has for Dad. After dating for three years, I know Tom well enough to know how traditional he is – traditional enough to wait and ask my father for my hand in marriage before proposing. I think again of those five days and nights we spent together in Cuba and hide a smile.

Mom, oblivious to this exchange, says, "Yes, yes. He'll come for a visit soon enough." She glances at the iPad again. "Tom, did Benni tell you that Mr. Manlapaz acquired an island off the coast of Boracay?"

By the time Tom finishes his extra helping of food, he needs to go. He has an early meeting at work tomorrow, and it's an hour drive back to his place in Toronto.

"Thanks for dinner, Mrs. Manlapaz. I'll see you next Monday?" Tom asks.

"Of course," Mom says. "Are you sure you don't want to come for a visit sooner? You're welcome any night of the week. I miss those days when you and Benni were in university. You used to be here more often."

"I'd love to, Mrs. Manlapaz, but it's such a far drive since I moved downtown. And since I've started taking on more responsibility in the family business, I find I hardly have any time these days between that and work at Deloitte." Tom stoops to kiss Mom on the cheek – an old habit for him now, after he learned to adjust to this traditional Filipino gesture for "hello" or "goodbye."

"If you say so," Mom says, "but don't let your parents run you ragged."

I pull Tom down the hall, away from Mom. She could talk forever if given the opportunity. "Thanks for coming tonight," I say at the door. "Sorry we didn't get any time alone together."

"No need to thank me, beautiful, or to apologize," Tom says. "We'll get more than enough time alone together tomorrow afternoon." He pulls me close and nibbles on my ear.

I push against him, glancing over my shoulder. "Not here, Tom, but maybe tomorrow." I smile. "We're still on for lunch then?"

"Absolutely," Tom says. "I'm looking forward to it. We have so much to talk about."

"Like?"

"Maria Benedictine," Tom says, before kissing my forehead. "You always want to know it all, but some things are better off left for later. We'll see each other tomorrow, okay?"

"Okay," I sigh, knowing full well that Tom follows his own agenda. He wouldn't tell me anything he wasn't ready to anyways.

Tom pulls me back for another kiss – long, lingering, and passionate – reminiscent of the days when we first started dating and could not keep our hands off each other. I'm pretty sure I know what he wants to discuss tomorrow judging from his amorous mood as of late and our frequent conversations about the future. He rests his forehead against mine, studying me before breaking into a smile. "I'll see you tomorrow, darling?" he asks one last time.

"Tomorrow," I say.

I leave the front door to find Mom playing on her iPad in front of the family room TV. "Hey," I say. "What happened to your Skype date with Dad tonight?"

"I don't think that's happening anymore," Mom says. "Something probably came up."

"Of course," I say. I reach up and let my hair down from its ponytail. I catch Mom studying me and pause. "What's with the scrutiny? Do you like what you see?" I do a pirouette.

"You look a little frumpy tonight, Benni," Mom says.

I pause mid-turn to look down at my T-shirt and shorts. "Seriously?"

"Yes, really. When your father was courting me, I would always dress nicely when he was around. None of this short shorts business. I'd at least be modest enough to wear pants or a nice skirt."

I stare at Mom's oily hair and the ratty housedress she donned as soon as Tom left and wonder when she stopped taking such meticulous care of herself. Though old pictures of her show a brooding face, hooded eyes, and draping hair, much of that woman is buried in her today. Now, at the age of sixty, her hair is dyed an unnatural black to hide the grey and cut short to avoid accentuating her double chin. Her favourite habits – eating and watching TV – maintain her figure, which can be summarized in one word: round. "Mom, these aren't short shorts. Besides, Tom and I have been dating for years. He's seen me in worse."

"Well, even if you and Tom have been dating for a while now, you shouldn't let go of yourself before you even get married. I approve of Tom. He's good for you. Who knows? Perhaps a ring will come any day now."

I study Mom's face. She's terrible at keeping secrets, and I wonder if she knows what Tom's been meaning to talk to me about. I wonder if Tom would ask for my hand in marriage without Dad here. I take Mom's comment as a promising hint, but shrug, not wanting to let her know that a ring is exactly what I've had in mind. "I'll be sure to put on more lipstick when Tom's around and, next time he visits, I'll wear my newest ball gown to welcome him to this palace of ours."

Mom ignores my comment. "You've done well, Benni. You've found a nice man, and you're ready to settle down. I'm happy you waited to move out like I told you to. You've saved up enough to get a really nice place. Actually, I saw one for sale just down the street recently."

I laugh. "Mom, when I move out, I won't be buying anywhere in Georgina. This place is a hellhole. There's nothing here."

"Your work is here."

"And great work that is," I say but quickly regret it.

Mom picks up the old reliable thread without hesitation. "Working for the town is good, Benni, but your father and I paid so much for you to go to a good university. When are you going to start aiming higher?"

I bite back the remark that Dad paid for my university, not Mom, and say instead, "My job has great benefits and pays enough."

"But you're a secretary."

I flinch at the word. "Administrative assistant," I correct her.

"Whatever it is, you can do so much more."

"Doing what? I have an English degree."

"With distinction. Didn't you always want to get into publishing? What happened to your goals?"

"Mom, I graduated from university, got a job, and even waited to move out…. I'm not sure what you're going on about. All my friends have moved out and moved on. They're living downtown, not at home with…" The iPad in Mom's lap starts beeping and blinking. Dad's profile picture pops up. We both stare at it for a second. "Are you going to answer it?" I finally ask.

Mom pats her tousled black hair before answering the call.

Dad's round face fills the frame. "Maria?" his voice crackles over the air. "Maria, can you hear me?"

"Yes, Ned, I'm here. Can you see me?"

"Yes. Oh, hi, Princess," Dad says, his face breaking into a smile. "What are you two doing up together?"

"Tom just left," I say. "Dad, we have a gorgeous view of you right now."

Dad is holding his tablet in his lap, giving us a close-up view of his double chin. "What?" He squints at the corner of the screen, no doubt studying the thumbnail image of himself.

"You have an intense chin shot going on."

"Are you referring to this old thing?" he asks, squeezing his chin further into his neck and flaring his nose.

"Ay, Ned, stop. That's so ugly," Mom says.

"Ugly?" Dad assumes a look of shock. "Maria, it's impossible for a stud muffin like me to look ugly." Dad pulls the tablet back, giving us a long view of himself as he makes a flexing pose with his flabby arms. "So, how have you two been?" he asks, returning the tablet to his lap.

"Good," I say. "Hey, Dad, why couldn't you come visit again? I didn't really get Mom's explanation."

"Ned, I told Benni about how busy you are at the fish farm," Mom says.

Dad's smile drops. "Yes, things are crazy here, Princess," he says. "I'm sorry I couldn't make it."

I shrug.

"Are you sure you don't want to come visit me here?" he asks, winking.

"No thanks, Dad."

"If you visit, you can finally meet the local spirits."

"As eager as I am to meet all the creepy ghosts you so often talk about, and despite how irresistible that fish farm of yours sounds, I think I'll pass. From what Mom says, it sounds like you can't wear shorts in that tropical heat."

"Plus, I have so much work to do here, right, Ned?" Mom says.

I stifle the urge to laugh – my automatic reaction whenever I hear Mom refer to her work-from-home part-time transcription gig. "Looks like there's a million reasons why we can't go, Dad. Maybe next time," I say. "For now, I'm going to bed. I'll leave you two night owls alone." I stoop to kiss Mom's cheek goodnight. "Goodnight, Dad," I say to the tablet.

"Goodnight, Princess," he says.

"*Muah*," I say, blowing him a kiss.

"*Muah*," I hear as I climb the stairs to bed.

2

MUTED MORNING LIGHT FILTERS THROUGH the shutters of the kitchen window, filling the room with the dull grey colour of dawn. I have half an hour before I need to leave for work.

I reread the text message Tom sent last night after he arrived home. "Good night, darling. I'm looking forward to lunch tomorrow. I think it's time I finally tell you what's been on my mind." I smile and tuck my cellphone away.

"Heading out for work?"

Startled, I turn to find Mom. "What are you doing up so early?" I ask.

"I was playing Bejeweled on my iPad last night after your dad and I finished talking," she says, turning on the TV. "I was on a streak. I turned it off at four o'clock, but then had a hard time sleeping. Too much stimulation, I suppose. I heard you moving around just as I was dozing off. I thought I'd come down and prepare lunch for you."

"Thanks, but I'm all right."

"I think we have some microwavables that you can bring to work," she says as she opens the freezer. "How about a Hungry-Man?" She pulls out the frozen dinner package.

"Mom, it's all right," I say again.

"I bought a box of Jersey Milk from Costco the other day," she says. "Why don't you bring a few to snack on later?"

"Don't worry about it."

Her house slippers *clip-clop* against the tiles as she walks to the computer room anyway, where all the chocolate is stored. I glance at the clock. It's six-forty a.m. "Mom, I'm leaving soon."

Mom re-emerges with three Jersey Milk chocolate bars in hand and places them on top of the Hungry-Man on the counter.

"Mom, I'm meeting Tom for lunch today."

"You're seeing him today?" Mom perks up.

I try not to read into her excitement. I change the subject, not wanting to show my own excitement prematurely. "What are you watching anyways?" I ask, pointing to the TV screen. It's on our local news station. "Is it necessary to have the TV on at six in the morning?"

"I was going to watch *Worldwide Star*. I didn't catch last night's new episode." On its sixth season, the reality talent show has captured the world's attention with its audience participation and Mom is no exception. She watches it religiously and records every episode in the off chance she misses it or – more often – to re-watch episodes again later. Mom continues talking when I don't respond, staring at the screen without seeming to register what she's seeing. "Your *Tita* Rosie updated her Facebook page again last night."

I fight the urge to walk away. It often feels like Mom speaks just for the sake of hearing her own voice. It's sad sometimes; almost as though she just speaks to know she's still there. Lacking material that would come from living a regular life out and about in the real world, she often reverts to repeating news about our relatives in the Philippines – the likes of which she gleans from Facbeook.

"Lisa is starring in another musical, *The Addams Family*, and Celeste is..."

"Is the newest leading lady in the nation's most popular daytime soap," I finish for her. "That's great, Mom. I saw *Tita* Rosie's post, too." This morning I have no interest in hearing about my celebrity relatives in the Philippines. It only makes life at home, and with Mom, feel that much more mundane.

"Oh, did you?" Mom looks disappointed that I got my news from Facebook before I heard it from her.

I feel guilty seeing Mom's downtrodden face and change the subject to something she usually has more to say about. "So, how was your talk with Dad last night?"

"Hmm?" Mom asks, focusing on the TV.

"How's Dad? Anything new?"

"What on earth could be new?" Mom asks.

"I don't know. What's going on with the business?"

"Look, that's just down the street," Mom says, turning the volume up on the TV.

"Georgina Giants let out a mighty yell after the Confederate flag was banned in school hallways this week," a news anchor says as she stands before the high school down the road. The screen cuts to previously-taped footage of a mousy teenage girl.

"To be told that using the Confederate flag is racist is itself a racist statement. What happened to freedom of expression? We live in Canada – not some third-world country where others can dictate what we can and cannot wear." The girl wears a trucker hat with the Confederate flag sewn on it. "We here in Georgina wear the flag to show our small-town pride and now folks are being racist to us white people by banning us from using it."

The newscast cuts back to the reporter. "As you know, this controversy comes hot on the heels of hate crime charges that were laid in Georgina after a man hung a skeleton, painted black, from a tree below a Confederate flag. The culprit's explanation of it being a 'Halloween decoration' didn't quite hold up, considering it happened in April. Back to the desk." The scene cuts to the anchorman, who is shaking his head in dismay.

"God, I hate Georgina," I say. I turn from the television, which is difficult considering the seventy-inch screen spans most of the wall.

"It's terrible how people in this area treat their Blacks," Mom says, shaking her head. Having been born in the Philippines and living as a stay-at-home mother in Canada, Mom doesn't understand middle-of-nowhere suburban culture. I don't bother to point out that Mom consistently misses the point of these attacks and the reason why these events are so relevant to her and I. Where there's racism against Black people, there's racism against all other visible minorities too.

I shrug, grabbing my purse and car keys. "Who knows? One day things may get better."

"That's the spirit."

"I'll see you later, Mom."

"So, you'll be home for dinner?"

"Maybe."

"Call and tell me. You know I don't like being home alone."

3.

"CAN YOU LAY OFF THE PARKING TICKETS for just a little while, Rick?" I ask. Rick, one of Georgina's bylaw officers, has just come in from another two-hour stint on the road to load his latest batch of tickets onto the server. "It's too nice outside to deal with so many grumpy people."

"The day is young and the city-goers are out. It's time to lay down the law. Anyways, why are you complaining? At least you can sit down and read those gossip rags behind your desk all day."

"First of all, I'm not reading gossip rags. I'm reading industry news," I say, waving the latest issue of *Quill & Quire*.

"Industry?" Rick snorts. "Look around you, doll. There's no industry here in Georgina."

"Second of all," I say, raising my voice to speak over him, "I'm the one who has to take the angry calls all day."

"I'm sorry," Rick says. "I can make it up to you." He wiggles his eyebrows.

"Ugh, Rick, spare me," I say, standing and stretching. "I'm going for lunch."

Rick perks up. "Are you going to Subway again? It's steak-and-cheese sub day."

"No, siree. I'm going to Timmies today. I'm meeting Tom."

"You're not done with that guy yet?" Rick asks, following me as I walk towards the back of the office.

"Be nice," I say, pulling out the mishmash of flyers and envelopes from my mail slot and extracting a recently-placed pay stub. I rip the envelope open and take a peek at the form. The number is the same every two weeks: another $1,400 added to my savings account. It's that much more towards a down payment for a house.

I had been planning on moving out since I was thirteen but, alas, the years passed and something always kept me back – the questionable job market, the sky-rocketing house prices, my mother. The dream has been deferred again and again – the one where I leave this backwards town and move into a gorgeous Toronto loft. It now only makes sense to wait a bit longer. Longer, that is, until Tom proposes.

As though reading my mind, Rick speaks up. "What are you waiting for, honey? A ring? Ditch him and take up with me. What's with all this in-race dating anyways?"

"Rick, how many times do I have to tell you that Tom and I aren't the same race?"

"Whatever. You all look the same to me. Especially when you stick together in herds."

"In herds, eh?"

"All I'm saying is that you need to mix it up. Try some vanilla, and you'll realize you've never had anything sweeter before."

I gag. "Even if I wanted vanilla, you're too old for me, Rick."

"Age is nothing but a number," Rick says, running his hands through his greying hair. "You don't have any unresolved daddy issues you want me to help with, do you?" He runs to catch up with me as I walk away. "Okay, that was a bit too much, but let's be serious. What do you think is going to happen if this guy gives you a ring? Happily ever after?"

I think about it for only a second. The question isn't what's going to happen after Tom and I get married because the possibilities are endless. I have a feeling the date can be set after today.

"A ticket out of this dump," I say, only half-joking.

"Buy your own ticket," Rick says. "You're a smart cookie, Benni. You read those *Queer Inquirer* magazines all day like a champ."

"It's *Quill & Quire*, Rick – a publishing magazine."

"That's exactly what I said. Regardless, you're bright, you've got a degree, and you've certainly got the interest. It's only a matter of time until the opportunity arrives. Tom's not the ticket holder."

"I know as well as you do that I can buy whatever ticket I damn well want, but I choose Tom. He and I will buy our ticket out together." I say, tossing my pay stub into my bag.

4.

TOM ASKED TO MEET AT THE NEARBY Tim Hortons. To be fair, I didn't expect my proposal to come over coffee and Timbits, but I'm willing to overlook the less-than-romantic environment. Tom is a practical man. He's already there by the time I arrive, sitting on a picnic bench outside nearest to his white BMW. The flowers are blooming nearby. Early cottage-goers passing through the streets of small-town Georgina stop by the shops on their way further up north. Across the street, antsy fishermen are readying their boats and testing the waters of Lake Simcoe, which have already begun flowing this spring.

I look at the food he's ordered with an appraising eye. "You upsized my French Vanilla. What's the special occasion?" I crack a smile, but Tom looks preoccupied.

"Thank you for coming, Benni."

"What is this, an interview?" I ask, trying to calm the fluttering in my stomach. *Relax*, I think. *This is Tom. You're ready for this.*

I sit across from him and he takes my hand. "I'm sorry. I don't know how to begin," he says. "I know I've been acting strange lately, but we've been dating for a long time." He looks into my eyes, and the intensity of his gaze makes me certain the statement will be followed by a ring. I'm already nodding my head, yes.

Tom's earnest words are followed by a, "But we just won't work out."

I stop nodding and stare.

"You know how traditional my parents are, Benni, and I'm their only child. Considering my age, my parents want me to start getting serious about my future. It's important for my family that my future wife be Chinese. You know that, right? It's important for them, it's important for our company, and ... I love you, but it's important for me."

I think of Tom's mother, who often comments on how close I look to being Chinese. After three years, I thought her remarks were all in good fun. The idea that my race is a point of contention is news to me.

"We're too old to play around anymore, Benni."

Play around. The words strike me. I think of all those nights on vacation; nights that seemed like pretty serious signs of commitment to me. I fancied the way we got up in the morning and got ready for the day, the way I imagined we would be getting ready for the day together every day for the rest of our lives.

The first thing I can think to say is, "But what were these questions you had for my dad?"

"Your dad?" Tom asks, a look of confusion crossing his face. "I was curious about his business, of course."

Of course. Why wouldn't Tom – who is always so practical and business-minded – want to ask my dad about work?

"Benni, you're hurting me," Tom says, and only then do I realize I am squeezing his hand.

I ease my grip. "You're joking, right? This is some kind of sick joke, right?"

Tom bites his lip. "Come on, Benni, you've always been so reasonable. You can't believe how much I love you, but I want to start taking on more of my father's responsibilities. I've been doing really well at the company, and I'm looking forward to doing more."

His ambition. His drive. The grounded, level-headed honesty I so much appreciated. "So, you're telling me that the only way for you to take on a share of your father's company is to break up with me?"

"Essentially, yes."

"I must be missing something. Your parents are telling you to breakup with me?"

"They're not really telling me. It's just understood."

"It's understood? Did I miss the memo?"

"Come on, Benni."

"Don't 'come on, Benni' me. We've clearly missed a few key fucking points in the past few years, haven't we?"

Tom flinches at the swear word. "Why are you acting like this?" he asks, looking around. "There are other people here, Benni." He takes my silent seething as compliance and nods at the children on the picnic bench behind me. "There are kids here."

Kids. He and I were supposed to have some kids of our own. We wanted two – a boy and a girl. I remember admiring his commitment when we talked about it. His ease in discussing the future showed a maturity I hadn't encountered in other men before he and I started dating. His consideration for the children behind me and complete lack of regard for the children we had planned infuriates me even more.

"Don't fucking tell me to keep it down," I say, raising my voice a notch higher. "What was the past three years then? A joke? A practice run? Clearly, it was a waste of time."

"A waste of time?" Tom flushes a red that colours his neck and cheeks in uneven blotches. "Christ, Benni, does everything have to be a process for you?"

"Are you kidding me? Mr. Analytical is talking to me about *process?* You're the one who colour-codes his goddamn underwear drawer. And just for the record, our relationship wasn't a process, but we sure as hell had a plan."

"I didn't know that the only way for our relationship to have meaning was for it to end in marriage."

"Oh, no, why would I want that? Clearly, all I wanted was

the chance to screw around with a prissy little mama's boy for three years."

Tom stands up and places his sunglasses on with a deliberation that only makes me angrier. "I should have listened to my parents when they said I was wasting my time with you. I don't know why I was so worried to have this conversation in the first place. Good riddance." Always the gentleman, he leaves a five-dollar tip on the picnic table for the Tim Hortons staff. Tom is a generous tipper by habit and tips so often wherever we go that he often forgets tips aren't required at Tim Hortons. I used to think it was endearing. Now, I see it for what it is: a pretentious send-off, similar to the one he's giving me.

"No, good riddance to you, dickwad," I yell after him.

He continues to his car.

"Tom, don't you walk away from me."

He steps into his car.

"Tom!"

He leaves.

I stand up and give the bench a good kick, ignoring the open-mouthed stares from the people around me. I yank my car door open, throw my bag inside, and turn the car on with as much force as though the key were stuck. Navigating out of the parking lot, I notice a brown-skinned, pimply-faced teen yelling at me from the sidewalk.

I slow the car and roll down my window. "What?"

"Your high beams are on!"

I struggle to find my high beam switch and turn it off, only after turning on and off my front and rear windshield wipers, too. "Thanks," I yell back.

He rolls his eyes and hitches his backpack over his shoulder. "Learn how to drive or go back to the dragon centre, chink."

"Are you kidding me?" I yell. I accelerate out of the parking lot, hopping the curb as I go.

The teen starts running. He is unidentifiable other than the fact that he wears his pants too low and his words are ironic because he looks as foreign as me.

I fight the urge to drive after the punk, hurling profanities. Instead, I take the road to work. "I'm okay," I say. "I'm okay." I grip the wheel tighter. "I'm okay," I say again, as though the words are a Band-Aid keeping all the jagged pieces of myself together.

I tell myself I'm okay all the way to work. Saying it keeps the Band-Aid on. Frankly, I'm too afraid to pause, peek, and see the blood.

I park my car and stare at the brown brick building where I've spent forty hours a week for the past two years of my life. The township sign is cracked and faded; it has been that way for as long as I can remember.

I've spent one hundred and four weeks in that building, waiting and saving so that Tom and I could plan our next steps together. One hundred and four weeks of work to achieve a now-impossible life. Now that Tom isn't here to take the next step with me, where am I supposed to go? Though I had every intention of going in, I can't bring myself to get out of the car.

I stare at the building and try to picture the rest of my life. It's uncharted territory that I now face alone. I begin to cry ugly sobs that leave me gasping for air.

I have my mother's once-slight figure, long chicken legs, and pale skin, while I have my Dad's slanted eyes and pointed nose. The difference in my appearance from that of an actual Filipina makes all the difference in how I'm stereotyped in this town. My skin dictates how others view my driving and speaking ability, and even my math and science capability. But, apparently, my skin colour simply isn't enough to determine my marriageability.

I knuckle my tears away, turn the car around, and drive back home.

5

"WHAT ARE YOU DOING BACK SO EARLY?" Mom asks as soon as I enter the house. If there's anything I can count on, it's Mom being home. Today, like every other day, she sits in the same ratty housedress with her headphones on and a laptop in front of her, typing a total of twenty words per minute as she transcribes tapes of customer service calls for a pharmaceutical company. A rerun of *Worldwide Star* is muted on the TV before her.

"I forgot something."

"Forgot what?" Mom tries to stand but is prevented by her headphone cord. She sits back down and rewinds the recording with great concentration.

"Don't worry about it," I say, heading upstairs. I hope that, just this once, Mom will leave well enough alone.

I sit at the foot of my single bed. I feel like the four walls of my nine-foot-squared room is closing in on me. I rummage around my purse for a smoke, forgetting for a minute that I threw my cigarettes away after Tom said smoking was a disgusting habit. I know I've hoped for too much when I hear Mom in her slippers climbing the stairs. I close my eyes. There is no privacy in this house. When I open my eyes again, Mom is standing in front of me with a hand on her hip.

"What's wrong with you?" she asks.

"Nothing. I'm fine."

"You are obviously not fine, Benni."

"I just feel sick," I say. I feel like I'm twelve again, when I'd come home saying I had a cold, but was really just trying to escape the girls at school who bullied me for looking different. Perhaps Mom remembers this too. "You're not a child anymore, Benni. What happened?"

I close my eyes and take a deep breath. "Tom and I split up."

I sense it rather than see it; Mom approaches and hugs me without hesitation. It's a maternal gesture I'm not about to reject and I cry into her shoulder, breathing in the smell of the well-worn, washed linen unique to Mom's housedresses.

"Why?" she asks.

"Because I'm not Chinese." I breathe the words out and cry harder. Part of me shudders at finding myself in this position of utmost vulnerability. Another part of me no longer cares. I am more inclined to agree with the latter. I sit, sobbing uncontrollably into my mother's shoulder.

"Well, Benni," her voice is muffled in my hair. "I know it's tough, but pull yourself together."

I pull away in the silence that follows. "What?" I ask.

"Look at you. You're a mess. Don't give Tom the benefit of seeing you so distraught."

I take a deep breath, pick myself up, straighten my clothes, then wipe my tears away with deliberation. I feel all the most secret parts of myself – my shattered heart and storm-swept mind – being locked away after having been on obscene display. I open my mouth to speak but realize that no words can bridge the gap between Mom and I. So, I close my mouth, walk out of the room, and head down to the kitchen to brew a pot of coffee. I'd forgotten my French Vanilla at Tim's.

The padding of Mom's slippers follows me down the stairs. "Benni, what's wrong with you? Why did you just walk out on me?"

My anger gathers momentum with Mom's turn of phrase. I get dumped, but somehow it ends with me walking out on her.

"Benni, don't ignore me." I can sense her coming up behind

me and feel the annoyance in her voice crawl up my back. "Just because Tom broke up with you, it doesn't mean you have to take it out on me."

Her words are the last push against a stuck door. I whirl around and see the fantastic hair and professionally made-up faces of *Worldwide Star* contestants flickering in the background. "Are you kidding me? For once, don't make this about you, Mom."

"Benni, if Tom could see you now, I'm sure he'd be smug over how much he's affected you."

"Tom can't see me right now, only you can, and just last night you were telling me I did a good job finding him."

"Except clearly Tom isn't who I thought he was, so don't bother. You don't need him."

I stare at Mom through throbbing eyes, wondering if she's joking. Her no-nonsense attitude is ludicrous in contrast to her housedress and oily hair. I turn away. "I don't need pointers from you about relationships, Mom. Maybe you can dismiss failed relationships easily, but I certainly can't."

"What on earth is that supposed to mean?"

"Hmm, let me think. How about Dad?"

Mom's look of surprise only serves to make me feel guilty and therefore angrier. "What are you talking about?" she asks.

"Dad just picked up and moved to the Philippines, and you didn't say anything about it. Were you trying not to look 'distraught'? If that's what you want me to do, it's not happening. I, for one, actually care if the person I love stays or goes."

"You're speaking nonsense, Benni."

"I'm not," I say. But just like that, I feel all the fight go out of me and am left empty. I'm barely able to lift my eyes to look at her and say, "Forget it. I'm tired, and I don't feel like talking. I think I just need a break. I need to go somewhere."

"We can go to the mall. You're already dressed. Fix yourself up and we'll go. I can change in a couple of minutes."

I can see Mom is making an effort to dispel the tension, and it only makes me feel that much worse. She and I never have, and never will, go out together like the mother and daughter duos often found on TV, where the mother is a more of a friend than a parent and the two are a pair – a partnership that can share confidences and hardships. "No, I don't want to go to the mall, Mom," I say.

"I'm not talking about the strip mall down the street. I was thinking of Upper Canada Mall. We can take a trip into Newmarket."

"No, I don't want to go to Newmarket. I don't want to be in York Region. I want to go away. Far away." I don't realize I'm pacing until I stop. "Maybe I'll go to the Philippines."

Mom snorts. "Why on earth would you want to go to the Philippines? You've never wanted to go before."

It's true. The natural progression of everyday life has eaten up my time, and I've been content to simply let it go on. But now that I want to be anywhere but here, the idea of going to the Philippines is becoming more and more appealing. "Well, I want to go now," I say.

"What do you mean?"

"I mean that I'm going. I'm sick of all this. I'm tired of Georgina. There's nothing here for me."

"You're acting rashly."

"I'll crash with Dad for a bit."

"Your father's enjoying himself in the Philippines, Benni. He has his fish farm to deal with right now. You've heard his stories. He's happy doing his own thing. You need to let men be by themselves." Mom takes my silence as license to continue. "You're ignoring the real problem, Benni. Maybe you just never realized Tom for who he was."

"We're not talking about Tom anymore. We're talking about the Philippines."

"But, Benni, how can you leave me here alone?"

The switch happens just like that – from a woman telling me to toughen up to a housewife in slippers and a housedress, unable to have a single dinner alone.

"I'm not leaving you, Mom. You can come too."

"How can I come? I have work to do."

It's my turn to snort. "That's your excuse? You get assignments once every three weeks, if that, then do your work at home during the commercial breaks of your daytime soap operas. I'm sure work can spare you. If I can go, you can go. But it's up to you. This isn't about you, Mom. I just need to go away somewhere – somewhere that's not here." I sigh. "Good talk, Mom. I'm jumping into the shower." I say this to end the conversation. Thankfully, this time, Mom doesn't argue.

6.

I LOG ONTO FACEBOOK AND CHECK Dad's profile. His cover photo is of a hilly expanse full of palm trees against an azure sky. I'm not sure where the picture was taken.

I study the last picture Dad posted. Taken almost half a year ago, it features a festive spread with a turkey at its centre. It was taken around New Year's Eve. Like every other photo on Dad's page, this photo has no caption or context – no one in it to explain where he was or who he was with. The photos are a mystery, much like my father.

Dad is a big man: six-foot-three, heavy set, with dark curly hair, a mocha complexion, and a booming voice. He was always a heavy man, but he carried it well. In the past five years, Dad has put on weight. His two-hundred-and-twenty pounds have become two-hundred-and-eighty, erring him on the side of fat rather than mass. He moved to the Philippines last year. When I asked him what happened to his job, he said he quit. "They were restructuring," he said. And since I didn't know anything about his job before, I don't ask anything about it now.

I scroll a bit further down to view Dad's feed. The last time I wrote on his page was two months ago – a generic "Happy Birthday, Dad." That, and a birthday phone call, was about as celebratory as I could get 13,211 kilometres away. Taking everything into consideration, next week seems as good as any to see my father again. It's been a long time.

I grab my cellphone and call Dad, not expecting him to pick up. The thirteen-hour time difference makes it just past midnight over there.

The phone seems to ring forever until the gruff voice of my father finally answers. "Hello?" he asks. The sound of clinking glass and cutlery fill the background.

"Dad?"

A long pause, and then, "Princess? Is that you?"

"Yeah, Dad, it's me. I just wanted to let you know that I booked a flight to Manila. I'm arriving sometime next week. I'll send you the flight info."

"To Manila?" Dad asks with surprise. "How come? Is your mother coming too?"

"Not that I know of. She says she has work to do."

"Why are you coming?"

His question rings with reluctance, but I'm going, whether he wants me or not. "I thought it'd be a good time to get together. It's slow in the office right now. Not quite summertime yet and all, you know…" I trail off and wait for him to reply. Laughter bubbles around him like white noise over the line.

"Of course. It would be good if your mother came with you, though. I can buy her a ticket."

"Sure, Dad. It would be nice for her to come too, but only if she can get the time off work, of course."

Dad ignores my sarcasm. "Are you okay?" he asks.

I'm surprised by the question. Dad's usually brimming with stories, but he's never been one to ask after any that aren't his own. "I'm fine. Tom and I just split up, but it was mutual." I can't keep my voice from cracking. "I'm pretty sad though," I add by way of explanation.

Dad, either out of foresight or habit, doesn't ask any questions. Instead, he simply says, "Well, then, it'll be good for you to get away." He pauses then adds, "you know what they say, Princess. You date the one you love and marry the one who loves you."

The next day, I receive confirmation in my inbox for Mom's ticket to Manila. Though Mom hems and haws, she finally calls her supervisor and asks for time off. As expected, he gives it to her without hesitation. We depart the next week.

7.

DURING OUR EIGHTEEN-HOUR FLIGHT, I tell Mom what happened with the kid outside of Tim Hortons, omitting the fact that Tim Hortons was the fateful place of my break up. "Can you believe what he said to me, Mom? God, I hate Georgina."

The first thing Mom asks is, "But what is a 'chink'?"

"It's a derogatory word for Chinese people," I say, already regretting my decision to share the story.

"But you're not Chinese."

"I look Chinese."

"Are you kidding me? You have *mestiza* features. It's the Spanish in you. As a *mestiza*, you're part of the ruling class."

"Maybe in the Philippines, Mom. But, in Georgina, I'm just another immigrant."

"But you're not an immigrant. You were born in Canada."

"That's beside the point, Mom. What can you expect from a town that still flies the Confederate flag in schools?"

"I never did understand that."

"What's there to understand? It's just the way things are." When it looks like Mom is about to argue, I cut her off. "Never mind," I say. We've had these conversations before, and I'm in no mood to have them again. The flight is long and cramped. My legs ache from being curled beneath me, and my heart aches from missing Tom.

Mom studies me. "Just you wait, Benni. When we land,

you're going to stand out as a beauty. Being North American makes you instantly desirable."

"Well, gee, it's a great confidence booster knowing I'll be much loved because of my Roots T-shirt."

"Brands are just one thing. You're also beautiful, if you didn't know. Trust me."

I don't reply, but inside I acknowledge that I wouldn't mind the change.

We stand upon landing, stooped and uncomfortable under the aircraft's low ceiling. We unload, following the crowd like cattle in a herd. We filter into Customs' large, fluorescent room with its white walls and tiles that have assumed a greyish tinge. Though there are six booths, all but one is for residents.

"This is clearly not a tourist-friendly country," I say as I watch the visitors' line build up.

Mom pauses in the doorway.

"Mom, what are we waiting for?"

"Should we line up as visitors or residents?" she asks.

"You're kidding, right? We should line up as visitors," I say, tugging her arm. "Let's go before the line gets too long."

"But we're Filipinos," Mom says, resisting.

"Yes, but we're Canadian citizens and therefore Canadian residents, not Filipino residents." I wave my passport for emphasis.

Mom's face brightens when she sees the passport. "Right. We're Canadians. We're visiting. Silly me." She walks forward with her chin raised and joins the visitors' line with no further hesitation, but it's too late. Despite having fewer visitors than residents to process, the one line has built up and the queue wraps around the scuffed walls. By the time we pass Customs, we've spent an hour and a half in line.

"Dad's probably frantic," I say.

Mom looks at me with a raised eyebrow.

"Well, maybe not frantic, but annoyed," I say, correcting myself. In all my twenty-five years, I have never once seen Dad frantic or uneasy.

A crush of Filipinos wait beyond Customs, offering baggage-carrying services, rides, or simply begging for money. The multiculturalism of Canada is lost. Instead, there is only one race here – Filipino – and I am aware that, like Mom said, we're different. I can't quite pinpoint it exactly, but it's a general sense of being an outsider in the crowd.

"Ready to go home yet?" Mom asks with a smile. "Is this what you expected?"

"Well, there's more Aéropostale around than I thought there'd be."

"It's all fake."

"How do you know?"

"Look closely," Mom says, pouting her lips in the direction of a woman dressed in what I presume is an Aéropostale T-shirt. Her shirt reads, "Aeropost."

"Oh," I say.

"Exactly. It's special to come from North America, Benni. Everyone wishes they came from there."

We push through the double doors of the airport to the outside. The heat is the first thing I notice. The warmth settles over us with our first steps towards the parking lot. I notice the smell next – a heady humidity mixed with sweat and garbage. It is not unpleasant. Even more Filipinos in dirty shirts and shorts lay outside on the ground around the airport's sliding doors. They sleep with ratty caps drawn over their eyes or fan themselves with woven mats.

The first thought I have is, *Home?* It's a question. This is the place where both Mom and Dad came from and where, by deduction, I must belong. As I found time and time again, I don't belong in Georgina. Perhaps I belong here instead. I try to greet the thought with all the gravity of a homecoming but feel only disoriented instead.

The second thought that comes to mind is, *foreign*. The packed airport, shouting people, heat, and smell are all unfamiliar. My entire life I operated under the idea that my place of origin was somewhere else – somewhere "over there." But here I am, and I am rootless.

We push through the crowded parking lot looking for Dad. We try our best not to look lost, moving away from outstretched hands and pointed stares. "Maybe Dad left. Maybe we took too long. I should've brought my phone," I say. While packing, I had decided against bringing my cellphone, thinking it would be good for me to be disconnected for a while. I wouldn't be able to take calls from Tom – even though he hasn't contacted me since the breakup – and I wouldn't be able to call him.

"If we can't find him, we can go back inside," Mom says. "We can use the payphones in there."

When we finally reach the end of the parking lot, we spot a squat man dressed in a light blue, short-sleeved dress shirt and jeans. He's middle aged and portly, shorter than Mom, and unremarkable in every way except for the homemade sign he holds that reads, "*Mabuhay* Manlapazes." We pause to read the sign and the van door behind him slides open.

"Maria Dychingco Manlapaz," a raspy voice calls. "Sister, it has been too long."

8.

"*A*TE ROSIE, YOU CAME!" MOM SAYS, referring to my aunt – or *Tita* – Rose with the Tagalog title of respect for an older sister.

"Of course. Why wouldn't I come?" Rose asks.

Rose – a round, busty woman – looks almost identical to Mom, but she has a deeper, huskier voice. Perhaps that, combined with the knowledge of her wealth, is why she seems almost immediately more glamorous than Mom, who seems even more small-town than usual with her black Crocs and a plastic bag full of snacks packed for the flight peeking out of her worn pleather handbag.

"I didn't think you ever left Forbes," Mom teases. Her smile is wide as she wraps her arms around her sister.

"I make exceptions for family," Rose says, hugging her back. "But where are my manners? Benni, my dear, I'm so glad to finally meet you. I'm so happy you and your mom are finally here. *Finally*," she says, stressing the word.

"I know. It's been a long time, *Ate*," Mom says.

"A long time? How about a lifetime? Quite literally, seeing as this is the first time I'm meeting my niece. How selfish of you to keep Benni from me for so long." Rose grabs my face and turns to Mom with a pout.

"*Ate,* stop being so *maarte,*" Mom says, laughing.

"Well, it's been more than a quarter of a century since I've last seen you."

"I know, but I couldn't just pick up and go. I have a job, you know." Mom stands a bit straighter.

"I know, you poor thing. Another reason why you should have stayed. But we can discuss this later." Rose turns to the squat man. "Jerry, be a dear and take Maria and Benni's bags."

Jerry deposits his sign in the car and returns for our luggage.

"Jerry, it's so good to see you again," Mom says. "I almost didn't recognize you."

"Thank you, *po*," Jerry says, using the customary title of respect. "It must have been my haircut that threw you off." He gestures at his receding hairline. "It's good to see you home again."

"Benni, this is your *Tita* Rosie's driver, Jerry," Mom explains. "Jerry has been with your *Tita* Rosie from the time she got married."

I reach out to shake his hand. He stares at it for a second as though not knowing what to do and extends his own as I'm already pulling mine away. We fumble hands and I flush in embarrassment as he turns to start the minivan.

Mom nudges me. "You don't shake hands with the help," she hisses.

"Thanks for the heads-up," I say.

"Jerry's practically family now," Rose says, oblivious to our exchange as she climbs into the back seat. We follow her lead. "He stayed with me, even after that *bruha* cursed our family to break it up and bewitched Carlo to fall in love with her. Carlo and that witch brought all the help with them. I wouldn't be surprised if that was witchcraft too. Wouldn't you agree, Jerry?" Rose turns to Mom. "Jerry was there. He can attest to it."

"*Opo*," Jerry says.

"Well, you're better off without him, *Ate*," Mom says.

"Certainly," Rose says, "and I'd choose Jerry over Carlo any day. He's far more helpful around the house. Who needs a good-for-nothing husband when you have help?"

Mom chuckles. "Speaking of good-for-nothing husbands, s*aan si* Ned? I thought he was going to pick us up."

"Change of plans, sister," Rose says. "Why? Are you not satisfied with plain old me?"

If Mom is disappointed, she doesn't show it. "Maybe you're old now, *Ate,* but you're anything but plain," she says.

"I guess we didn't have to stress about Dad worrying after all," I say, forcing a laugh. Even if Mom is unsurprised, I'm disappointed. In this foreign country, Dad's presence was the one thing I was counting on.

We begin the drive to Rose's house in Forbes Park, which will be our home base for most of our visit to the Philippines.

"Sister, where is Ned staying if he doesn't have a house here?" Rose asks.

"He's been travelling so much that it would have been a waste to buy a place. When he needs to camp out for a long time, he stays with his mom at the hospital in Iloilo. But Iloilo's so far out; I thought Forbes would be a nicer, more central place for Benni's first visit."

"Hmm," Rose says.

"But if it's too much trouble...."

"Sister, it's never too much trouble," Rose cuts Mom off. "I wouldn't have you anywhere else." She reaches over and squeezes Mom's hand.

We drive by dingy storefronts, littered streets, whirring tricycle taxis, and jeepneys packed with passengers. Here and there, a bright KFC or Pizza Hut sign dots the landscape. Mom inquires after street names. When she recognizes one, she smiles, nods, and points out the familiar sights. When she gets one wrong, she shakes her head and says, partly to us, but mainly, I suspect, to herself, "Well, it's been a long time."

"Have you noticed all the billboards, Benni? They all feature light-skinned models," Mom says after a time.

"Mom, it's all the same woman."

"Benni's right, Maria," Rose says. "It's Vanessa Hernandez

on most of these billboards. She's huge right now; one of our biggest pop stars."

"And she's *mestiza*," Mom says, determined to make her point. Rose arches an eyebrow.

"Benni doesn't believe that being *mestiza* is special here," Mom explains.

"Oh, darling, your mom is right," Rose says. She turns to survey me. "Honey, you could be a model here."

"Because of my skin colour?" I ask.

"And because you're pretty," Rose says, winking.

We fall silent after leaving Manila and entering a highway that is shaded by palm tree after towering palm tree. The car ride feels filled with waiting; we wait for the silence to pass and for all the things that need to be said.

"Really, though, *Ate*," Mom says after a time, "how come Ned didn't come? Is he there yet?"

"*Oo*," says Rose. "He arrived earlier this afternoon."

"Has he been drinking?"

"I don't know, sister," Rose replies, with a pause so slight as to be unnoticeable if not for the fact that it has been there all along.

"I know," Mom says. "I know my husband."

The rest of the ride continues in silence.

9.

ROSE'S SUBURB, FORBES PARK, IS GUARDED by manned kiosks to monitor traffic in and out. I let out a low whistle. "That's some security," I say as we drive through, studying the guards' rifles.

"We in Forbes like our privacy," Rose says. "It keeps the busybodies out."

The streets are narrow and crowded inside the subdivision, but each house is extravagant and custom-made. Within the already private suburb, we slow down before another set of bleached stucco walls and wrought-iron gates. Jerry idles before the gate to wave at an armed guard hidden in camouflage amongst the trees. The guard unlocks the gate and holds it open.

The driveway we enter is a lengthy promenade, but I'm distracted from further observations upon spotting a pacing figure by the house's arched front doors. The figure grows larger the closer we get until I make it out to be my own very rotund father.

When Jerry parks the minivan, I slide the door open and meet Dad at a sprint. Despite distance, time, and how much ambiguity rests in between, I never feel any less excited to see Dad again than when he first started travelling for work.

"Princess," Dad yells, his face flushed. He crushes me in a hug and nearly burns my forehead with the cigarette dangling from his lips. "It's good to see you. Did you have a good flight?"

"It was fine. Long. We thought you'd pick us up from the airport."

"Did you? But I thought it would be better to give you your very first taste of the Philippines by having a driver pick you up."

"That would've been nice if you sent a stretch limo, but I'm sure you could've easily driven the minivan." I wait for his response, but realize he's not listening. He's turned away, watching Mom walk towards us with her hand shielding her eyes from the spotlights facing the driveway.

"Hi, Ned," she says.

"Maria," he replies.

They kiss – a peck on the lips.

"Did you like the stretch limo I sent?" Dad asks, winking at me to show he'd been listening after all.

"Loved it," Mom says without a smile. "Why are you outside?"

"I'm having a smoke," Dad says, waving his cigarette. "Can't smoke inside."

"I see. Well, I don't want to keep the Consuelos waiting," Mom says, motioning at Rose walking ahead to the front door.

"Of course. Go ahead. I'll see you inside," Dad says.

I want to wait for Dad, but Mom is already walking away. I follow her.

A lady opens the doors from inside the house before we reach the entrance. The heavy wooden doors with stained glass inserts dwarf the small woman at two times her height. "Good evening *po*," she says with a smile. She wears a starched grey dress and a crisp white apron. "Come in, *po*," she says, stepping aside.

We enter into the Consuelos's foyer. I know my relatives are wealthy – Mom talks about it often enough – but it's one thing to know it and another thing to see it. A heavily polished grand piano with an all-glass top stands at the foyer's center. Curving twin staircases frame it, stretching along the expansive marble floors. Just beside the door, a black onyx leopard with a diamond-studded nose and ruby eyes stretches perpetually with its yawning gold mouth. The mansion is a far cry from our house in Georgina, where the largest piece of décor is the TV when Mom leaves it on the nature channel by accident.

Immediately in front of us stand my cousin, his wife, and their two kids. Though we have never met, I am privy to enough intimate knowledge about them from Mom's dinnertime gossip to identify them on sight.

Rose takes the lead, introducing me to her son, Ariel, first. Ariel, my TV-star cousin, is even prettier in real life than in the magazine photos he shares online. His pink lips are glossed, and his soft powdery skin and pointed features would look more suitable on a woman.

"My family," Ariel says, sighing and clasping his slender hands by his chest. "It has been too long." He throws his arms out and swoops like a butterfly towards Mom for a hug and kiss.

"Ariel, it's so good to see you," Mom says. "You look as young as ever. You must have had work done."

I'm embarrassed by Mom's frankness, but must admit Ariel looks well-preserved. Forty-five is by no means old, but it's bizarre that he still looks the same as he did on his TV show, *Dance, Dance Pinoy*, which he did when he was nineteen.

Ariel smiles. "I'll never tell," he sings. "But my gorgeousness is one matter among many for us to discuss later. *Tita* Maria, this is Celeste."

"Pleasure to meet you, *Tita*." Celeste steps forward to kiss us. She is a natural and graceful beauty, with light-brown hair, milky-white skin, sharp features, and full lips.

After Ariel honours his wife with the first introduction, he introduces us to his children. The young woman standing beside Celeste is her eldest daughter, Lisa. Lisa is a close reproduction of her mother, though her wraithlike figure and dark bags accentuate the gaunt delicacy of her face, and her darker complexion must surely be a token from her birth father – a man who purportedly left Celeste shortly after Lisa's birth and well before Celeste's rise to fame.

"And last but not least," Ariel says, raising the hands he laid on Celeste and Lisa's shoulders, "is my Gia!" He picks up the littlest Consuelo and, though she's tall for a seven-year-old, holds her at his hip like a toddler. "I'm so happy my kids finally get to meet you," Ariel says. "I've told them all about their *Lola* Maria and *Tita* Maria."

"Please, call me Benni," I say. I notice their puzzled looks and clarify: "It's short for Benedictine, my second name."

"Ah, right. I almost forgot that your full name is Maria Benedictine," Ariel says. "You must be very blessed having been named after the Catholic order."

"That's what my wife likes to believe," Dad says as he re-enters the house, "but she's really named after my favourite drink – B&B – Bénédictine and brandy." He grins and nudges me.

"How charming," Rose says. "So, Benni, how do you like the Philippines so far?" Her abrupt change of subject and her distaste for the previous topic is clear.

"I'm not too sure, *Tita*. I haven't seen much of it yet. From what I have seen, though, it's beautiful," I say, gesturing at the foyer.

"You'll be able to see more of it soon, I hope." Rose says. "In the meantime, we have a special meal planned for you tonight."

"Great," I say, though all I want right now is sleep.

"Dinner is still being prepared, but we can wait by the dining room," Ariel says. "I promise we won't keep you up too long tonight." He ushers us into an antechamber with plush green sofas and bowls of lychee atop mahogany side tables.

I lean against a wooden column near one of the sofas as Lisa strikes up a conversation. "So, *Ate* Benni, what do you do? Are you still in school?" she asks.

"No, I graduated years ago. I work in an administrative capacity for my local municipality now," I say. It's the crap I've learned to spew to make my job sound at least somewhat dignified. My job seems even less glamorous than usual in this multimillion-dollar home. "What about you?"

"I'm studying part-time, but devote most of my time to musicals. School will take a bit longer for me, what with all the acting, but my mom is pretty set on me finishing my undergrad."

I count backwards in my head. According to North American standards, Lisa, at twenty-two, should be done all her schooling by now. I feel a tinge of resentment at Mom. Our relatives' lifestyle proves that, contrary to what Mom pushed on me during my turbulent teen years, stability and following the status quo aren't the only routes to happiness and success. "My mom was the same," I say. "She had a well-worn adage of her own while I was growing up: 'A good education is key to getting a good job.' What are you studying?"

"Performing arts."

"A little superfluous since you're already doing it, no?"

"You think?" Lisa asks. As we chat, her eyes wander the room, trace patterns on the floor, and settle on my ankle. "*Ate* Benni, is that a real tattoo?"

Dad, sitting on a sofa nearby, joins us before I can hide the band around my left ankle. "You have a tattoo? Since when?" he asks.

"Sorry, *Ate* Benni, I didn't mean to call attention to it," Lisa says.

"But when did you get it?" Dad asks. "Is it real?"

"I got it years ago, Dad, when I turned eighteen."

"What does it say?" Dad doesn't seem at all disconcerted that his daughter has had a tattoo for almost a decade that he didn't know about.

"It's my name," I say with hot cheeks.

"Your name?" Lisa asks. "Why...?"

"How did your mother react?" Dad asks, cutting her off. He seems pleased by my tattoo and the rebellion it suggests. He prides himself on being a free spirit and party animal and I think he may be proud that his daughter is following in his steps.

I avoid the awkward, too-personal question of "why" with relief. "She cried," I say.

The response puts an end to Dad's questions, but it doesn't stop him from patting me on the back.

10.

ARIEL INTERRUPTS THE CHATTER WITH A clap of his hands. "My beautiful family, it is time to eat." I wonder if he talks this way even when visitors aren't around. He bows and two helpers open the doors behind him to reveal the dining room. The dining table is set with embossed silver cutlery, gold plates, and bouquets of fresh red roses.

I follow the Consuelos past the table and through the glass doors at the far end of the room. We exit onto a wide terrace overlooking a kidney-shaped pool. Several food-laden tables span the space and are illuminated by tall burning lanterns. I watch the Consuelos before grabbing my food. They handle their gold-rimmed dishes as though they are at the most casual of family dinners.

"Ned, must you smoke near the food?" Mom calls across the balcony.

Dad has lit another cigarette, and it dangles from his lips as he leans over the *lechon,* a suckling pig that has been roasted and is surrounded by a medley of colourful grilled vegetables. "We're outside," he protests. His clenched lips muffles his speech.

"Please finish it over there," Mom says, pointing him to the corner.

I follow Dad to the railing. He drapes his arm around my shoulder and puffs on the cigarette hanging from his thin lips. "This is something different, eh, Princess?" he says as we take in the view of the table laden with food, the torch-lit balcony, and the vast and lush backyard.

"You can say that again."

"This is something different, eh, Princess?"

I elbow Dad in the ribs as he chortles with laughter. "Care if I bum one, Dad?" I ask, looking at his cigarette. I began smoking because I loved the smell that lingered on my fingertips afterwards. It reminded me of earlier, easier times, like the days around Christmas when Dad still hung around. If not for Tom, I would never have regretted picking it up. The musty, smoky smell of Dad's clothes and the scent of Marlboro in the air makes me feel nostalgic for this time before it's even passed.

"Are you crazy? Do you know what your mom would do to me if she found out I let you?" Dad pretends to stab himself in the neck with the lit cigarette and winces.

I laugh, enjoying the casual way Dad and I chat. One thing I've always loved about Dad is that, when he is here, he is most certainly here – jovial, present, and lively. "I'm not five, Dad," I say.

"I never said you were five. Obviously, I know you're fifteen."

I get one more elbow jab in before Mom calls us to attention. I join everyone at the buffet, filling a bowl with steaming hot *arroz caldo* – a flavourful chicken congee – and grabbing another small plate for *lechon* and *pancit palabok* – noodles topped with shrimp, pork, tofu, and scallions.

As I approach the dining room doors, Rose falls into step beside me. "Is that all you're eating, Benni?" she asks. "By the amount you eat, one would almost think you have the same problem as Lisa." I pause as Rose glances at Lisa in the dining room. Lisa's skeletal hands look almost transparent around the fork she uses to poke at her salad. "I can't understand girls these days," Rose says, shaking her head. "I keep telling Lisa that she's beautiful, but she never thinks she's beautiful enough."

I'm surprised by Rose's frankness. Before we arrived, Mom mentioned Lisa's on-and-off battle with an eating disorder – a common illness for aspiring female stars – but I assumed such issues were private. I'm sure the conversation is uncomfortable for Lisa, who can likely hear us from where we're standing.

"What's your reason for not eating, Benni?" Rose asks.

"I'm sorry, *Tita* Rosie. I guess I ate too much on the plane. I'm still full."

"Full? Did you know that we were never allowed to say that we were full at Assumption College? We had to say, 'I'm satisfied' instead. The nuns used to say, 'Pigs are full, but young ladies are satisfied.'"

Feeling my soup bowl cooling in my hand, I curtsey and say, "Well, then, I suppose I'm satisfied."

"Did I hear you say you were satisfied?" Mom asks when we finally join everyone at the table. The smile on her face is one of genuine enjoyment. Her plate is laden with food. Mom hasn't been to a dinner this fancy for as long as I can remember. "That brings me back. At Assumption College, the nuns tried to instill good manners and etiquette into their girls by training us to say things like, 'I'm satisfied.' It was important, especially since it was such a top-notch school and only the children of the prestigious and wealthy attended."

"Yes, Assumption girls were great," Dad says as he joins us at the table. "Nothing like St. Joe's girls, or St. Mary's, if you know what I mean."

Lisa giggles.

"Ah, this young lady knows what I'm referring to. Do St. Joe's girls still have the same notorious reputation as they did before?"

"*Opo*," Lisa says.

"Well, there are always girls for playing and girls for marrying." Dad winks.

"Yes, yes, Ned," Mom says. "We have no need for your raunchy humour at the dinner table."

"I'm just complimenting and agreeing with you," Dad says, but he mimes zipping his lips. And so we eat, polite and proper, in relative silence for the rest of the meal.

11.

A RIEL STANDS FOR OUR ATTENTION AS scoops of rich chocolate ice cream topped with gold candy sprinkles are set before us for our final course. "Family, we would like to offer you some sweet entertainment to accompany your sweet dessert," he says. "Gia's going to sing for you."

Gia, who has moved to sit on Lisa's lap, resists. She buries her face in Lisa's chest with a coy smile that makes her refusal seem more put on than anything else.

"Gia, baby," Ariel pouts. "Come on now."

Gia peeks back at us, blinks, and then broadens her shoulders and breaks into a Tagalog song. I don't understand any of it. Her singing is confident for a girl of seven, but her tone sounds average and boastful. When she finishes, I clap and smile along with the rest as she eyes us in seeming measurement of our enthusiasm. Once our appreciation is assured, she hides her face against Lisa's chest again and refuses to turn around until her caregiver picks her up.

"She's shy," Ariel says. "We're trying to open her up a bit more."

"She's doing well as is," Mom says. "Ariel, you have a family of stars."

"*Tita,* you're too kind, but I like to think we're a regular family, just like everyone else." Ariel grasps Celeste's hand, beaming at the one-time singer, one-time model, and now, TV star.

Here, the house, dinner, family, and, heck, even the little girl seem only to question when, not if, praise will be given. I offer the praise in excess – it costs nothing – but find myself wondering when the show will end and we can go to bed. I'd like to go to my room, but I don't have one here yet. I'd like to feel like I'm home, but I haven't found it here. My cheeks hurt from smiling with an enthusiasm I don't mean.

I study a large painting hanging on the wall at the foot of the dining-room table. It's a lifelike portrait of an elderly Filipina in Filipiniana garb – the butterfly sleeves of her white *terno* dress exaggeratedly puffed. Her hair is short, and her face is stern and unforgiving. I wonder who she is.

My attention is drawn when everyone stands up from the table. "Are you sure, Ariel?" Mom asks. "It would be nice to go to bed, but it would be even nicer to see this beautiful place first."

"Of course. I'll show you to your room after I give you the private tour." Ariel turns to the Consuelos. "Do you guys want to come?"

"No," Lisa says, yawning.

"Okay, say good night to the Manlapazes then."

We kiss everyone goodnight.

"It's good to see you again, sister," Rose says, giving Mom a fierce hug.

We depart the dining room with Ariel and his shining TV personality. I pull out my camera. It feels natural as Ariel readies us to view his house as one would a tourist attraction.

I am lost as soon as the tour starts. We wind our way through a series of hallways and doors. Even if I were in dire need, it would be impossible for me to trace our steps back to the dining area. I view and photograph each new room and wing as a unit unto itself. Each is glamorous to the point of fantastic.

Ariel brings us into Celeste's wing with its hardwood corridor and echoing walls. Her washroom is complete with a small garden (*click*, goes my camera), a large Jacuzzi (*click*), and an auto-flush toilet with a gold-plated seat (*click*). "Oprah has the exact same toilet in her room," Ariel says (*click, click, click*).

Ariel's wing is more modern, though visibly smaller than Celeste's. Whereas Celeste's wing spans an entire side of the house, Ariel's consists only of three rooms and a bathroom. Even his bed is a smaller queen-sized bed while Celeste's is a large king.

"Ariel, why is it necessary for you and Celeste to have separate wings?" Mom asks. Her question is ironic considering she and Dad live in separate countries.

"Sometimes Celeste and I like our space during the day. I do my own thing in my wing, and she does her own thing in hers. We see each other in the evenings."

Ariel seems diminished. Put in his place in his smaller room, he stands by his smaller bed and tries to explain why he and his wife sleep apart. Perhaps the distinction is only fair. After all, despite Ariel's inheritance, almost all of Ariel and Celeste's money comes from her more successful career. And yet, despite my contemporary North American upbringing and feministic education, seeing a man – the traditional head of the family – placed in such a lesser role, disconcerts me. It is so divorced from my ideal of a happy, healthy, regular marriage that it is uncomfortable to see. When I pictured marrying Tom, I looked forward to cooking for him, cleaning for him, and overall just being a woman for him. There is none of that here.

"Ariel, who wears the pants in your relationship?" Mom asks.

Though I'd usually find Mom's bluntness embarrassing, her questions don't bother me, posed as they are during Ariel's private showing. I'd just taken pictures of Celeste's toilet, after all. Our voyeuristic eyes and prying questions feel like a natural part of our all-access VIP tour.

Though I'm not uncomfortable with Mom's question, I am uncomfortable hearing Ariel's response. "Who wears the pants in the relationship?" he asks. "Well, Celeste and I are woman and man – two equal beings, just as God created us. Of course she has more control than I in some things, and in others, I have more control than she. She usually makes the decisions about finances, investments, and the maintenance of our assets, while I have a lot of input on how the house is kept and run. We're quite progressive, you see."

Ariel's long-winded answer is painful to hear. I'm happy when Dad puts an end to it. "Ariel, you two don't sleep together at night?" he asks, apparently still hung up on the reality that this husband and wife have separate wings. His question is no less intrusive than Mom's, but Ariel pounces on the new subject, regaining his smiling composure with an actor's cool experience.

"Of course we spend nights together," he says. As he talks, he guides us from one hallway to the next before we finally stop in front of yet another double door. Ariel pauses, exhales a contented sigh, and throws the doors open into yet another bedroom. The room's bed, sofas, divans, and pillows are covered in heavy red velvet and leather. "This is our little love nest. Celeste and I spend most nights here." Ariel winks. "And some mornings and afternoons, too."

Thankfully, we're saved the details of Ariel's sex life by the appearance of one of the help carrying red bath balls and rose petals. "Sorry, *po*," the young lady says when she sees us. She backs away from us with her head bowed and her arms full.

"Not to worry. We're leaving now anyways. You can proceed," Ariel says. As we leave the room, he looks back and whispers, "We should give her time. We need to ready the room." He winks again.

"Atta boy," Dad says, smacking Ariel on the back. "Distance makes the heart grow fonder. Maria and I know that well enough if you know what I mean. Isn't that right, Maria?" He nudges Mom.

"Don't be naughty, Ned," Mom says, giggling.

I gag. "I don't need to hear this," I say.

In light of my creeping jet lag and our awkward conversation topics, I'm relieved when the tour ends.

"I hope it's okay that we put the three of you in the same room," Ariel says as we approach doors leading off a first-floor hallway. "I thought you might be more comfortable all together."

I try to hide my dismay at the thought of enduring two weeks of Mom and Dad snoring, but I am mollified when Ariel opens the door. We enter into another small antechamber that branches off towards two separate rooms. The guest room is really a guest apartment.

"The help brought your luggage in already, so please unpack and make yourselves at home. Unfortunately, the three of you will have to share one bathroom, which branches off the main quarters," Ariel says, gesturing towards it.

The main room is large with a king-sized bed on one side and a shuttered window overlooking the pool on the opposite wall.

"Benni, your bed is in the other room. It's not as large as this one, but hopefully it'll do."

"I'm sure it's great," I say, heading over to see my room while Dad asks Ariel if the windows open. I have no doubt he'd love to sneak a late-night smoke without going outside, but he'd be hard put doing it with Mom around.

Mom follows me out in time to see my reaction to my room. Though not as small as Ariel said it would be, it's cold, dark, and devoid of windows. Heavy pink drapes surround a canopied double bed, complementing the rose-coloured walls and imposing oak furniture. A wicker rocking chair, standing watch in a shadowy corner by the foot of the bed, completes the mood. It calls to mind the countless horror stories I've heard that occur in the Philippines: the dark omens, restless ghosts, mischievous dwarves, and haunted possessions that seem to be the status quo of life on the islands.

"This room is a bit spooky," I say, staring at the rocking chair in particular.

"It's not too bad," Mom says, but I can tell she's stifling a laugh. "It's cozy, see?" She sits in the rocker. It flings her back with a moan. When she finally rises, dishevelled after fighting against the chair, she breaks into uncontrollable giggles. "Well, just hope it doesn't move at night." Its solitary cushion remains crumpled as though it is being sat on by someone we can't see.

"Everything all right?" Ariel peeks in.

"Benni's spooked by the rocker," Mom says, still red from laughing.

"Oh." Ariel's smile stiffens as though he is unused to anything but praise.

"It's just a bit creepy, like a rocker out of a horror movie," I say. I only realize after that I may have been too candid, lulled into brief comfort by the humour Mom's found in the situation. I try to soften my tone. "It just looks old and…"

"It's antique," he rushes to say.

"Oh, Ariel, don't take offence." Mom pokes the rocker until it groans again. "Look at this thing. Is it yours?"

"No, it was Celeste's grandmother's."

"Is Celeste's grandmother still alive?" I ask, knowing the answer must be no. A rocking chair like that doesn't sit in a dark, windowless room without a deceased owner to haunt it.

"Yes. She lives in California."

"And yet at night you can still hear the rocker go, *cree-chee*, *cree-chee*, though no one is around to move it." Dad's voice precedes him as he creeps into the room.

"*Ay*, Ned, stop making up stories," Mom says, reaching out to swat his shoulder.

Dad dodges her attack. "But it's true. I've slept in rooms like this before. They have a certain vibe to them. The air is a little colder. The darkness is a little heavier."

I shiver, having noticed the room actually does feel a bit chillier than normal.

"*Palabiro ka, Tito* Ned," Ariel says. "Don't worry, Benni. If you hear anything unusual tonight, it'll just be your Dad."

"That's a given," Mom says. "He's so big, his footsteps sound like an earthquake."

"And yours sound like a tsunami, my dainty bride," Dad says.

I haven't seen Mom and Dad act this playful together in a long time. Perhaps Ariel senses the intimacy of the moment too, because he moves to the door.

"You two must be exhausted," he says to Mom and I. "What time is it in Toronto now?" His TV personality has ebbed, and his announcer's voice has relaxed. He now sounds like everyone else, like us.

"I think we're thirteen hours behind, making it eleven a.m. now," I say.

"So you haven't slept in over a day. You'll probably be jet-lagged for a while then. Don't worry; we'll take it easy on you. I assure you most of your visit will consist of eating, eating, and more eating anyways."

"Just the way I like it," Mom says.

"Just like a true Dychingco. I'll let the three of you get settled now. We really are so glad to have you all here." Without any showiness, Ariel kisses Mom and I on the cheek, shakes Dad's hand, and retreats.

12.

MOM TURNS TO ME AFTER DAD excuses himself for a smoke. "So, what do you think of your relatives?" she asks.

"They're nice," I say. My mind is barely functioning; the day's travel is catching up with me, and I'm exhausted.

Mom peeks behind her shoulder, verifying we're alone. "So, did you notice that Ariel is a tad flamboyant?" Mom asks, raising an eyebrow.

"Mom, now is definitely not the time to discuss this," I say.

"But Benni, he's as *arte* as a woman."

Despite how rude I feel Mom is being, I can't help but laugh. The Filipino word, *arte*, usually used to describe a high-maintenance fussy woman, is the perfect word for Ariel.

"Maybe you didn't get why I was surprised by Ariel's marriage, but surely you get it now."

I shrug, though Mom's dinner-table gossip is certainly more intriguing now that I've actually met the people she's talking about. "Who cares why Ariel married Celeste? He could have had a million reasons – to maintain a certain image, for her money, or maybe for, you know, love."

Mom waves her hand dismissively at the latter.

"What I'm curious to know is why Celeste married Ariel."

Mom looks at me as though I'm talking nonsense. "What do you mean?"

"I mean, why would Celeste marry Ariel? What would her incentive be? Love?"

"Maybe. Or convenience."

"What's the convenience? She's wealthier than him."

"Sometimes, you just want someone of your own to make a home with."

I think of Tom and don't press the matter further.

"Anyways, tell me everything," Mom says. "Did you talk to your relatives a lot? I saw you talking to Lisa before dinner. I hope you didn't say anything bad."

"What could I possibly say that would be bad?" I laugh. "We talked about work, school, and our drug habits."

"I'm not kidding. The things you may find normal in North America can easily offend Filipino sensibility. Be careful of what you say and how you act."

"I'm sure they're not much different from us, Mom."

"You'd be surprised."

"Or maybe you'd be surprised. Is the Philippines even the same as you remember it? You haven't been back in decades."

It doesn't seem like Mom hears me; at least, she doesn't respond. Instead, she says, "It's been a long day. I think we both need some rest," as she turns to leave.

"Why did you leave?" I ask before she goes.

"What do you mean?"

"Why did you move to Canada? Look at all this."

Mom turns to take in the antiquated pink room.

"Well, not necessarily this bedroom, but everything else – the house, the bejewelled decorations, the people to do everything for you. It's awesome."

"*Ate* Rosie got a lot of her wealth from her divorce, and the rest of the stuff was bought with Ariel and Celeste's money."

"But you kind of lived like this, right?"

"Kind of, but we didn't have such a big house. We had help, but everyone has help here. Even the help have help sometimes."

"Still, why leave?"

"I don't know, Benni. I like doing things for myself. *Ate* Rosie doesn't work. She just sits at the computer, checks Facebook all day, and simmers in anger over her bewitched husband." I think of Mom working in front of the TV all day and providing me with verbal updates from Facebook at night. Perhaps she guesses what I'm thinking about, because she adds, "At least I have the option in Canada to do something if I wanted to. Here, in the Philippines, you can't. You don't have the option to do anything at all as a woman. At least you're not supposed to. It's not proper."

This is the most progressive, North American comment I've heard Mom ever make, but I think of all the years she spent at home raising me and waiting for her husband to return and wonder if she's benefited at all from such ideals.

"What's not proper?" Dad asks, peeking in.

"I was just telling Benni how it's not usual for women to work in the Philippines. Mind you, Benni, the mindset has changed. For my generation, it was not common for us women to work. In this regard, at least, I liked breaking the rules. Who'd want to sit around waiting all day for the men to come home?"

"*If* we come home," Dad says, winking.

I'm sure he means to be playful, but Mom's look makes him pause. "You're right," Mom says. "If you come home."

I expect to fall asleep quickly when I get into bed, but I don't. Perhaps it's the unfamiliar atmosphere, imposing room, or cacophonous sound of Mom and Dad's snoring that is audible even two closed doors away. I wake throughout the night, unable to get comfortable. After what feels like hours of fitful sleep, I grab my music player, plug in my earphones, and turn it on. I don't usually listen to music at night but figure it can't hurt.

And then I hear another sound as the music begins to play. *Cree-chee.*

I freeze. My exhausted mind struggles to make sense of the foreign nighttime noises.

Cree-chee.

I remove my earphones and stare at the rocker. I stare at it for so long without blinking that coloured dots pollute my eyes, and I can't tell if I'm seeing spots or movement anymore. I put my earphones back in my ears.

Cree-chee.

I close my eyes and force myself to sleep.

13.

ROSE TASKS JERRY WITH TAKING Mom and Dad out to their old haunts the next day. "It'll be good for you to become reacquainted with your country, sister," she says.

"Will you be good to go in an hour, Benni?" Mom asks.

I look up from my slumped position on the sofa. The jet lag has caught up with me, and my poor sleep last night makes it feel like I'm functioning on my thirty-sixth hour of no sleep. "What? No. Why?"

"Aren't you coming?" she asks.

"No. Why?" I ask again. "I was thinking of napping."

"Don't leave me to do this alone, Benni," Mom says.

"Alone?" I want to protest. We're not in Canada anymore; we're in the Philippines. Even here, on vacation surrounded by family, I am still being accused of abandoning my mother. "Dad will be with you."

Mom glances at Dad, furtive and almost shy. I can see, just this once, why Mom doesn't want to do this alone. It's too much – this re-acquaintance with her husband, this mapping of new and old ground.

"Give me an hour," I grumble as I rise.

Not a single car passes on the road. The sprawling ground is fenced-off with a low-roofed building in old-Spanish fashion spanning the length of the enclosure. We stand on the grounds of Assumption: the all-girls school Mom and Rose attended.

It looks like an ancient monument to an earlier time of harder education.

Inside the grounds, our footsteps echo in the silence. I feel as though, at any minute, a bell will ring and girls will flood out of the school's doors.

"Let's go," Dad says. "I don't think anyone's here."

"If no one's here, then why was the gate unlocked?" Mom asks. "Let's look around."

Dad looks at me and rolls his eyes. We've shared this look countless times whenever Mom says something stupid or juvenile. But I'm with Mom on this one; I'm already looking and wandering around.

"Don't wander too far, Benni," Mom calls, but she doesn't sound too concerned. We're inside a gated all-girls' school and convent, after all.

I approach a door marked by a hand-carved sign that says *Banyo*. It's one Tagalog word I understand: "Washroom." I open the door to find beige tiles and an aged toilet and sink. I step into the washroom and am startled by the movement of my reflection in a mirror over the basin. I remember ghost stories about Assumption that Mom had told me when I was a child. Assumption was an old, haunted place, "filled mostly with kind ghosts, though," she had assured me. "It attracted the spirits of old nuns or girls who thought of Assumption as their home." One hall had been filled with the sound of footsteps and clicking rosary beads from the ghost of a long-passed nun. Another girl who'd passed away still appeared in every class picture until graduation. "The scariest story I've heard by far, though," Mom had said, "is of Assumption's haunted washroom. All the girls hated going in there because it gave them a creepy feeling. One girl was so afraid that she'd recite the 'Our Father' every time she went in. One time, though, when she looked into the mirror, she saw the face of an old crone repeating the 'Our Father' along with her in a mocking voice."

"I thought there were only kind ghosts in Assumption?" I had asked.

"I said there were *mostly* kind ghosts in Assumption. I hated that story," Mom had said, her cheeks trembling and leaving an even deeper impression on my seven-year-old mind. "God's supposed to protect you." She had, in that moment, seemed to forget that she was the mother and I was her impressionable child. "What does it mean if a ghost isn't even scared of the 'Our Father'?"

Mom's contemplation marked me. From then on, a small part of me had wondered what the point of praying was when even God couldn't scare away the scariest of ghosts.

I close the washroom door with a shudder. Mom never said which washroom here was haunted, but I don't want to take the risk. My shivers tell me it's possible this could be the washroom from the story.

I round a corner of the building to find a winding, stone-paved path lined by beautiful Egyptian star clusters and bright orange bougainvillea. It feels stiller here, away from the wandering voices of my parents. I spot a slight figure in the distance – a child, a small girl I think, dressed in white with her back to me. My footsteps resonate across the yard, but she doesn't stir. The closer I get to her, the more distinct she becomes. Her dress falls around her in white waves and her brown hair is fixed in an old-fashioned coif. No one else is nearby, and I wonder what this girl is doing here alone.

"Hello?" I ask. The longer her silence draws on, the colder I feel. "Excuse me?" I try again. I become as still as the girl. Goosebumps crawl up my arms. I hear footsteps behind me.

"Benni, what are you doing here?"

Mom's voice startles me into taking a couple of steps forward. "There's a..." I realize then that the girl is a statue. Her porcelain hair has faded into a weather-beaten brown, and her skirts are chipped and dirtied. "I thought she was real. I was spooked."

"She does look real," Mom says, squinting at the statue. "A bit on the short side, though, don't you think?"

I circle to the front of the statue. It's a rosy-cheeked white child with tight, wavy hair and a white smock. Her hand rests on a lamb standing next to her.

"Who is this?" I ask, suddenly not sure if it's a girl or a boy. "Is it Jesus as a boy?"

Mom keeps a statuette of Jesus as a boy on display in our living room in Canada because he wears a crown of real gold and there is gold thread embroidered along the hem of his velvet robe. He looks too girlish, though, with cheeks too pale, hair too blonde, and lips too pink. One of my earliest memories involve coming upon the statuette late at night. It left me with such a terrifying impression that I avoided that part of the house for a long time afterwards. I never understood why the artist made Jesus look the way he did, but Mom had explained that being blonde, fair, and fine-featured was a Filipino's interpretation of true beauty. Rendering Jesus in that fashion was, therefore, the artist's way of paying homage to God.

"No, this is definitely a girl. Look at her long lashes." Mom points out the heavy brown eyelashes painted on the tops and bottoms of the statue's eyes. They are dark compared to her weatherworn hair and look like spiders climbing out of her lids. "Maybe it's an idol for a saint."

"Does Assumption have a patron saint?"

"Not that I know of, but that may have changed."

"Or maybe the statue was erected in memory of one of Assumption's students who died young." Dad joins us, a cigarette in hand. "It must have been a tragic death for a statue to be erected. Poor girl," he says, shaking his head.

"You're really awful, Ned. I don't know where you get your ideas from."

"I'm a great storyteller, that's all."

"A great liar, perhaps," Mom says.

"My darling Maria, you should know by now that all my stories are true."

We leave the girl with her lamb. She is a sight to see and a sight we saw – nothing more than that. The fright she gave me was fleeting – the questions of who she is or was remain unanswered. The Philippines contains too many unanswerable questions to linger long on any one in particular.

We turn another corner of the building to find a fenced-in play area with swings. I spot a rusted structure at the back of the enclosed yard and approach to see it more closely. It's a large metal heart, at least two times my height, cracked and rusting. Within its metal structure are three smaller, suspended hearts. Metal-crafted words of HOPE, LOVE, and CHARITY are soldered within each one. Verdant vines grow in a tangle be-neath the structure. It's framed by two cactuses – surprisingly dangerous plants for a playground.

I approach the cactus on the right and reach my hand out to trace its scars. Names are etched into this cactus's skin with nails or pens: "Cora," "Gloria," "Loren," and "Mixi," among a few others. The cactus on the left is bare. Only the one on the right bears the names of girls who've been here. I use my thumbnail to scratch my name, fresh and bleeding, into the skin of the cactus on the right. As antiquated as the school feels, I like seeing my name on this living thing. It marks my place, as if I belong here, connecting me to a history of hope, love, and charity.

"Hope, love, and charity. Our three values."

The unfamiliar voice startles me. I turn to find a crooked nun standing at the entrance of the enclosure. Her arthritic fingers grip the back of a wooden chair with wheels. Mom and Dad are nowhere in sight. I flush, aware that I've been caught defacing convent property.

The nun shuffles to me, pushing the chair before her for bal-ance. "I've thought of getting a walker," she says in well-enun-ciated English.

I look up at her face guiltily, having been caught staring at her chair for too long. Her face is a map of cracks and valleys – a delicate web that shows how long she's done her time here on Earth. Cracks converge, more valleys form, and I realize she's smiling at me.

"But this thing is as good as any walker." The nun pats the worn chair and almost loses her balance as one of its wheels skip over a rock.

I rush forward, bridging the gap between her and I, and grasp her knobby elbow to keep her from falling.

"I'm okay," the nun says, drawing herself up to her full, osteoporotic height of four-foot-ten.

I release her arm.

"Are you here alone?"

It's her first question, and I realize I've allowed her to carry the entire conversation herself since I was caught vandalizing the cactus. I clear my throat before speaking, reluctant to break the silence and the mesmerizing effect of her distinct shuffling, her squeaking chair, and her calming voice. "No. I'm visiting with my parents though I don't know where they've gone."

"Ah, I see. Let me find them with you."

Now that we're standing side by side, she begins to turn the chair in a slow semi-circle towards the entrance of the enclosure. I prepare myself for a long walk.

"Usually visitors have reasons for coming," the nun says after a minute. "Have you ever been here before?"

"No, Sister," I say, recalling Mom's habit of referring to anyone of stature or rank by their proper title. "But my mother and grandmother used to attend Assumption."

"Is that so? What's your mother's name? I've been here a long, long time."

"My mother's name is Maria Manlapaz. Her maiden name is Dychingco. My grandmother's name was Amelia Dychingco. Her maiden name was Chengcuenca."

"Ah, yes. I remember Maria though I never taught her personally. And your grandmother.... Well, she's an old girl indeed. She was here with her sisters, right?"

"Yes," I say, though I hardly know anything about my maternal grandmother. I didn't even know she had sisters.

"Yes, it was a tragic tale. I began here as a nun just as she graduated. Amelia and I were about the same age, but her sisters were younger and stayed longer. Time has truly flown. How is she now?"

"She passed away before I was born."

The nun shakes her head. "Oh, Lord," she signs herself with the cross. "May her soul rest in peace. Too young, too young," she says, though when my grandmother died she was nearly eighty. "I always wonder where the girls go after they graduate, but I wondered about the Chengcuenca sisters in particular. They lived well, right?"

"Yes, I think so," I say, wondering if it's a graver sin to lie to a nun.

"That's good. The Chengcuenca family was always special."

"I'm sorry to ask, Sister, but why is that so?"

"You don't know?" the nun asks, raising her eyebrows in surprise.

"I suppose my grandmother's history never came up."

"It's important to know where you come from. Thankfully, I can tell you, and it seems we have a bit of time." At the pace she's walking, we have only just reached the enclosure's entrance. "As I'm sure you know, Assumption girls were often from wealth or power. The Chengcuencas were part of the wealthiest and most powerful of Philippine circles. They were actually one of Assumption's primary funders, and the Chengcuenca girls were some of the first girls to attend Assumption College."

I hadn't heard of this wealth before. I knew Rose was rich because of her ex-husband's money, but much of Mom's childhood sounded middle class and average.

"The Chengcuencas were charitable people but, poor souls,

their wealth, as it so often does, begot envy. Your great-grand-parents were murdered." The nun shakes her head and kisses her rosary, ignoring my look of shock. "They were shot in their own home. It seemed to be a random house invasion, but who knows how true that story was. It was lucky that the Chengcuenca children were playing outside at the time and avoided their parents' fate. In the end, though, money was needed here or there, properties needed to be paid for, debts accounted for, and all the Chengcuenca's power and wealth disappeared. None of the children were old enough to under-stand what was happening or to stop their home from being taken from them."

"Were there no family members to take care of them?"

"The kids were too many, and the other Chengcuencas lived in Spain. Since the Chengcuencas were old girls though, the nuns took them in. All their fees were waived, and they studied and lived in Assumption until they were of age."

"So my grandmother was in a family full of girls. That's fortunate."

"Oh, no, there were Chengcuenca boys, too, but they were placed into orphanages."

"That's horrible."

"It is, but Assumption's an all-girls school, dear."

"So, what happened to the boys? Did they go to good fam-ilies?"

"Not that I know of. No one really wanted to adopt children over the age of five. That's the way it is, even now. So the boys ended up on the streets. They had hard lives."

"That's terrible."

"Such is the way of the world. We are products of our cir-cumstances."

The nun's statement strikes me. I often wondered growing up if I would have been different if only I'd been born into a Canadian family, or one where Mom worked full-time and Dad stuck around like normal parents did.

The nun takes my silence as a pause for more and says, "Such is the way of life." She allows another moment of silence to pass. "Shall we move along?" she finally asks.

I hadn't realized I'd stopped walking.

I expect to find more walkways and flowers around the final corner of the school, but instead, I find two brown bungalows. Mom and Dad stand beneath the narrow strip of shade that the roof of the main building provides.

"Where on earth were you?" Dad yells, his hand shielding his eyes. Dark sweat rings his neck. "How could you heartless harlot leave us out here for so long? What were you doing?" He spots the nun. "Oh, sorry, Sister. *Kamusta po kayo?*"

"Sorry to keep you two waiting. Your daughter and I were having a nice chat."

Despite the depressing nature of our chat, I smile.

"That's quite all right, Sister," Mom says.

"Maria Dychingco, you look exactly the same," the nun says. "I'm so pleased to see you again."

"Thank you, Sister," Mom says. She looks so happy at being recognized that I decide not to share that I told the Sister her name earlier. "Sister, this is my husband, Eduardo."

"Pleasure to meet you, Eduardo. I apologize for being the heartless harlot that caused you to wait here for so long." The nun smiles and turns back to Mom, ignoring Dad's blushing face. "I knew your mother when she attended school here, Maria. You're just as beautiful as I remember her to be. Your resemblance to her is uncanny."

Mom beams. "Where are you heading, Sister?"

"I'm just going to my dorm," the nun says, pointing to one of the bungalows across from us.

"We'll walk you," Mom offers.

The nun protests but eventually accepts our accompaniment. We approach the brown bungalow furthest from us at a snail's pace, and with each step I am filled with an overwhelming sadness at the thought of leaving. Assumption fills me with a longing to belong and a sense of having missed an important rite of passage. Generations of women in my family attended Assumption College before me. An irrational part of me believes that, had I attended Assumption, I'd have gained nobility and history in a world where currently I have none. The one chance to do so, however, has passed. Having already finished school, I can never belong to the college in my own right or have a history of my own here.

"What a sweet nun," Mom says after we leave her. "And so cute, too."

"Poor old thing," Dad adds. "I'm going to send her a walker."

The thought is nice, but I know the likelihood of Dad sending the nun a walker is next to none.

"Anyways, I don't mean to break up the party, but I'm melting. Let's move on," he says, turning to the gate.

Assumption days are over.

14.

A S WE DRIVE AWAY FROM ASSUMPTION, Dad points out a low-rise apartment building at the edge of a busy street. "Look, that's one of Mommy's apartments," he says.

"What do you mean?" I ask. The building is a nondescript rectangle with beige metal balconies. It has the universal look of quickly built housing.

"Daddy sent home a lot of cash when he worked for the United States government during the Second World War," Dad says. "He was the breadwinner, but Mommy was the bread baker. She invested all the money. She built this apartment and a few others for extra income when *Kuya* Miguel and I were in our teens." Dad's older brother, Miguel, was his best friend and partner in crime growing up. "We were still gathering rent from this building's tenants until recently."

"And then what happened?"

"Mommy sold the building to invest in the hospital and to help out with Daddy's nursing home fees."

"It's too bad you sold it. I would've liked to live here. Actually, I've been thinking of moving here," I say, putting words to the nagging feeling I've had since entering Assumption.

Dad snorts. "You? Here?"

"What's so good about Canada?" I ask, voicing for the first time what I've been wondering since Tom and I split up.

"I'm there," Mom says.

"What's so good about Canada that you want to live there?"

I ask Mom. "It seems everything is here. Your sister, your…"
I'm about to say "your husband" when Mom cuts me off.

"You're there," she says.

"Well, that solves the problem. We can move here together."

"Moving isn't so easy, Benni," Dad says.

"Says the man who moves every other year," I say. Not
wanting to sour the moment, I move on. "Anyways, owning
property would've certainly taken care of some of the hassle."

"It's not a nice place anymore. Look at it." We've already
passed the building, but Dad cranes his neck to look at it one
more time. "It was nicer when I lived there, that's for sure."

"You lived there? Why weren't you living with *Lola* Ofelia?"

"I was attending the University of the Philippines. Living in
the apartment was like living on campus, I guess."

"Really?" I say, unable to mask my sudden flare of anger at
this new revelation. I attended a nearby university because I
was forbidden to live on campus. I always thought the strict
rule against moving out before marriage was a Filipino thing,
but apparently it was just a Mom and Dad thing.

"*Kuya* Miguel lived with me too."

"You guys were roommates?"

"No, he lived in the apartment beside mine. He got the
best unit – the corner one," Dad says, as though not living in
the corner unit makes up for the hypocrisy of his and Mom's
longstanding rules.

"Sounds like a tough life. Pretty unfair that you kept me from
moving out all these years." I know I sound childish, picking
fights that ended years ago. But seeing snippets of Mom and
Dad's childhood makes me feel how much less colourful mine
has been in comparison.

"Canada's a free country last I checked, Benni," Dad says.
"You could've gone off on your own if you wanted to."

"And then who would've been home with Mom?"

"Your mother's a grown woman," Dad says, but Mom doesn't
respond, and we drop the subject.

Not for the first time today, I feel the pang of loss. Even if Dad and Mom say life is more dangerous in the Philippines, so far all it sounds like is an easier, more expansive lifestyle than the harried everyday of Canada. I didn't get to live on campus or in my own bachelor apartment. I didn't live in a place where my family built and owned multiple properties or where people chauffeured me around and cooked my meals. No, I got to live in a bland, small-town suburb where the idea of excitement is meeting your boyfriend at Tim Hortons for lunch only to go home to your lonely mother at the end of the night.

As though detecting the tension in the car, Jerry speaks up. "Here we are," he says.

"What is this?" I ask, staring blankly at the church before us.

"It's St. Mary the Queen Parish – the church where your mother and I got married," Dad says, sounding tired from our confrontation.

"It looks much the same, except for all this construction," Mom says. Scaffolding climbs the church's walls. The parking lot is pitted and, in some places, stripped. Ever since we arrived in the Philippines, Mom has been saying that things look the same, other than this or that change.

"I think they're making improvements," Jerry says.

Mom sniffs as though to say the church can't be improved from the church it was in her marital splendour. For all of Mom's stories of growing up in a century-old cloistered convent, the church she chose to marry in is a modern, art deco building done in shades of blue.

I walk into the church and find a strong sense of familiarity. It gives me a jolt to realize that the church where Mom and Dad married is similar to my childhood church in Georgina — the church where I had thought Tom and I would marry. I turn in the aisle to view the entire building and notice a second-floor balcony at the back. Blue metal is worked into the outline of crosses below its banister.

"Stay right here," I say, pacing along the back of the church until I reach a knee-high gate to the steps upstairs. I hop the gate and take the steps by two. Diffused light streams onto the second floor from three stained glass windows. I pull out my camera, crouch down before the wire cross at the centre of the balcony, and aim the camera lens through it. Mom and Dad wander the aisle below me.

"Mom, Dad, smile," I call.

They turn.

Almost twenty-six years ago, Mom and Dad's wedding photographer took a picture much like this one after their vows were spoken and the church cleared. Mom, dressed in white lace, and Dad, in his bell-bottomed tux, smiled up as they were framed by the cross. The older I get, the more Mom and Dad look like children playing pretend on their wedding day. Married at twenty-four – younger than I am now – they looked innocent and unaware. I find it sad seeing them, so many decades later, turned toward me with nostalgic smiles on their faces after a day of fantasizing how life would've been if only they had stayed, or perhaps made different choices, or said different vows.

"How did you know that we took a photo like this before?" Dad asks.

"I've seen the photos, of course," I say. I centre Mom and Dad in the cross's narrow bottom. I zoom out to fit their bulk.

"Now, let's take one together," he says, opening his arms wide.

"We won't fit," I say, "and there's no one else here to take our photo."

"We could ask Jerry," Mom suggests.

"It's all right. It's too much hassle," Dad says.

I watch him lower his arms and walk away.

15.

I SPEND THE FIRST FEW MINUTES of our drive from St. Mary's with my fingers braced against the seat in front of me. Jerry manoeuvres the minivan through thick crowds, along tight roads, and around sharp corners. It feels like we're on a roller coaster hurtling around unfenced edges.

Dad sits sideways in the passenger seat so he can look back and forth between the front and rear windows. His smile grows with each turn. "This area looks familiar," he says. "I think I crashed *Kuya* Miguel's bike somewhere near here." Growing up, Miguel taught Dad how to use all his dangerous toys – guns, motorcycles, and women – but he settled down as the years progressed while Dad continued living the same wild life of his teens. We used to see Miguel, his wife, and my cousins often when I was a kid since they only live forty-five minutes south of us in Ontario. But we hardly see them anymore.

"When did this happen?" I ask.

"Many years ago. I borrowed *Kuya* Miguel's bike to take a girl out on a date."

"I suppose your date wasn't with Mom, right?" Whenever Dad shares one of his bad-boy stories, Mom makes it clear that, no matter what Dad did when they were younger, she was always a lady. God forbid she ride on his motorcycle, where her back end would be exposed for others to see.

"No, I wasn't on a date with your mom. I was on a date with another woman. This one always wore the tightest hip-huggers.

All the guys would turn to look when she walked by. When she'd sit on the back of a bike her..."

"Ned, what's the point of this story?" Mom asks.

"Anyways," Dad continues, "we were riding on a busy road much like this one. I was taking the turns quickly..."

"Why? Were you trying to impress her, Dad?"

"No, why would I try to impress her?" Dad scoffs. "I'm naturally impressive. Anyways, I was taking the turns quickly when we hit a pothole in the road. It was unexpected. You could hardly see it from the bike."

"Though if you were driving properly, you probably could have avoided it," Mom says.

"So we hit the pothole and the bike spins out. I remember hurtling towards a building and thinking to myself, 'This is it. We're going to die and end up taking a whole bunch of other people in the building with us.' And then the bike's front wheel hit a jeepney that somehow snuck through all the mayhem, and we came to a complete stop."

"Was anyone in the jeepney hurt?"

"The jeepney was empty except for the driver. He had a bit of whiplash. We were pretty lucky."

"And the girl?"

"She was bruised and shaken but otherwise okay."

"And then what happened?"

Dad shrugs. "I don't know. The bike wasn't drivable, so I called *Kuya* Miguel to come get me. He was furious that I totalled his bike, but he couldn't be too mad after seeing the state we were in."

"Did you ever go out with that girl again?"

Dad smiles but doesn't reply.

Just beyond the minivan's windows, a mess of people go about their business in a country lacking enforced traffic rules or vehicle safety measures.

"Can I drive?" Dad asks, turning to Jerry.

Jerry smiles. "Of course, *po*. If you want."

Dad grasps the door handle in anticipation, as though ready to exit the minivan immediately and take the wheel.

"Ned, you think you can drive like you could before, but..."

"What do you mean? I drive everywhere. I've driven us twenty-four hours straight to Florida. I've taken overnight drives to Ottawa after ten-hour flights. I've..."

"That was long ago, Ned, when you were younger. You don't even drive here anymore. And now you want to drive after telling us the story of how you crashed on a road similar to this one and almost killed yourself and your passenger? You want to take the wheel with me and our daughter in the minivan? Do you want to kill us all? Just sit still."

Dad removes his hand from the door handle and stares forward without responding. The car falls into silence. I lean back in my seat and close my eyes. The car's movement makes me feel as though I'm on a boat riding in circles on violent waves. It's enough to make me want to vomit.

The silence doesn't last long with Dad in the car. "Hey, Princess," Dad says.

I open my eyes to find him turned around again, addressing me in particular.

"Did I ever tell you about the time *Kuya* Miguel and I were driving along Manila's city streets late at night?"

"Of course," Mom says, "if you two were together, then you surely got in some sort of trouble."

"I don't remember exactly which road it was, Princess," Dad says, ignoring Mom, "but it was late at night, and hardly any cars were around. *Kuya* Miguel was driving and I was in the passenger's seat. I was the first one to spot her – a blonde woman jogging, wearing a sports bra and tight shorts. She had a nice, fit body..."

"Oh, God," Mom groans. "Is there no end to the stories of hot young things in tight pants with their underwear showing? You're an old, grown man, for heaven's sake."

"Well, I'm just telling it like it is," Dad says, acknowledging

Mom again. "If she were a dumpy old crone in baggy clothes, we probably wouldn't have stopped. As it was, after I pointed her out to *Kuya* Miguel, we rolled down the window and said hello."

"'Said hello?'" Mom snorts. "Is that what you call whistles and catcalls?"

"Well, no matter what you want to call it, we greeted her and offered her a ride. She stood out, and it wasn't a safe place or time for any girl to be jogging."

"You're a pair of knights in shining armor, aren't you?" Mom says.

"Of course." Dad nods, smiles and, intentionally or not, misses the sarcasm in Mom's voice. "Anyway, you wouldn't believe what we saw." He pauses, waiting for us to ask him more.

"What did you see? That she was actually a man?" Mom asks.

"No. We slowed down until we were level with her, but her face was hidden by her hair. I kept calling out to her, asking her to join us, until she stopped. We parked the car, sure she would come in, but she just turned toward us." Dad rubs away goosebumps that have sprouted along his arms. "And she had no face."

Mom snorts again. "No face? How could she have no face?"

"I don't know. It was just a…" Dad struggles to find words to describe the faceless jogger. "A dark hole. A blankness. We didn't have to say anything to each other. *Kuya* Miguel floored the gas pedal, and we were out of there. We never drove through that road late at night again."

"Good. That serves you two right. At least that was one less headache for your mother."

"What a silly story," I say. "A woman with no face? How is that even possible?"

"I don't know how it's possible, but I know what we saw. That place was rumoured to be haunted, too."

The minivan finally falls into a comfortable silence with Mom's refusal forgotten and Dad's latest story bizarre enough to provide food for thought. I keep my eyes closed, avoiding thoughts of reckless Filipino drivers or faceless jogging spirits.

The next thing I know, it's dark outside, there are no street lights in sight, and we're still in the minivan.

"I'm sure it's close," Dad says.

"Or did we pass it?" Mom asks.

"No, I'm sure it's further along."

"How can you tell? Everything is dark. We wouldn't know if we missed a turn."

"It's a brightly lit corner."

"Or it *was* a brightly lit corner."

I blink the sleep from my eyes. "Where are we?" I ask. It feels like I've woken up in a dream.

"Carmona," Mom says.

"I see," I say, but I can't see anything at all. The name of our location has no meaning or presence for me.

"We're visiting Dad's cousin," Mom explains.

"Cousin? Which cousin?" Though a talkative man by nature, Dad never mentioned much about his extended family in his many stories.

"A Manlapaz cousin."

"A Manlapaz cousin? Are you close to him?"

"Her," Dad corrects me.

"Her!" The idea of a female Manlapaz is appalling when I think of my stern grandfather, raucous boy cousins, or Dad and all of his alpha-male endeavours with Miguel. I had naively assumed all of my relations on Dad's side were men until now.

"Yes, *her,* and we are – or at least were – very close to her. We used to see each other every weekend when we were kids. She was a tomboy and fit in with us well. I haven't spoken to her in years though."

"She kept them in line," Mom says. "You wouldn't want to cross her. She's as loud as your father, if not louder, and ten times stronger, I'm sure."

"Hey, now. Watch what you say about these guns," Dad says, flexing an arm.

"Easy there, stud." Mom laughs.

We fall silent again with Dad on alert. It feels odd counting time in long, dark, empty seconds without the markers of trees, street lights, or lines on the road passing us by. Just when I'm also about to ask if we missed our destination, we come upon one streetlight, and then another, a pothole here, a guardrail there, a stoplight, and then…

"Here! Turn here!" Dad exclaims.

Jerry makes a tight right turn onto a narrow street. Gated houses line one side of the road, mirrored by parked cars along the other.

"Drive slowly," Dad says. His hand is raised and ready to signal a halt at any moment. The houses we pass are far older and more worn than those in Forbes Park. "Wait, slow down," Dad says.

Jerry complies, though the minivan is barely inching forward.

I study the gates, trying to glean from small details which one would contain Dad's closest female cousin, until I realize Dad's not even looking at the houses. Instead, he's gazing at the opposite side of the road where a lady with flowing black hair is getting out of a parked SUV. The closer we get to her, the brighter she becomes. The minivan's beams frame her as she crosses the street.

"Ned, what are you doing? Is that her?" Mom asks.

"I don't know," Dad says. "I can't see her face." Under the minivan's lights, the lady's features are washed out into white skin and black hair. Dad waves at Jerry. "Put the headlights on low. They're blinding in this darkness."

Jerry lowers the headlights, throwing the lady into soft, yellow relief, but her face is hidden now in a curtain of hair as she bends to look at her cellphone.

Dad reaches for the door handle.

"Wait, Ned."

Dad glances back at Mom.

"What if it's not her? This woman could be crazy. She could have a knife."

I laugh, but it's more out of habit than mirth. Though Mom's over-exaggeration often ruins her credibility, it's hard to know what exaggeration is while we idle on this dark street before a faceless woman. While Mom worries about knives, I worry about ghosts, so I strain forward in my seat in the hopes of seeing the woman's face. In most stories I've heard, ghosts confront people alone, but Dad and Miguel were together the night they saw the faceless jogger. Are we all seeing a ghost together?

Never one to heed advice, Dad gets out of the car. He forgets to close the door, and the silence of outside seeps into the minivan.

Dad steps forward, metres away from the lady who is still fidgeting with her phone. "Hey!" he calls.

She doesn't turn around. It's as though she hasn't heard him.

"Hey, stop!" Dad yells.

The woman keeps walking. She crosses us like an image. I can't hear her footsteps on the road or the sound of her voice, though her phone is at her ear now. Do ghosts use technology? I've never heard of a ghost with a cellphone before.

"Melissa, is that you? It's Ned."

The woman turns. Her face is thrown into sharp relief, revealing a long, hooked nose, wide mouth, and slanted eyebrows that make her look angry. I think for a moment that she will lash out at Dad after all with a knife, a hex, or a string of curses.

The moment passes. The woman still does not speak. She squints her eyes against the van's headlights.

"Ned," Dad says again, though he sounds unsure of who he actually is. "Eduardo Manlapaz."

"Ned? *Puñeta!*" Her voice is brash in the night.

A lanky boy emerges from a house on the right. The squeaking sound of the rusty gate calls everyone's attention.

"Bobby, it's okay. I know this man," she says.

The boy stops but doesn't leave, squinting at Dad from behind the wrought iron.

"I can't believe you," Melissa says, running forward to smack Dad's arm with such force that we hear its contact in the minivan. "*Pu-ñe-ta*!" With each syllable she hits him again.

"What? What did I do?" Dad protests.

"I called Bobby for help. I thought you were following me."

"We were."

"When you turned off your lights, I thought, 'Surely I will be mugged or hurt tonight.'"

"We didn't turn off our headlights. We only dimmed them."

Melissa lets out a roar and continues beating Dad. We watch transfixed as Dad puts up a feeble fight. His hands are ineffectual shields against the blows.

"Mrs. Manlapaz, maybe you should help him," Jerry says.

Mom climbs out of the minivan, but Melissa doesn't notice or stop her assault until Mom walks in front of the minivan's headlights and throws the road into momentary darkness. Melissa squints at Mom's backlit figure.

"Melissa, leave some for me," Mom calls.

"Maria!" Melissa yells. She runs to Mom, gathering her in a fierce embrace before pulling back to look her over. "You look just the same as always."

"Just the same, except a few pounds heavier," Mom says.

"Hardly a couple."

Mom laughs, smoothing her hands over her figure, which is a far cry from the ninety-five pounds she weighed when she and Dad married.

"Let's get off the road. Come in. Tell your driver to park. I didn't even know you two were in town." Melissa waves to the boy by the gate. "*Hoy*, Bobby, get some coffee ready." She turns back to Mom and Dad, casting another glance over to the minivan. "Are you two alone?"

"No, our daughter is in the minivan," Mom says. "We just

stopped over from a visit to St. Mary the Queen Parish. Benni, come out."

Without needing further instruction, Jerry pulls over to wait for us on the side of the road. I fix my hair and straighten my clothes before stepping outside. With Jerry parked, we're left in relative darkness as introductions are made.

Before Mom can say anything, Melissa points a knobby finger at me. "You, young woman, look just like someone I know, but I can't put my finger on it."

"Melissa, this is our daughter, Maria Benedictine," Mom says.

"Hello, it's nice to meet you," I say. I move forward to kiss Melissa's cheek, but she places a hand on my shoulder to keep me at arm's length.

She lays a finger on my nose. "There's something about your nose that makes me feel like I've seen it before. Ned, you must know who I'm talking about."

"No." Dad shrugs.

"Typical man," Melissa grunts.

I tilt my head, hoping to receive more light from the nearby streetlight to end Melissa's close scrutiny.

"You look like…" Melissa trails off before snapping her fingers. "Aha! You look like *Lola* Baday. Holy camoly, Eduardo. You've created a small *Lola* Baday."

Dad looks at me as though seeing me for the first time. "You're right, Melissa," he says in wonderment. "You do look like *Lola* Baday, Benni. I never noticed it before."

"Once again, I must point out Exhibit A – your typical man," Melissa says, gesturing at Dad and rolling her eyes.

"Who is *Lola* Baday?" I ask.

"She was our grandmother," Dad says. "Your great-grandmother, Benni."

"I'm sure I have a picture of her in a photo album somewhere," Melissa says. "Come in, and I'll show you."

"Melissa, it's kind of you to offer us a drink, but we can't stay long," Mom says.

"Nonsense. I'm sure you can stay for coffee at least."

"Coffee isn't necessary."

"Maria, don't make me beat you, too. You've arrived home from God-knows-where, after disappearing since God-knows-when, without a word of warning for God-knows-why. I'm already ticked off that I couldn't have dinner with you, so you better take the coffee." Melissa raises her eyes to the sky every time she says "God," making it look like she's gone into a prolonged and violent fit during her speech.

Dad smiles at Mom, shrugs, and follows Melissa inside.

16.

WE PASS THROUGH A SMALL, UNLIT yard scattered with stones and crawling vines. The garden is a wild patch of grass and flowers. We enter into Melissa's brightly-lit foyer before she ushers us into a small sunroom where we take our seats on a mishmash of plush velvet sofas, hardback chairs, and plaid recliners. Bobby enters carrying a tray loaded with a coffee pot and mugs and sets them on the coffee table before leaving us alone.

Melissa re-enters shortly after with four leather-bound albums. "I must have a picture of *Lola* Baday here somewhere," she says, dropping the albums on the floor. Two albums splay open, revealing ordered rows of black-and-white photographs tinged yellow. Melissa flips through album pages, making the book a blur of fading faces in her hands. "*Lola* Baday, *Lola* Baday, *Lola* Baday," she says, almost like an invocation. Her hair settles around her in disarray. Melissa notices us watching her when she is halfway through the second album. "What are you doing? You," she points at Dad, "you, and you," she says, pointing at Mom and I, "drink some coffee. Drink and enjoy!"

By the time Dad pours coffee for us, Melissa's finished looking through all four albums. She stands to take the pot from Dad before he can set it down.

"It's really odd that I don't have a picture of *Lola* Baday," she says, pouring herself a cup of coffee. "I could've sworn I had one somewhere." She squints at me and holds a hand up as though to frame me in her vision. "Benni, you are the spitting image of our grandmother, as absent from family record as she may be. I'm tempted to take a photo of you and put it in our album. I'll label it 'Lola Baday' and pour some coffee on it to make it look old. No one will be any the wiser that I don't seem to have any pictures of her at all." She flops onto a plaid recliner across the table from us, slopping coffee over her cup's rim. She catches the spill using the palm of her hand. "Are your coffees okay?" she asks. "Would you like anything else? Something to snack on, perhaps?"

"Not unless you have something hard. Rum, vodka, or brandy, perhaps?" Dad asks.

Melissa laughs. "Funny one, Ned. You're a real joker. Though I do remember your preferred drink of choice from when you weren't such an old man. B&B. Bénédictine and brandy, right? Coincidence that that's your name?" she asks, turning to me with a wink. "I think not." She settles further into her recliner. "Anyway, when did you all arrive? When are you leaving? And how long has it been since you've been home?"

"Benni and I just arrived," Mom says. "We'll be leaving in a few weeks, and it's been twenty-six years since we've last been home." Both Mom and Dad fail to mention that Dad's been living here for more than a year, and the conversation barrels on.

"Twenty-six years? Why did you wait so long?" Melissa asks. "I must say, Ned, I never took you and Maria for the sea-going types – the ones who would jump ship and never look back."

"Are you kidding me? You know I always wanted to leave the Philippines," Dad says. But that's news to me. As far as my recollection goes, Dad always wanted to return here. I had always assumed he donned rose-coloured glasses of nostalgia for the Philippines the moment he left. "And what a world there is to see, Melissa.... The pyramids in Egypt and the glaciers in Alaska, the canals of Venice and the Alhambra in

Granada, the cars in Monaco and the ladies in Vegas." Dad smacks his lips. "There's so much to see and so many lives to live beyond Manila."

I do a mental check of all the places Dad mentions as he speaks. He's been all over the world: North and South America, Asia, Africa, Europe, Australia, and Antartica. I have the souvenirs to prove it: a little plastic pyramid, a stuffed Penguin toy, casino chips, postcards with foreign stamps, and more hotel stationery than I can count. He's been everywhere, but the most exotic place Mom and I have ever been is here.

"You make it sound grand, but you're missing out on a lot, Ned," Melissa says, throwing an arm out in a showcase gesture of her darkened sunroom. "Especially living in Canada. What do you do in Canada anyways? Ice skate? Build snowmen? You can skate in our malls, for goodness' sake. I bet they don't have skating rinks in the malls in Canada."

I think of Georgina, where the idea of fun for most people I know is a bush party in the summer and Netflix in the winter.

"No. We don't have skating rinks in the malls, but it's only because we have plenty of space for them naturally outside," Dad says. "Anyways, I can't build snowmen in the mall. So there."

I've never seen Dad build a snowman in my life. My winter memories consist of him complaining about the bitter cold as he smoked in his undershirt and boxers with his belly resting over the railing of our back deck.

"Actually, I think SM Mall had a promo recently where they made fake snow for snow angels and snowmen, so you're really not gaining anything in Canada after all. The Philippines has everything – fun, food, and family – though somehow you managed to convince your dad to leave with you before he passed away and Miguel to follow you shortly after. All that good Manlapaz blood, gone, and not a word from you men since you left."

"Oh, Melissa, what would you expect from the Manlapaz men? Daily phone calls?" Mom laughs. What she doesn't say is that even she and I – Dad's wife and daughter – don't hear regularly from him.

"Typical men," Melissa scoffs again. "I suppose not. I do wish you all stayed though. Tell me how you've been."

Dad gives Melissa a summary of our lives, and the lives of Miguel and my grandmother, failing to mention that he's lived anywhere but Canada in the past ten years. It's surreal hearing the surface stories I've told him about my school, work, and hobbies repeated almost verbatim by Dad with such ease. I'm surprised to learn he'd listened at all, and though I know better, I could almost be convinced that he'd been there for it all, too.

Like a typical man, perhaps, Dad doesn't ask about Melissa's family when he's done but instead sets his cup down with a deep sigh and says, "I suppose we should be going now. We shouldn't stay too long with the driver waiting outside."

"I suppose it's getting late," Melissa says. "I wish you told me you were coming so we could've spent more time together. I would have invited you all over for dinner."

"It's okay. It's just nice to say hello," Dad says.

"Of course. I'm glad you came," Melissa says, walking with us to the foyer. "I'm sorry you didn't get to see *Lola* Baday, Benni. You'll just have to believe me when I say that you look just like her."

"It's okay. Maybe next time," I say, but I can't imagine we'll ever meet again.

Dad paces behind Melissa as if he is trying to trace and re-trace his steps for memory later. He stops. "Melissa, isn't that *Lola* Baday?" he asks, pointing at a wall displaying multiple portraits.

"Ned, you're right! I can't believe I overlooked this." Melissa laughs. "I see it so often that I tend to forget it's here. I knew she was in the house somewhere. Benni, meet *Lola* Baday. Doesn't she look just like you?" Melissa points at the large centre portrait. Its colours are faded and dusty. Baday, old and matronly, is seated beside a thin, dark man in a black suit. She wears the traditional Filipiniana dress with its puffed sleeves and bodacious skirt. I try to find my face in her face, my features in her stern ones.

"I suppose she does look like me," I say, and yet I'm not sure if she does or if I just want her to.

Dad moves me beside the portrait. "You're the spitting image of her, Princess. I can't believe I didn't notice it before. I remember *Lola* Baday so clearly now. She was a smiley-eyed, pale-skinned woman with sharp features and a laughing mouth, just like you."

There isn't a hint of a smile on Baday's face. I've never heard of her before today. Though I can't find any resemblance between Baday and myself, it's nice to think I may look like someone in the family. I study Baday again. "It's nice to know where my features come from," I say. "I guess I wasn't switched at birth after all."

"Who told you that?" Melissa asks.

"My Manlapaz cousins," I say, remembering Miguel's kids and the days we used to see each other regularly. "They told me that the nurses switched me in the hospital. They said Mom's real baby lost her ID, and since they used to put all newborns in one room, they accidentally picked up another baby with missing ID and gave her to Mom instead. They said my parents decided to keep me since they didn't figure out what happened until later, but that's why I look so different from all the other Manlapazes. They would say, 'All the nurses used to call you "China Doll," just like your mom said, but they called you that because you're really Chinese,'" I mimic their teasing voices. Though humorous now, my cousins' cajoling used to really worry me. I could never find the resemblance between myself and my relatives, with my curly hair, my fair skin, and my pointed features, all of which was so unlike any of the Dychingcos or Manlapazes.

"That's an awful thing to tell a child. Sounds like the work of Miguel's kids, all right," Melissa says.

"Manlapaz cousins," Dad says grinning. "Aren't they just the worst?"

Melissa punches Dad's arm. "Well, no fear, Benni. You're Manlapaz through and through."

There are seven enlarged photos surrounding my great-grand-parents' portrait – wedding photos of couples and graduation photos of those who presumably stayed single. Though they must have all been relatively young when these photos were taken, the women look stern and handsome and the men wizened and gaunt. The faded portraits give the impression of an infinite amount of time and wisdom having passed and gone before reaching us today; surely, I have never been able to muster such a regal look. Their assured smiles and strong countenances convince me that uncertainty must be a modern disease.

"Is this Mommy and Daddy?" Dad asks, pointing at the furthest portrait on the left.

"That's them," Melissa says.

"I thought I knew those faces," Dad says, gazing at his parents. "That's your *Lola* Ofelia and *Lolo* Pepe, Benni, and *Lolo* Pepe's six siblings."

"I didn't know he had so many, and *Lola* Ofelia looked so young when she married. I can't wait to meet her."

"You haven't brought Benni to visit your mother yet, Ned?" Melissa asks, rounding on Dad.

"We haven't had time to bring Benni there yet. She's only been here a day. Anyway, seeing Mommy is as fun as stubbing a toe. You know how she can be."

"That's no excuse, Ned. After twenty-six years, it's import-ant to go, and it's important for Benni, too. Benni, it's good to know where you come from and how you ended up where you are now." Melissa pats Dad's back. "Next time you come back, Ned, let me know. Say hi to your mom for me when you go, and send my love to those in Canada. Benni, if you're ever in the area, be sure to knock on my door. You can stay here. We'll have lots of fun." She gives me a tight hug. It's as if we've known each other all our lives.

Though we only stayed for half an hour, it hurts to leave a place where I found my blood. I suppose a silly part of me always felt like a misplaced child, unrelated to my family and heritage. Here, in this packed room, I can find my face in another's, and I'm so happy to see its reflection.

We climb into the minivan and don't speak again until we've turned off Melissa's street.

"It's funny," Dad says, turning to look at me again. "I never thought you looked like *Lola* Baday before, but you really do."

"I couldn't tell from the portrait."

"Don't worry. The portrait doesn't show much, but I remember her well, and you're just like her in looks and personality. She was stubborn and adventurous just like you."

I nod, though I'll never know if it's true.

"Come to think of it, you kind of look like Melissa, too," Mom says.

"And you act just as weird," Dad says.

"She's an odd one, isn't she?" Mom laughs.

"You've been here for a while, Dad," I say, voicing something that's been bugging me since we arrived at Melissa's house. "Why didn't you visit her earlier? You let her believe you've been away for so long." I can't quite bring myself to say what's been bugging me most: *you made it sound like you were around for me when you weren't.*

Dad shrugs. "I guess I never made the time when I first moved back. And, as time progressed, I wanted to return with you two." Dad turns and smiles at me. "A man needs to return in all his splendour after leaving his home country the way I did. You're my crown, Benni, and your mom's my sceptre. Can't arrive properly without that, right?"

Mom clucks her tongue. "Smooth talker *naman*. What a line."

"There's a difference between a line and the truth."

"Sure." Mom laughs. "Keep going."

I close my eyes as Jerry drives back to Forbes Park, only half-listening to Mom and Dad's banter. Both Melissa and the old nun had said, "It's good to know where you come from." Though I know now who I may look like, I still feel too detached from a history that happened leagues away from what's supposed to be my home. I can't help but think of how eerie Melissa seemed on the street, like a figment, a spirit, a shade of a person, a ghost. She was only made real when we approached her, spoke to her, and connected her in relation to Dad's past. That's what history does for you. It makes things real. If I don't have a real history of my own, does that mean I'm hardly real myself? And how do I go about getting one?

I think of the apartments we passed earlier today and set my mind on change. It's time for something different; it's time for a move.

17

LISA AND I EAT BREAKFAST AT a small table on the balcony. The rest of the family eats inside. "Who wants to be outside?" Ariel asked when we invited him to join our table. He says the last word with distaste. "It's too warm outside."

The weather is a welcome change though. It's eight a.m., but it already feels like a sunny, summer day even if I would still be wearing long-sleeved shirts in Georgina at this time of year.

Breakfast is delicious. Though we occasionally eat Filipino food in Canada when Mom feels the urge to cook, I have never eaten our current breakfast dish, *tapa*, a dried, marinated beef served with rice and egg. Our meal comes with homemade *lemoncita* – a sweeter, Philippine variation of lemonade – that is served in cold glasses wrapped in knitted doilies.

"Are you ready for another exciting day in the Philippines, *Ate* Benni?" Lisa asks.

"Sure am. Where to today?"

"The cemetery. The place everyone is dying to visit, of course."

"Oh, Lisa, be nice," Ariel says, peeking his head out to check on us. "Benni should pay her respects to Mama Melia and Papa Addie." Though said in a matter-of-fact tone without judgment, Ariel's justification for the day's itinerary is sobering. "Not to worry, Benni. We'll try to find more entertaining ways for you to pass your time after." He winks.

We leave after breakfast. I watch the outside blur to green as we drive by the palm trees and crawling vines that surround the Forbes Park houses. The complex's security guards, with their guns holstered just beneath the crease of their elbows, peer inside the packed vehicle. There are no seat belt laws or maximum occupancy numbers enforced here. Ride where you can and do what you need to do: this is the unspoken maxim of a country filled with people who can't afford caution.

Travelling from Forbes Park to Manila Memorial Park, where my maternal grandparents are buried, is like going from one gated community to another. Between the quiet streets of the Forbes Park complex and the quiet walks of the park stand two gates and the Philippines' throbbing arteries. The ride between is fast-paced, and I can't help but appreciate the luxurious comfort of our drive after catching glimpses of the hawking vendors and overcrowded jeepneys clogging those arteries.

Manila Memorial Park is clean and old and full of looming tombstones that jut out of manicured lawns. Mom and Rose's parents, Mama Melia and Papa Addie, rest in a marble box raised above ground. Their full names, Amelia Chengcuenca Dychingco and Adolfo Dychingco, are transcribed on the grave in raised gold lettering.

We clear a way for Mom upon arrival so she can see the tomb first. She has twenty-six years to account for; she already has tears in her eyes.

She moves forward and pats the front of the grave before gently tracing her fingers over the names. "It's dusty," she remarks. Rose and Ariel are already chattering about the lack of care the graves receive from their paid caretakers. Mom doesn't join the conversation. She slides her hand along the tomb's surface, bringing it to a stop at the back of the grave. She bends down. "Hi, Mommy," she whispers, as though greeting Mama Melia again on a hospital bed.

Mom was fresh off a plane from Canada the last time she saw her mother. She returned just in time to visit the hospital and see her mother die.

"It's Maria. I'm home, and Ned and Benni are here, too."

The fragility of the moment is uncomfortable to watch. Ariel and Rose chatter on.

Mom turns to me. "This is where her head is," she says, patting the back of the grave. "And this is where her feet are," she says, gesturing to the plaque before us.

"I hate cemeteries," Dad whispers to me. "Cremate me when I die."

"We are cremating you, Dad, but you know how I feel about that."

Only a few months earlier in Canada, Mom had purchased glass cubbyholes for her and Dad in a bright room of the nearby Catholic mausoleum. She had chosen both cubbyholes at eye level to the bench beside it, "so people can talk to us when they visit." I had tried to protest, preferring burials to burnings, but Mom had been adamant about her decision. "If we're buried," she'd said, "you will always remember how we are laid. You'll know where we are in our graves. You'll never be able to move on."

Dad approaches the grave. "Hello, *po*," he says, addressing Papa Addie's side of the stone. "It's Eduardo."

Papa Addie died when Mom was twenty-two. The first time Dad met him was in his casket.

Dad falls silent, but I wonder if he's carrying on his greetings in his head, relating an account of all the promises he couldn't pay in person in regards to Mom's well-being.

We cluster around the back of the grave, where Mama Melia and Papa Addie's heads rest, for a family picture. Mom smiles, but tears are in her eyes. I can't decide whether to smile or frown. I settle on a grim face, my arms crossed as I peek over Mom's shoulder. When we gather around the camera's screen to see the photo after, I realize I look as closed off as I feel. The trip has made me see how detached I look, and it doesn't look good. Beyond that, the grave looks the same as it does in Mom and Dad's wedding album. I recall, as though superimposed on the present moment, the image of my newlywed parents – a bouquet in Mom's hands brought the day after her wedding to lay down before her father. The snapshot is the last photo in the album. Though it seems a little out of place after the wedding photos, the marble slab asserts its place in family memory. The bouquet in Mom's hand says, "This is my father," the moment before she lays it at his grave.

After so many years of seeing the photographed gravesite in family record, I stand now before the real thing. Children, grandchildren, and great-grandchildren congregate around it with a mixture of jubilant arrival and suitable solemnity. Seeing the grave seems to confirm everything I have ever seen or heard about the Philippines. Before this moment, the tomb itself was no more than a photograph, just as Mom and Dad's stories were no more than words. Standing here now, in solid stone, the tomb makes real all that was said before. A place like the Philippines, from all the stories my parents told, really does exist. A history that contains my parents really did happen here. People really did come before me – people who shared my blood and lived and breathed as I live and breathe. And everything about the place seems to ask, "So what are you going to do about it?"

18.

I CHANGE MY CLOTHES WHEN WE RETURN from the cemetery, having found the growing afternoon heat stifling despite my linen blouse and denim skirt. I pull on a yellow spaghetti-strap baby-doll top and pair it with fitted khaki shorts before joining Mom and Rose where they lounge in the living room.

"There's my gorgeous niece," Rose says from her seat. She doesn't hide the once-over she's giving me, or her approval at what she sees. She draws me into a tight hug when I reach her. "Benni, you're beautiful and sexy, just like I was at your age."

Mom laughs. "Of course, you can't give a compliment without taking one."

"I'm only telling the truth. If I said I was sexy now, then you'd know I was telling a lie." Rose runs her hands over her hefty figure. She wears a frumpy green shirt with a red apple on the front that says, "Bite me." I'm surprised at the homeliness of her outfit considering her wealth.

Mom turns to me with an air of gravity. "Benni, I suppose what you're wearing is fine," she says in a way that makes it clear that she thinks the exact opposite.

"Pardon?" I ask, taken aback by the switch in topic.

"*Ay nako*, don't listen to Mother Superior over here, Benni. She's just being her typical nun-in-waiting self. If you've got it, hon, flaunt it. That's what I always say. God only knows how long you'll have those legs for." Rose gives my thigh a slap.

Mom's lips draw into a tight line. "Your outfit would be fine in Canada, Benni, but the Philippines is more conservative, remember? People don't usually wear sleeveless tops here, for example. Why not keep that nice blouse on that you were wearing earlier or wear something like what you wore yesterday?"

"Not in this heat," I say. I regretted my wardrobe choice yesterday while we traversed Mom and Dad's old haunts. I thought the light blue T-shirt would deflect the sun, but it only served to further accentuate sweat stains.

"It's fine. She's changing anyways," someone says behind me.

I turn to find Lisa leaning against the patio door. "Is that so?" I ask.

"Of course. You look great, *Ate* Benni, but my dad said we'd have something exciting planned for you this afternoon, didn't he? We're going swimming today at the Manila Golf and Country Club. We can't let you get bored on your second day here." Lisa smiles, halting my protest that I don't need to be entertained. "Come to my room, *Ate* Benni. I have some sarongs you can borrow if you didn't bring any."

"Go on," Rose says, smiling at Mom's evident look of relief at having avoided a fight.

I follow Lisa to her room through a meandering route of stairs, doors, and hallways. It feels like every room here must be accessed by a circuitous route of some sort. Upon entering her room, we're faced with a floor-to-ceiling closet – to the left is a queen-sized bed, and to the right is a makeup counter leading to a bathroom as big as the bedroom.

"Come on in," Lisa says, tossing me a blue sarong and floppy sunhat. "You need to protect yourself from the sun." She pushes her shirt up to change into her bathing suit.

"Lisa, what's that?" I ask, pointing to the script of raised ink on her hip bone. I speak before noting the way she is turning to hide it. I'm embarrassed at having called attention to something I shouldn't have seen. "Never mind," I say, averting my eyes.

"Are you referring to this?" Lisa asks, lowering the band of her shorts further to reveal a tattoo, raw and puffy on her hip. "I got it a few nights ago. A friend did it for me in his basement. You're the first to know."

I try to make out the foreign characters. "What does it say?"

"It says 'family.' It's written in the Tagalog alphabet."

"I didn't even know there was a Tagalog alphabet."

"Yeah, before the colonization and Americanization of the Philippine school system, we had our own alphabet."

"So, it says 'family,'" I repeat.

"Yes, 'family.'" Lisa smiles. "By the way, I hope you didn't mind me jumping in there earlier when you were talking to your mom. I just find it funny how things like clothes and bodies can become such topics of conversation. It's all so silly, isn't it?"

"No problem at all," I say, studying Lisa's pronounced cheekbones and pale pallor. "It is funny."

We hear a knock on the door. Lisa pats her waistband and gives me a look. "Remember, we keep this between you and I for now," she says, as if we're girls trading secrets during recess.

A small, dark girl dressed in the help's uniform peeks around the door. "Um, Miss Lisa," she says, "do you need any help getting ready, *po? Inday* Rose said I should check to see if you need anything."

Lisa studies the girl. "Who are you? Are you new?"

"Um, y-yes, Miss Lisa. I'm new," the girl stammers.

"Okay, the first thing you need to know is that no one calls me 'Miss Lisa.' 'Lisa' is fine."

"Oh, okay," the girl says, her eyes darting about as though looking for a pen and paper to take notes.

"Second of all, I don't need help getting dressed, unless it's for a big occasion. I can dress myself all on my own, thank you very much. Oh, but *Ate* Benni, do you need anything?"

"Nope, I'm good," I say, wondering what the girl could possibly do to help us dress. If movies are a show of anything, we have far less laces to do up than the wealthy women of the nineteenth-century who seemed to require all the assistance in the world.

"Okay then, *po*. I brought these just in case you needed any refreshments." The girl nudges the door open to reveal two sweating glasses of mango juice on a silver tray accompanied by fresh mango slices.

"Thank you. You can put it there," Lisa says, gesturing to her desk.

"This is amazing," I say, after the help leaves and I sample the mango. "Now this is wealth worth having." I nod to the juice in one hand and mango slice in the other. The mango is fresh and sweet, picked at just the right time so as not to taste sour or overripe.

"Are there no mangos in Canada?"

"Certainly not ones served to you at home on silver platters. I love it here."

"I'm glad you do," Lisa says, smiling, "and I'm happy you're here. It's nice to have a relative close to my age to talk to."

I smile back, realizing that I've never had a relative to confide in before either.

While Lisa chatters on about bathing-suit styles and colours, I think about her tattoo. For some reason, the fact that she chose the word "family," of all words, makes me feel more rootless than ever. She chose to etch "family" into her skin, as told through the unique history of the place where she was born and raised. I chose to tattoo myself with my name in my handwriting. It's a word without secrets or history – a word that is individualistic and nothing else. Suddenly, I think my tattoo is vulgar.

I wonder what circumstances in our lives led Lisa and I to identify ourselves so differently. Lisa is from the same family as I, and yet seems to have a firmer grasp, or at least a deeper appreciation, of what "family" means. Thinking of Lisa's secret, I wonder if I'm too far off to learn the meaning behind "family," too.

19.

JERRY DRIVES LISA, GIA, GIA'S *YAYA* – or nanny – and I to the Manila Golf and Country Club. The drive is short. We take a right at the end of the street, a left, and another right, before coming upon the gated club entrance.

Jerry rolls down the minivan's window at the club's security booth and Lisa leans forward to speak to the guard. "Carlo Consuelo," she says, flashing a card. The guard nods and a man emerges to open the front gates.

"Who's Carlo Consuelo?" I ask. The name is unfamiliar.

"My *Lolo*. Memberships to the Manila Golf and Country Club can only be inherited, so membership won't pass to my dad until after *Lolo* passes away. My *Lolo*'s very nice about this though; he lets all of us come here whenever we want."

Jerry pulls up to the front of the club. It's a widespread building with a copper-green roof, a manicured lawn speckled with fountains and ponds, and glimpses of an eighteen-hole golf course around the back. He idles at the front of the building until we're safely inside.

"This is the one place where Jerry doesn't need to follow us," Lisa says.

"Follow you?" I ask.

"You could call Jerry our driver and bodyguard. He carries a gun and accompanies us most places, but he doesn't need to come in here. Security's so tight here that only those with membership or who are close to those with membership can attend. We don't need to be watched here."

Lisa leads the way through the building, which is a maze of halls and doors. Glass inserts allow glimpses into a ballroom, bowling alley, dance studio, gym, indoor tennis and badminton court, and various restaurants and dining rooms. She leads us right to the back, where we exit onto a serene patio, complete with a pool equipped with laneways and a waterslide.

"This place is amazing," I say, as Lisa sets her towel down on a lounger beneath a poolside gazebo. "Do you come here often?"

"Hardly," Lisa says.

"Gia, come here and I'll put your sunscreen on," Gia's *yaya* says. She must be hot in her pressed dress and apron.

"No," Gia yells. She's already stripped to her ruffled two-piece bathing suit and scattered her clothes along the poolside, her *yaya* trailing behind her to pick up the mess.

"Gia, baby, you need to put your sunscreen on," her *yaya* says again.

"No, I'm going into the pool!" Gia inches toward the water's edge.

"Gia, baby, you need to put on your floaters. You don't know how to swim."

"I hate floaters." Gia pouts and stomps her feet.

"Gia, baby," Lisa coos, "put your sunscreen on. Do you want to get dark like *yaya*?" She speaks about Gia's *yaya* as though she's not there. Indeed, in the sun, the woman's skin does look especially dark in contrast to her light grey uniform.

Gia surveys her *yaya* as though considering the possibility. After a minute more of stamping and stomping, she consents to her *yaya*'s careful application of sunscreen and floaters.

After stripping to my bathing suit, I turn to join Gia in the pool. Though I assumed Lisa was waiting for me, she remains reclined on her chaise. "Aren't you going to swim?" I ask.

"I don't like to get wet," she says as she applies more sunscreen. She looks even skinnier in her two-piece bathing suit and wraparound sarong.

I glance from her to the pool, not understanding how one could resist the draw of water so inviting in a country so hot. "Anyways, if I wanted to swim, I could've swum at home." I recall the kidney-sized pool in the Consuelos' backyard and wonder why we came here. The Consuelos' pool at home is almost as big and just as nice as this one, but it does lack a water slide. "So, why come in the first place?" I ask.

"I wanted to bring you out."

I shrug and start towards the waterslide.

"*Ate* Benni," Lisa calls from under the shade. "Aren't you going to reapply your sunscreen?"

"We already applied sunscreen before we got here," I say. "There's no need to apply more. And besides, I need to darken up a bit."

"Who would ever want to get darker?" Lisa asks. Her sun hat is drawn low on her head, and her toes are tucked into the square shade over the lounger.

"I think tans are gorgeous," I say. "Everyone wants one in Canada. It means you've been somewhere."

I spend half an hour in the water trying to bond with Gia. Unfortunately, Gia's idea of bonding with someone involves bossing that person around. I comply with her demands of when and how to ride the waterslide, where to stand, and what to pretend to be with waning enthusiasm. I leave the pool after Gia throws a fit when I suggest that I'm a fellow mermaid princess instead of her recommended seal. I am not Gia's *yaya*; the poor woman can keep her tedious job.

I rejoin Lisa by the poolside, dragging one of the loungers out so I can recline in the sun.

"Have fun?" Lisa asks with a smile.

"Sure," I say, careful to mask the fact that I think "Gia baby" is a brat.

"*Ate* Benni, look at that cutie," Lisa says, peering at the other side of the pool from under the brim of her hat. "I wonder what family he's from. I haven't seen him around before."

I follow her gaze to find a couple of young men who had arrived while I was swimming. One is in the process of receiving drinks from a waitress from the comfort of his lounger while the other adjusts the umbrella.

"He looks Chinese," I say, assuming Lisa's looking at the slight, pale-skinned man. The other is darker-skinned and wears a plain white uniform. I haven't seen much of the Philippines, but from what I've seen as we passed through the streets, there's only one race in two varieties – Filipino, light and dark.

"I doubt he is. Most club families are of Spanish descent. He's cute though, don't you think?"

I study him. He's short with an undefined chest, spiky hair, and tiny eyes that may be squinting in the sun or may just be small. He looks average to me. I think of Tom, who said I wasn't marriage material because I wasn't Chinese. Everywhere I'm either too brown or too yellow. Mom was right in saying things are different here.

"Sure," I say, shrugging.

The man glances over at us, as if sensing we're talking about him. He stands up, stretches, and saunters to the edge of the pool. If I'm not attracted by his looks, I'm even less attracted by his attitude. He sips from his glass, calls his help over to hold his drink – because God forbid he take the two steps to the table to put it down himself – and dives into the water. All of this is performed as if he is bestowing a great favour on us – as if he's conscious we see him, and we're lucky to look.

"*Ate* Benni, I think he's swimming here."

Sure enough, the man emerges on our side of the pool. His once spiked-up hair is plastered down into an unattractive bowl cut. "*Kamusta*, ladies," he says.

"Hello," Lisa replies.

"How are you today?" he asks.

"We're good," Lisa says.

"And how are you?" he asks, looking at me in particular. He speaks English well, but his triumphant air does nothing to help him win points in my estimation.

"Fine," I reply.

"Do you two come here often?"

"I do with my sister," Lisa says, nodding at Gia. "*Ate* Benni is visiting from Canada though."

"Ah, I knew you must be a visitor. How do you like the Philippines so far?"

"It's good."

"I see." The man seems put off by my brief responses. He pauses, puffs his chest slightly, and says, "My name is Abe, by the way. Abe Razon." He raises an eyebrow. "What family are you from?"

I'm appalled by his question. It's not even posed as the simple question, "what is your name?" It blatantly regards our lineage.

"Ah, Razon," Lisa says, interpreting whatever Abe is trying to convey with the raised eyebrow. "We're Consuelos."

"You as well?" he asks me.

"Nope." It's all I'm willing to give this obstinate and intrusive fool.

My single-word response ends his line of questioning, and, after some additional strained chatter, Abe finally leaves.

"*Ate* Benni, how could you do that?"

It is only after Lisa asks that I feel a tinge of guilt at my bad manners. "He seemed like a prick," I say. "What's up with all those questions about which family we're from?"

"That's how men are here. Especially men that belong to the country club," Lisa says, laughing at my bewildered expression.

Abe, who's emerging from the opposite side of the pool, hears, and shoots us a look of disgust. He leaves the poolside shortly after with the haughtiest look I have yet seen on such an unattractive man.

"He was a bit of a prick, but, then again, he can be. He's a *Razon*," Lisa says, stressing the last name again.

"What does it matter if he's a Razon?"

"It matters because he's part of the second-richest family in the Philippines."

"How do you know how wealthy he is?"

"You just know these things here. Plus, *Forbes* publishes the list annually. The Razon's have seven-and-a-half billion to their name."

"Seven-and-a-half … what?" I splutter at the figure. I can't even imagine that much money. I glance across the pool to see if Abe is still there, and a pang of regret courses through me. I should have been nicer. "So, who's the richest family?" I ask.

"The Sanchezes." She wrinkles her nose. "I hate the Sanchezes."

"Maybe all the richest families are made up of pricks."

"I hope not because we're on the list."

"Oh," I say, not knowing how to react. Somehow, my first thoughts of *Where the hell have you been all my life?* and *Can you adopt me?* seem inappropriate. "Well, I'm sorry if I ruined things for you with that guy, Lisa."

"It's fine. He was clearly more interested in you. And there's plenty more where that came from anyways. What's your type, though, *Ate* Benni?"

"You mean what's my type if not featureless, spineless men with lots of money?" I ask, pulling my lounger over to sit beside her in the shade. I order another mango slushie and consider her question. I only liked Filipinos when I was in high school because I was trying as hard as possible to disassociate myself from the hostility I encountered when people assumed I was Chinese. But Filipinos were scarce, and I was turned off of Filipino men after one told me that Filipinos were the "blacks of the Asian race in Canada," whatever that meant. In university, I preferred white men. If I wasn't Filipino or Chinese, then I could at least be North American. But my own insecurities got the best of me. I always assumed a white man would never want me, what with all the embarrassing stereotypes floating around. Whenever one did, I wondered if he was only curious about being with an Asian woman. Finally, after university, I ended up with Tom. He was Asian but was as Canadianized as I was, with a family still cultural enough to eat rice regularly. Above all, I loved the security I felt with Tom. It was as though I'd found someone in-between, like me.

"I don't know. Maybe black guys or brown guys," I say. I laugh at the look on Lisa's face. "To be quite honest," I say, to ease her mind, "I'd be happy with anyone as long as they are happy with me and we're happy together. That's important."

"Happiness," Lisa says. "That's a vague requirement if I've ever heard of one."

20.

J ERRY WAITS FOR US IN THE COUNTRY CLUB parking lot.
"*Opo*," I hear him say as we close the minivan door. He
glances at me in the rearview mirror as he snaps his cellphone
shut. "That was *Inday* Rose. We have to make one stop before
going home."

"Where to?" Lisa asks.

"Makati."

"What do we need to do in Makati?"

"We need to pick up *Señor* Ned." The way he says it makes
it clear that we're not going on a good trip. Perhaps Lisa hears
it too because she doesn't ask any questions.

It doesn't stop Gia from piping up though. "Why is *Tito*
Ned in Makati?" she asks. She grows cross when Jerry doesn't
answer. "Why? Why? Why is he there? Where did he go?"

"He went to meet some friends," Jerry says.

"Friends? Then why didn't we go with him? Did he go to a
party?" Gia asks.

"Hush, baby," Lisa says, glancing at me.

The ride lasts half an hour but feels longer. Gia grows impatient after fifteen minutes, and Lisa pulls out her cellphone
for her to play with. Gia flips the cover open and shut the
rest of the way there. Her pink nails click against the plastic.
The sound is maddening. I focus on Jerry's creased eyebrows
in the rear-view mirror, but it doesn't stop me from noticing
Lisa biting her lip as she reads the street signs we pass. I try

to ignore the tight feeling growing in my chest – the kind you have when you wake up and know, just by feeling it, that it's bound to be a bad day.

As soon as we enter a seedy part of Makati, I know I've hoped for too much when keeping my eyes strained for Dad among the more reputable-looking shops and restaurants we drove by half an hour before. I expect to spot Dad's location easily; I look for a bar among the cramped tin houses we pass. Instead, we stop at a nondescript, unmarked shack. Barefoot brown men with missing teeth and stained undershirts drink outside. The place lacks even the air of camaraderie that comes with alcohol. The men drink with bleary-eyed determination. They don't talk. They don't look at each other.

"This is it?" I hear myself ask. "This is where he is?" I turn to look at Lisa, but she avoids my gaze.

The air in the car is still and stale. Jerry raises his phone to his ear. The volume on the phone is turned up. We hear it ringing.

"Yes?" Dad's voice fills the car.

"*Señor* Ned, we're here to pick you up."

"Who is this?"

"Jerry, *po*."

"Why are you here?"

"*Inday* Rose asked me to get you. Mrs. Manlapaz is looking for you. Come out, *po*."

Dad utters a string of curses in Tagalog. "If I must," he says. The phone beeps when he hangs up.

Dad emerges from the shack in his white undershirt, his knobby knees bared beneath house shorts. The sight of his pasty-white skin, bulging belly, and skinny legs, which seem to suffer beneath his weight, would be comical if not for where we are and why we're here. He puffs on a cigarette in one hand and shields his eyes from the dull sunlight with the other.

I throw the minivan door open before he reaches us.

He looks surprised to see us, but regains his composure. He throws his cigarette away and squeezes into the backseat beside me. "Fancy seeing you girls here," he says with that easy smile I've always loved. He throws an arm around my shoulder. "Did you have a good day today, Princess?"

"Yes," I say, but it's all I can manage.

"Are you happy to see your dad?" he asks. His eyes are red-rimmed and watery.

"Of course," I say, but I don't convince anyone, not even myself.

The car is thick with the smell of cigarettes and alcohol. "Where are we going?" Dad asks.

No one answers. Not even Gia speaks anymore.

Jerry finally says, "We're going back to *Inday* Rose's, *Señor* Ned."

Dad makes a noise that sounds like a cross between strangulation and protest.

All I can think of are Lisa's pitying eyes, unable to so much as glance our way, and my own eyes start to sting. "Do you have another place you'd like to go? Perhaps another bar?" I only vaguely regret saying this in front of everybody's averted gazes since I'm preoccupied with keeping my own gaze clear. I expect Dad to say something back, but he pulls out his pack of cigarettes instead. He takes a cigarette out and readies it for lighting.

"I don't think you should smoke in here," I say.

Dad's mouth works furiously. I wonder what he's going to say, but he lowers his cigarette without a word, and I see that it is hopelessly chewed, the filter crushed.

21.

DAD EXITS THE MINIVAN FIRST when we return to the Consuelos'. If he planned on a quiet entrance, his plans are thwarted. Mom and Rose are in the foyer.

Mom sits on the piano bench, her face as still and unreadable as the black onyx leopard by the front door. Rose stands beside her, fretting with the piano, brushing her hands along its top as though to rid the immaculate surface of invisible dust.

Dad stops in the doorway when he sees Mom. Lisa and I stop just in time to avoid hitting him, but Gia bumps into his legs. "Hey," she wails but falls silent when she realizes no one else is talking.

"Sorry I took so long," Dad says, his voice steady except for when he hiccups at the end. "I was held…"

"Don't." The movement of Mom's lips are so imperceptible that, for a second, I think Rose is speaking.

My parents rarely fought. They were not often together. I can only recall a couple of fights from when I was younger. I never really knew how they began. Mom would say something and Dad would blow up, storm about the house, bang cupboards, slam doors, and take up as much room angry as he occupied when happy. At these times, Mom would be the calm, quiet voice of reason, hushing him when he got too loud. The next day, Mom would tell me everything was fine. Never before have I seen Mom angry like this.

"Maria, darling…"

"Don't," Mom says, her tone quieter than before.

"Maria…"

Mom stands. The piano bench scrapes against the marble floor. The sound echoes in the vastness of the hall. She walks away to the guest apartment.

Dad watches her for a moment before his shoulders slump. It's a sudden transformation with just a curve of the spine. He goes from upright to defeated in seconds. He follows Mom.

I watch my parents retreat to the only place I could have disappeared to on my own. Where do I hide now? Where can I be alone?

Rose and Lisa look at me as though realizing the same thing. "So, how was swimming?" Rose asks, just as we hear the bedroom door slam.

I flinch.

"What's wrong with you?" I hear Mom yell through the door.

"It's so nice outside," Rose says, clapping her hands as though to hide Mom's yelling. "Why don't we go outside?"

We exit through the walkout basement to the poolside patio and assemble under the shade. Rose orders a round of fresh *calamansi* juice from the help. It is only after the scraping of our chairs cease that we realize the guest bedroom window is open and we can hear the murmurs of Mom and Dad's voices. The sound is unintelligible but insistent. I see the realization – then embarrassment – dawn on Rose's face and can read the struggle there. To suggest moving locations now would be awkward – an acknowledgement of the fight and of our earlier attempt to escape it – and Rose is nothing if not tactful and therefore gentle with my feelings.

"So, Benni, tell me about yourself," Rose says, her voice raised to block out the murmurings from above. "We haven't really had a chance to get acquainted yet. Do you have a boyfriend?"

The question, though typical of an aunt to ask, is almost unbearable. At almost every turn, in almost every situation in the past two days, I am reminded in some small way of my breakup with Tom. "No," I say.

Rose attributes my shortness to the situation unfolding above us. "Why not? A beauty like you shouldn't be single."

I shrug.

"Well, not to worry. You'll find a nice man here without a problem. If you stay long enough at the country club, you'll meet more than a few eligible bachelors in no time."

"Enough!" Mom yells loud enough for us to hear outside.

Lisa jumps into the conversation. "Funny you say that, *Lola*," she says in a raised voice as well. "We met someone at the country club today."

"Really? Who?" I appreciate Rose's feigned look of interest despite the fact that our attention is on the conversation upstairs.

"Abe Razon," Lisa says.

"Abe Razon!" Rose repeats as though announcing a prize on a game show.

"Yes. He seemed awfully interested in *Ate* Benni."

"Is that so? He's a catch, Benni. I've been trying to arrange a chance meeting between him and Lisa for ages. Wouldn't it be nice to settle down, find a nice man, and get married? I tell Lisa that now's the time to start thinking about such things."

"Enough! Enough, enough, enough!" Mom's shouting is so insistent that our conversation comes to an abrupt stop. There's a pause, and then a door slams.

"Well, that's enough," I say, standing up with a scrape of my chair. "Thank you so much for today, but I think I'm going to rest for a bit."

They don't say anything to stop me, and it's only when I reach the bottom of the basement stairs that I realize I don't know where to go. Mom and Dad are in our guest suite, and the last thing I want to do is join them.

Just when I'm about to turn around, Mom walks down the stairs. "Where are you going?" she asks. Her voice is hoarse, as though she's lost a bit of it screaming.

"I wanted to shower."

"Go ahead. Your dad is in the room still, but he's not using the bathroom."

"Where are you going?"

"I was looking for *Ate* Rosie."

"She's in the backyard with Lisa."

"Okay," Mom says and continues past me.

"Wait, Mom. Are you okay?"

Mom looks at me as though she is not sure what to say. Then she smiles and says, "I'm fine, Benni. Every couple has their differences."

"Are you kidding me? What the hell was that?"

Mom sighs, and again I see that split-second change happen in the curve of her spine and then in the curve of her lips. "Benni, I can't talk right now. I just can't. We're supposed to be on vacation, aren't we?"

I nod. All I know is that I can't talk right now either, so I climb the stairs past her.

Before turning down the hall toward our guest apartment, I hear Mom's voice greeting Rose on the patio. "Why hello, family!" she sings, false and cheery. She can barely hide the cracks we'd heard in it before, but I already know no one will acknowledge it anyways.

I open the door to our guest apartment as quietly as possible. I peek into Mom and Dad's room where the master ensuite is located. Dad sits on the edge of the bed with his back to me, looking out the window at the pool below. You can't see Mom and Rose from here, but Mom's voice still carries in murmurs. An outbreak of laughter suggests a party is happening that we aren't invited to. I wonder how Mom does it.

Dad fingers an unlit cigarette. He brings it to his lips as though forgetting it's not lit. He places his hand down again. He doesn't turn around, but asks, "Did you hear everything?"

The way he asks me, I feel like he is laying himself in my hands with trust that I won't be angry. My spine bows. A sudden weight on the back of my neck makes me sigh and say, "Not everything, but enough."

Enough, enough, enough.

I wait for Dad to say something more – a sorry at this point would be appreciated – but he says nothing and shrill laughter rises in the air and strikes our ears.

Dad lifts the cigarette to his mouth again.

"It's not lit, Dad. Go smoke outside."

I head to the washroom, wishing Dad wasn't there.

22.

I WAKE TO FIND MY HAIR DRIED and matted after forgetting to comb it out last night after my shower. I shower again in the ensuite and peek outside the bathroom afterward to confirm that no one's around before emerging naked with my towel in hand to dry myself.

I hear hammering outside and see a shift of light at the window. Someone must be working in the backyard. The hammering stops as soon as I emerge. I wait for the noise to resume. When I don't hear anything, I wrap myself in the towel and tiptoe forward. I peer through the window slats and see a small flutter; it's the blink of someone's eye looking back at me.

I yell and drop to the floor, gripping the towel to my chest.

The banging resumes outside just as Ariel rushes in.

I cower lower on the floor. "I'm naked!" I yell.

"What happened?" Ariel asks as he covers his eyes.

"Someone outside was watching me."

Ariel strides to the window and pulls the blinds up, forgetting that I am undressed on the floor. I squint to see two of Rose's "boys" – the term she uses in reference to her male help – near the window setting up a folding table.

"You must have just seen them moving about. They've been asked to work there."

Mom comes to the door.

"It's okay. False alarm," I say, though I know what I saw. It was a still figure with a blinking eye, but I'm ashamed of the scene I've caused.

Ariel pats my head as he passes me on his way out the door. "Oh, Benni," he says, as though he's just humoured an attention-seeking child.

"Need help?" Mom asks, offering a hand to pull me up.

"I'm okay," I say, pushing myself up from the floor with as much dignity as I can muster.

"You better be careful, Benni. The help are paid to be here. They're workers, not family. And, to them, you're very exotic. You know that. Just watch out next time, okay?"

I grab my clothes and change in my windowless bedroom.

All eyes turn on me when I enter the breakfast room where brunch is being served.

"How are you feeling, Princess?" Dad asks with a smile.

I shrug. "Sorry about that," I say, addressing the table. "I thought…"

"It's okay, Benni," Rose interrupts, "I asked my boys to assemble the new patio set outside. I forgot you might be in the main guest room. I'll make sure they work elsewhere while the apartment is occupied."

"There's no need to do that," I say, taking the empty seat beside Dad.

Dad throws an arm around my shoulders. I stiffen when I smell fresh alcohol on his breath and realize that a mid-morning buzz is behind his easy demeanor. "Hey, Princess, do you know what I realized?" he asks.

"What?"

"We haven't taken you out yet."

"We've only been here for three days, and I've already visited plenty of places." I eye him as I say this; the seedy bar in Makati is first and foremost on my mind of recently visited locales.

"No, we haven't taken you out though, as in out partying.

Philippine nightlife is a beast to behold. I'll take you one time. We'll have some drinks and have some fun."

"Not everybody needs alcohol to enjoy themselves, Eduardo," Mom says.

Dad's arm falls from my shoulders, and a chill settles over the table. "My apologies for having a conversation with my daughter," Dad says. "I need a smoke," he mutters, standing up.

The atmosphere around the table is subdued after Dad leaves. I excuse myself as soon as I've finished eating and wander by the poolside where Dad has taken up camp on one of the patio chairs. I want to ask Dad if he even remembers yesterday but stop when I catch sight of his slumped shoulders. He stares out at the backyard. The grass beyond the pool is dry, parched by the relentless sun.

Instead of a reprimand, I find myself saying, "Tough crowd, huh?"

Dad swipes a hand over his brow. "That's family for you, eh, Princess? It's just too hot here sometimes."

I can't tell if he's referring to the weather or our family; I am left with an overwhelming sadness staring at his profile. His once strong jaw, stern eyes, and handsome face had gone to flab and waste. Studying Dad now, I see a void – a space I can't address, a loss I can't yet face.

I shrug and turn to leave. If I were to be honest with myself, I feel like Dad's right. It's just too hot here sometimes.

Dad lights another cigarette and swings his feet up onto the coffee table. "Hey, Princess?" I pause as he looks out at the wilting backyard with studied nonchalance. "You didn't have to apologize to us about this morning, you know? Don't ever feel embarrassed, or ashamed, or shy with us. Don't ever think you have to prove something to us, or act a certain way, or keep your thoughts to yourself. We're your family. And the only place where you can be yourself is where your family is."

"Same to you, Dad," I say automatically, the way I'd say, "Good, and you?" to a stranger who asks "How do you do?"

Only after I say it do I realize that I mean it. It's a reconciliation of sorts – the closest I can get right now to saying, "I still love you."

Dad's eyes seek mine, but I turn to go before he can say anything more.

23.

I MEET LISA ON MY WAY BACK IN and realize she's been absent during brunch this morning. She's especially pale today. The bags beneath her eyes look too dark to be real.

Lisa sees me studying her and laughs. "Don't mind me. I just came back from set. We're putting on the musical version of *The Addams Family*. I'm Wednesday."

"Very nice."

"Well, it's not quite Morticia, but I'm getting there. I was just heading to my room to take this makeup off. Want to come with me?"

"Sure," I say, falling into step beside her. "Tell me more about this musical."

"The musical appeared on Broadway earlier. We're always a bit behind here in that regard, but it's all good fun. It's something to do to pass the time," Lisa says. "You can say I was kind of born into it, I guess."

"You're being modest. I saw that article *Tita* Rosie posted on Facebook last month. You're listed among the top ten rising stars in the Philippines this year, aren't you?"

"For sure, but I wonder how much of that is because of me or because of my parents."

"Who cares? It's awesome."

Lisa snorts.

"Don't you enjoy it?" I ask.

"Sure. Again, it passes the time. I was born to be a star," Lisa says with a sarcastic note in her voice. "Although sometimes I wonder what it would be like to be something different, like a librarian or an accountant."

It's my turn to snort. "You're onstage thinking about becoming an accountant?"

Lisa smiles. "I don't know. Something different. Something anonymous. Something that doesn't require me to smile all the time."

"You sound like a reverse Superman. Superman by day, closet Clark Kent at night."

Lisa laughs. "I guess you can say that though I'd hardly consider myself Superman. I don't think I'm terribly good at acting, to be honest."

"That's impossible. I'm sure you're great."

"Oh well. Who knows? Maybe I'll even be in the real papers one day, not just some online zine. Let's hope they say something good."

We fall silent, but it's a comfortable silence. I like Lisa's modesty and the easy conversation we share.

We enter her room and she goes to her vanity to remove the dark smudges under her eyes.

"I'm glad I caught you," I say after a while. "I wanted to apologize. I'm sorry you had to see my dad like that yesterday."

"Don't apologize, *Ate* Benni."

"No, really. I'm sorry I had to see my dad that way, too. It's embarrassing for him and for me."

"I don't think you should be embarrassed. We all have our moments. I like your dad. He reminds me of my daddy."

"*Kuya* Ariel?"

"No, your dad reminds me of my birth father, or at least what I remember of him."

I recall Mom's speculations about Lisa's birth father – that he was likely a good-for-nothing man that left Celeste in the lurch – and am almost offended by what she's said other than the fact that she's said it so fondly. "I haven't heard too much about your birth father," I say. From the whispered way Mom spoke of him, I always thought the subject was off limits.

"He was a great man. Like your dad, he was always the life of the party, friendly, jolly, and he always made my mother laugh. It was terrible when he died."

"He's dead?" I ask, failing to hide my surprise.

"He died when I was five. You didn't know?"

"I had no clue."

"I guess you wouldn't have heard about it. My mom doesn't talk about him often. I'm sure she still misses him though. My mom and real daddy? Now that was real love. She wasn't happy for a long time after he passed away. It was hard for both of us. Don't get me wrong; my mom loves Ariel, but I don't think you ever get over a loss like that, right?" She ends the statement as a question, leaving me to wonder if I've ever experienced, or even witnessed, that kind of love before.

"How did he die, if you don't mind my asking?"

"His family owned a *hacienda* – a mishmash collection of farm land – and he was on his way to the bank to deposit a cheque for one hundred dollars. Thereabouts, people knew who you were and what you owned, and I guess someone tracked his schedule. He was robbed and murdered for that one hundred dollars." Lisa laughs, but nothing about her story is funny, and the sound is jarring and angry instead. "The culprit was never found. The cheque was never cashed. It couldn't have been; it was in my daddy's name. My mom could have stayed on the *hacienda* with his family, I suppose. She did for a while, simply because she couldn't bring herself to do anything after he died. She was twenty-one, in love, and heartbroken. She was even younger than I am now. She talks about my daddy still sometimes. He was a great man," Lisa says again. After a pause, she shakes her head and looks at me with wide eyes, almost unsure of how our conversation led this way. "Anyway, your father reminds me of him. He's always laughing and lively, like a warm spot in a cold room, you know?"

I nod, looking at this girl who seems to have it all.

"It's good you're here. At least you two get some time to-gether, right? I could only ever wish to have more time with my daddy," she says.

24

WE CONGREGATE IN THE GAME ROOM later that evening. The help sets up a card table, and Rose, Mom, and Dad play *mahjong*, which is a game that uses small, carved ivory tiles. "*Mahjong* is almost like poker," Mom explains, "There are three suits – sticks, balls, and characters. You need to create certain combinations using them in order to have *mahjong*."

The game is quiet and unexciting to watch, except when Mom or Rose break into giggles or shrieks at unexpected winning hands. Dad gets up for a smoke break or two, but otherwise, he sits in contented silence, studying his tiles and sipping a cold beer. Celeste, Ariel, Lisa, and I spread out amongst the couches, with Gia playing quietly for once with gold pieces of a custom-made Monopoly board. Ariel flips through channels on the floor-to-ceiling, wall-to-wall projector-screen TV while the rest of us also nurse cold beers – an awful Filipino brew called Red Horse.

The shows Ariel flips through are gaudy and loud; the unfamiliar language jars my ears. Shows range from over-emotional Philippine dramas with lots of crying to rambunctious game shows. No matter the channel, everyone looks too powdery white, the women's voices are too high, and the men's clothes are too tight.

Ariel pauses on one channel where the camera cuts between a woman sobbing on a kitchen floor and a man shedding silent tears on a balcony overlooking a full moon. "This is Celeste's channel: FSUTV. It's too bad we didn't tune in earlier. Her show would've been on."

"That would've been neat to see," I say.

"*Hoy*, Ariel, why don't you show Benni some of your *Dance, Dance Pinoy* clips?" Rose calls from the *mahjong* table.

"Certainly," Ariel says, requiring no encouragement. He flips to an Internet browser on the smart TV and pulls up YouTube.

"My son is so *guapo*," Rose gushes as Ariel types "Ariel Consuelo" into the search bar. A number of hits come back.

Ariel clicks on the first link: "Dance, Dance Pinoy Consuelo." The sound of an audience cheering and Gloria Estafan's "Rhythm Is Gonna Get You" fills the room. The screen displays a pixelated video of a man's legs in dress pants and dress shoes performing complicated steps to the beat. The camera zooms out, revealing the man to be none other than Ariel. He looks exactly the same, though his gelled, flat-top haircut in the video à la Jason Priestly is styled into a conservative *au naturel* side-swipe tonight.

Gia drops the Monopoly pieces and jumps up, mirroring her onscreen father's dance moves.

"Good job, baby," Ariel says, delighted. "You've learned the moves."

Celeste's glazed look and Gia's imitation confirms my suspicions that the Consuelos watch these videos often.

"Good work, G..." Lisa is saying, but she is cut off by Ariel.

"Hush, hush, it's starting now," he says.

"*Magandang gabi, Pilipinas!*" onscreen Ariel shouts. He draws the greeting out like a sports announcer, albeit a flamboyant one. The crowd cheers as Ariel pauses to wink and smile at the camera for a prolonged period of time. I hunker down to watch the video's remaining three minutes and ten seconds.

If I thought the dramas with all the crying and game shows with all the shrill voices were overwhelming, they are nothing compared to the spectacle of Ariel humming, bobbing, and laughing along to the video of his 1990s self.

My hope that the barrage on our senses will end with the current video proves futile. Ariel seems to grow only more enamoured with himself as the video plays on, and we're subjected to five more *Dance, Dance Pinoy* videos, including one that is a full-length episode. Mom, Dad, and Rose are lucky enough to retire to bed after the end of their game. Celeste nods off on the couch adjacent to ours, Gia and Ariel dance together, and Lisa seems to be feeling pretty good after her third Red Horse.

"These *Dance, Dance Pinoy* videos are awesome," I finally say. "What comes up if you Google yourself? Have you ever tried?" The suggestion doesn't take us away from Ariel-related content, but at least it gives us a respite from the videos.

"I'm not too sure what comes up, Benni. I haven't tried." The idea that Ariel hasn't Googled himself at least once surprises me, but I believe it upon seeing the gleam of excitement in his eyes at the prospect.

Ariel opens a new browser screen and types his name into Google. The first result on the list is a gallery of "Ariel and Celeste" images. The second is a fan site for Celeste that mentions Ariel. The third is an article about the Consuelo family on Wikipedia. Just below that, the image results for Ariel show thumbnails of him on *Dance, Dance Pinoy*. The latest news and headlines mentioning Ariel follow next.

"That article is fairly recent," I say, seeing the date before the title.

"What is that?" Ariel gasps, startling Celeste awake.

Celeste reads the headline and snorts. It was posted the day before: "ARIEL CONSUELO: GAY."

Ariel's reaction draws everyone's attention. "This is preposterous," Ariel splutters, his colour rising. "Who would write such a thing?"

"Wow. *Phil Star Biz*, Dad," Lisa says, letting out a low whistle.

"What is *Phil Star Biz*?" I ask.

"It's the Philippine equivalent of *People Magazine*," Celeste says. "Ariel, let's read it."

Ariel looks like he'd rather go back to watching YouTube videos, but he complies and clicks on the link. The article pops up and everyone falls silent as they read.

The old *Dance, Dance Pinoy* hunk Ariel Consuelo is currently the centre of intense scrutiny, along with his friend Sam Paolo, of possibly being gay. Both are good-looking men, nice, quiet, and have been spotted giving each other starry looks when in each other's company. It is very hard not to think that they are gay, and a couple, too. Sam Paolo has not yet had a serious relationship with a woman. What could Celeste possibly think?

The article is followed by photos of Ariel with an equally-groomed man sitting down to lunch, entering the country club, and swimming together.

Ariel opens and closes his mouth, speechless for once, until Celeste's laughter rouses him. "The old *Dance, Dance Pinoy* hunk?" is the first thing he says. Then, "This is ridiculous. I hardly ever see Sam. How can we be *gay* together?" Ariel spits the word out with disgust.

"It looks like you two really are gazing at each other with starry looks in that photo though," Celeste says.

Ariel turns to her, "You certainly don't believe…"

"Of course not, darling. *Phil Star Biz* probably just wrote this because Sam has a movie coming out next month. It's more about him than you. See, he hasn't even had a serious relationship with a woman." Celeste giggles again. "I'm sure nothing will come of it. It must be a slow news week. Don't think anything of it. It's late, anyways. Let's go to bed."

She takes the remote from him and turns the TV off. Then, she leads him away as he mutters, "I can't believe they called me 'old'."

25.

ICAN'T SLEEP DESPITE IT BEING well past midnight. I toss and turn in my room until I can't stand it anymore and get out of bed. Earlier today, Rose showed me a library in the house. It is only a matter of finding it again. It's somewhere on the first floor. I am curious to see what kind of novels have made its way into the library here – what popular stories have formed the collective Filipino consciousness, but haven't reached Canada.

I pad barefoot along the halls like a ghost in the dark. At this time of night, with no lights around, the ornate frames in the hallway look like black, blank boxes leading to nowhere. All I can hear is my breath, and all I can feel is the cold marble on my feet. I turn corner after corner and am about to give up until I see a thin ribbon of light below one of the double doors. I assume I have as good a chance as any of finding the library through those doors, and I push them open.

The light and sound is disorienting. My senses are flooded, and I blink to regain vision. It sounds as though I've walked into a room with a Philippine drama blaring; voices are raised and combative. It is only when I can see again that I realize my mistake. I've walked right into the love nest.

"I may as well be gay for all the action I'm getting," Ariel yells across a rose-strewn coverlet. He's stripped down to his boxers, and his skinny chest heaves as he faces Celeste standing at the opposite side of the bed.

"What part of 'I don't want to' do you not understand?" Celeste asks, her arms tight around her, clutching her pink silk robe. "I. Don't. Want. To." She says each word louder as she goes. Neither of them have noticed that I've entered the room.

"You never want to," Ariel yells. "For God's sake, woman, you're my wife."

I edge to the door.

"I'm your wife, not your mistress. What part of our marriage agreement did you not understand? Do you think I married you because I'm attracted to you?" She stops as soon as I stub my toe on the door.

I bite back a curse and keep my eyes closed; if I can't see them, maybe they can't see me. I feel someone rush past me – a breeze of disturbed air – and turn around. I open my eyes to find Celeste alone in the room, staring at the empty space beside me where Ariel fled. "I'm sorry," I say, backing away. "I didn't mean to.... I just... I was looking for the library, and..."

Celeste sighs and sits down on the bed, crushing rose petals beneath her.

"I'll just go."

"No need to go now."

"I'm sorry," I say again.

Celeste shrugs.

"Are you okay?"

She shrugs again. Her eyes are still closed; her arms still crossed around her chest.

I feel awkward leaving now, without her saying if she's fine or not. I approach.

Her eyes fly open. She studies me before breaking into a wary smile. "Every couple has their differences," she says, reminding me of Mom the day before. She rolls her shoulders back to ease them. "Don't look at me like that," she says, laughing. "It's true."

I try to reassemble my contrary expression into a look that is more neutral. "I'm sorry," I say again. "I was just thinking of something my mom said the other day."

"No problem," Celeste says, closing her eyes again. She stays quiet for so long that I start looking around, thinking again of how to escape, before she says, "I used to have a husband."

I glance at her, but she's not looking at me.

"I used to have a husband, whom I really, so very truly, loved. When he died, I felt I died, too." Celeste says all this with the air of a storyteller unsure of the ending of her story. "After he died, I lived so long in misery, pain, and anger. I never wanted to love again. The days passed, the years stretched on, and I made something of myself – all alone – without him." For the first time, she looks at me, and I am startled by the clarity of her gaze. "But each day passed alone. Lisa didn't have a father, and look at what happens when you're alone too long in the Philippines – and in show business in particular." She laughs, gesturing aimlessly. "Rumours. I wanted a man just to have one. Not to love, but to be there to stop all the speculation, to keep things steady, and to create that picture of a perfect family. That's all I ever really needed. Not love. Is that so bad?"

I don't reply, but it sounds terrible to me.

"Have you ever been in love, Benni?"

I nod, thinking of Tom. "I have. I mean, I was in love once."

"I suppose it didn't end well if you're talking in the past tense. Love can only take you so far. At the end of the day, you need stability and mutual understanding. That's what Ariel and I have most of the time."

I think of Tom again. Didn't I love him because he offered stability and what I thought was mutual understanding? I realize with a start that Celeste and I are not that different; my reasons for loving Tom are the same as Celeste's reasons for being with Ariel.

"You see," Celeste says, smiling. "You understand. You pick your life and you live it. It's just a question of what kind of life you want to live, isn't it?"

26.

THE REPORTERS APPEAR EARLY THE NEXT morning in the form of a phone call from Forbes Park's front gates. We are sitting around the breakfast table when one of the help brings Ariel the phone. Compared to last night, he seems his usual composed self. Neither he nor I acknowledge that I was party to his marital spat last night.

"Yes?" Ariel answers the phone with polite curiosity. "Speaking." He pauses for a second, a look of puzzlement on his face. "What? No. Who is this?" Another pause. "A reporter from where?" By the time Ariel hangs up, his composure is lost, and we are left watching him for more information. "It was a reporter from *Phil Peeps* at the front gate, asking about the allegations in *Phil Star Biz*," Ariel explains through clenched teeth.

"*Phil Peeps* is nothing," Celeste says with a wave of her hand. "A piddly small online zine run by students at the University of the Philippines. Don't think anything of it, dear. We'll just tell the gates to be a little more diligent from now on, but I doubt anyone else will show up."

But someone else does show up. This time at the Consuelos' front door. The visitor is announced by the new help that offered Lisa and I assistance the other day. She approaches us in the game room, unable to mask her nervousness as she clears her throat to call our attention. "*Señor* Ariel?" she asks, when her throat-clearing goes unnoticed.

"Yes?" Ariel asks, his attention still focused on the tenth rerun of *Dance, Dance Pinoy* we are watching today.

"A Mr. Christopher is here to see Miss Lisa." Her eyes dart to Lisa at the use of the "Miss." Evidently, she is afraid to drop it in current company.

"Christopher?" Lisa asks. "I don't know anyone named Christopher."

We don't have to wait long to find out more about the mysterious Christopher. He pushes into the room with a recorder in hand. "Sorry to interrupt you under false pretenses, Mr. Consuelo," he says, "but I'm from the *Phil Daily*, and I was hoping to ask you a few questions about your relationship with Mr. Sam Paolo."

Ariel stands and faces the reporter. He is breathing heavily; his face is an angry red. "Out," he yells. "Get out of my house. Out! Jerry!"

His call for Jerry is unnecessary. As soon as Ariel raised his voice, Jerry appeared with his shirt tucked to expose his gun. He grabs Christopher by the arm and drags him away.

We sit frozen, staring at Ariel. His heaving chest seems to be the only thing moving in the room. "You," he says, pointing at the help. "You are fired."

The girl begins crying. "I'm sorry, *Señor* Ariel. I only started working here this week. I didn't know. Please, *Señor*. I need the job. My mother … my father … I'm sorry."

It feels like she cries for a long time. We don't do anything. On the one hand, it feels so wrong. I think of the steel-tight labour unions back in Canada – one of which I belong to as a municipal employee – that protect workers from being fired even in extreme cases of unproductivity. On the other hand, it feels worse to intrude. This is Ariel's house, this is how he runs it, and here, he has every right to hire or fire his employees. I just wish the girl wouldn't cry like this in front of us; it's an awkward display for all involved. Jerry returns and escorts her out.

Ariel sits down only after she leaves. He turns to face the TV.

Celeste, who's remained sitting the entire time with her feet curled under her – a picture of utmost comfort – opens her mouth to speak. Her hand is already raised in a gesture of dismissal.

"Don't," Ariel says. "Just don't." His pretty face is a mask of silent suffering.

The house phone rings the rest of the day; the Consuelos' number has been leaked. After Ariel's unceremonious dismissal of the girl who admitted Christopher, the rest of the help know better than to bring the phone in. After a while, they just stop answering it, but the ringing phone fills the marbled halls from noon until night.

That night, at the dinner table, Celeste breaches the subject that's been on everyone's minds. "Maybe you should make a statement. Address the rumours and let the reporters know they're wrong."

Ariel gazes at Celeste across the table. His look is inscrutable before he glances at me. It's a quick glance, lasting no more than half a second, but it adds meaning to his words when he says, "I could. I can just reconfirm that you and I are happily married, and there is no foundation at all to these rumours. I can say that these rumours are cruel and hurting the perfect equilibrium of our marriage and our family."

"Exactly," Celeste says.

Ariel sighs and swipes a hand across his eyes. "I could," Ariel says again, "and I will, but I don't want the kids home while this is happening. One reporter already used Lisa as a decoy. Who knows how long this will last. Kids," he says, looking at Lisa and Gia. The bags beneath his eyes are pronounced. "How do you two feel about going to Boracay?"

27.

ARRANGEMENTS ARE MADE FOR GIA, her *yaya,* and Lisa to accompany Dad, Mom, and I on our trip to the island paradise, Boracay. Rose decides to come too to keep Mom company. The Consuelos are taking the one-hour flight to Boracay straight from Manila. Though Ariel offers us flights free of charge, Mom suggests we take the opportunity to fly to Iloilo instead to visit Dad's mother, Ofelia, then drive over to Boracay from there.

Mom always said that my grandmother, Ofelia, was a formidable match for my father. "We're placed on this earth to be closer to God, and one of the ways we do that is through suffering," Mom said. "Your father was born to your *Lola* Ofelia as her burden, I'm sure, and your *Lola* Ofelia was chosen to be your father's mother for the same reason. God's funny like that." For as long as I could remember, Dad and Ofelia would get into vicious verbal disputes for one reason or another, even while countries apart. These led to silences that lasted months, sometimes even years, at a time. Mom once told me about a time that the fighting got so bad in the Philippines that hospital staff thought it best to clear the top floor of the facility so the yelling wouldn't be heard by patients. My grandmother, despite her advanced age, managed the hospital well, but could never manage her youngest, wildest son. Similar incidents grew in frequency until Ofelia fell ill five years ago.

First, Ofelia started putting on weight in a puffy, bloated sort of way. She lost the function of her legs soon after. It began with a limp, as though she'd sprained an ankle, progressed to a hobble, and deteriorated into complete loss of mobility. She got a scooter to move around, but still refused to see a doctor despite the dozens of doctors on hand to provide medical advice.

Mom speculated that Ofelia waited out of stubbornness, while Dad complained that she did it to torment him. Whatever the reason, by the time Ofelia was diagnosed a year later, the damage was irreparable and her legs were permanently paralyzed. The reason for paralysis? Ofelia, a Type 1 diabetic, stopped her insulin shots. When asked why, she said that the act of pricking herself every day – "hurting herself," she said – was tiresome. So she skipped one day, and then another, and then one more, until it became a habit to forget. She returned to daily insulin shots after diagnosis, but remained paralyzed and retained her unwieldy weight.

Talk of Ofelia's ailment at home since then ceased when the reason for it was discovered, along with all mention of Ofelia herself from either Mom or Dad. It was as though the ordeal had been so trying that everyone exhausted the will to fight.

Things did seem to improve once Dad moved back to the Philippines last year, though. Dad mentioned visiting Ofelia often, at least.

Now, here in Iloilo, Dad shows off his mother's assets. "This is our family hospital. Mommy sold all her real estate and invested in this. It's less glamorous living on top of a hospital than in a penthouse suite of a condominium, but I suppose it's more philanthropic," Dad says.

The hospital is a four-storey building that takes up a good portion of the block and sports the universal blue "H" like a tiara. Dad leads us inside, standing tall in his jean shorts and stained undershirt.

Inside, it is cramped with nurses in white dresses, doctors in white lab coats, and the old and sick in white beds and steel wheelchairs. Dad brings us to the bottom of a curving plaster staircase that winds its way four floors up. "Up we go to the penthouse suite," he says.

"Ned, there must be an elevator in this building," Mom says, looking weary before the climb even begins. "How are patients brought from floor to floor?"

"Runners carry them on beds if need be. Come on, my darling bride."

"You really expect us to climb these stairs?" Mom asks. Though we're only halfway up the first flight, she's already paused to catch her breath.

"It's good exercise. Three more flights to go."

Mom, usually so careful to avoid germs, throws all caution to the wind and grabs the stair's railing as though onto a lifeline. Dad and I wait for her at the top of the stairs and greet her with enthusiastic applause when she emerges. "You're really awful, Ned," Mom says, her round face red and sweaty.

Our celebration is interrupted by the creak of the doors behind us opening. I turn, expecting to see my grandmother, only to find a petite lady in a three-piece dress suit, her hair cropped into an edgy pixie cut and dyed a brassy brown. I expect her to say something, but she seems frozen, her gaze transfixed on Dad.

I turn to look at Mom and Dad but they, too, are staring at the woman with looks of surprise. I clear my throat, startling the lady into action.

"Eddie," she says, her voice sounding choked.

"Sarah, what are you doing here?" Dad asks.

"Eddie, it's been so long," the lady named Sarah says.

"But what are you doing here?" Dad asks again. He does not sound rude, but instead genuinely confused.

"I was visiting your mother," Sarah says. "But I'm sorry. Where are my manners?" She extends her hand. "My name is Sarah. I'm an old classmate of Eddi– Eduardo's. You must be his wife, Maria."

"I am," Mom says, shaking her hand.

"And this is my daughter, Benni," Dad says.

"Hello," I say, waving. She seems to have forgotten to shake my hand as she studies Dad's face.

"Well, I think we'll be going in now," Dad says, inching forward.

"Of course," Sarah says, and then she rummages in her clutch purse. "Before you go, take this. Please. Call me sometime. It would be nice to catch up after all these years."

Mom stares at the card in Sarah's hand while Dad looks at Mom, seeming to gauge her reaction. I grab the card to end the awkward, lingering moment.

"Thanks," I say, before following Mom and Dad inside.

The industrial doors of the stairwell lead into a room that abandons linoleum and metal for hardwood and gold. The opulence of the room is striking compared to the minimalistic utilitarianism of the hospital below.

"Sarah, have you forgotten something?" The voice that asks is followed by the hefty figure of my grandmother on a shining red scooter emerging from behind wooden latticework to the left. "Eduardo, it's you," the woman stops. "And you have guests with you. Eduardo, you should have told me in advance that you were coming. I would have had the help cook something."

"Mommy, what was Sarah doing here?" Dad asks.

"She was visiting," Ofelia says.

"Why?"

"Why? Because I'm an old lady and I like to see old friends," she replies. "You should contact her sometime, Eduardo." Ofelia angles her scooter at Mom without missing a beat. "Hello, Maria," she says, putting an end to the subject of Sarah.

"Hi, Mommy," Mom says, stepping forward to kiss Ofelia's cheek. "It's good to see you again. We thought it would be nice to stop over on our way to Boracay."

"Ah, Boracay, *maganda doon*," Ofelia says. She turns her

scooter towards me. "Maria Benedictine, it's so nice to finally meet you. Come, kiss your *Lola*."

Our meeting is so unlike the fanfare that was our meeting with the Consuelos or the suspenseful episode that accompanied our meeting with Melissa. Though Ofelia is my closest blood relative after my parents, she greets me with the professionalism and distance of a doctor. As I bend forward to kiss her, I am surprised that the fleshy meat she assumed when refusing treatment feels tough and unmalleable rather than like mere loose fat. After seeing my grandmother for all of two minutes, I am unsurprised at Dad's conflict with her; she is so different from my affectionate father.

"You have quite a place here, Mommy," Mom says.

"I do, and yet you've never bothered to visit."

"Now, now, Mommy," Dad says. "There's no need to act that way. As soon as we found out we were passing through Iloilo, Maria and I thought, 'We must visit Mommy.'" Dad turns to me and smiles. "The hospital is a great place to kick back and grab a cold drink." Dad doesn't notice the rigid silence that greets this statement. "Speaking of drinks, do you have anything in the fridge?" Without waiting for a response, Dad pads around the corner.

Ofelia invites us into the kitchen after him. A rectangular room stretches behind the latticework. The main portion of the room serves as a dinette and kitchen, while the back is the family room. Ofelia asks us to take mango juice from the fridge, but Dad refuses one in favour of a beer. We sit around the kitchen table with our attention focused on Dad as the most reliable source of conversation.

"So, Eduardo, how is my *apo*?" It's an odd question to ask Dad, considering I'm sitting right here. Dad glances at me.

"I've been well, *Lola* Ofelia," I say. The answer seems sufficient because she doesn't ask anything more.

"So, how have you been, Mommy?" Mom asks after a moment of silence.

"Well, I'm sure you can see how I've been," Ofelia says, gesturing at her scooter. "I was walking the last time you saw me."

Dad makes an impatient cluck at the back of his throat. "Well, Mommy, it's your fault. How could you just stop taking your insulin? It's madness."

"Is it madness or unhappiness, Eduardo? And either way, whose fault is that?"

"Madness or unhappiness," Dad says, standing up. "I think I'd know what that's like, too, now wouldn't I? I'm going for a smoke." He rummages in the fridge for another beer before he goes.

Awkwardness fills the spot Dad left behind. The sour tone lingers and is made even worse when Ofelia tries to dispel it with a dry laugh. "That Eduardo," she says, but her tone is short of endearing. It's clear that everyone shares a singular wish to part from current company. Dad's relentless search for alcohol has brought us into unfriendly territory, but without him we cannot leave. There's too much tension in this place and too much left unsaid about Dad's life. "Please, have more juice," Ofelia says.

"It's okay," Mom says. "We should go soon."

"We may as well get comfortable while we're waiting for Eduardo. He's taken his drinks out with him."

We can see Dad on the balcony from here, smoking and drinking with his back to us, his face looking out on a grey, grey sky.

"He shouldn't be too long," Mom says, but her admission sounds like a betrayal considering he's brought two beers outside.

The silence grows more awkward the longer it draws on. I spy a bookshelf in the corner of the family room and stand up. "*Lola* Ofelia, would you mind if I take a look at your books?"

"By all means, go ahead."

"Benni loves to read," Mom says. The topic is neutral – a white flag in what feels like a battle zone.

Ofelia ignores the signal. "So, I guess Eduardo's back on the booze," she says when I reach the bookshelf. It's more of a statement than a question. Dad's habits are a source of contention in our family, but loyalties become cloudy when it comes to discussing it with this cold grandmother of mine.

I scan the books on the shelf. It's filled with mass-market paperbacks of old westerns and sci-fi novels. I skim the titles and my eyes settle on four thin hardcover books; they are old St. John's Academy yearbooks

Ofelia takes Mom's silence as a green light to keep talking. "I really don't understand Eduardo. He treats his health with such disregard that sometimes I wonder about him."

"It's ironic hearing you speak of treating health with disregard. You're the one who stopped taking your insulin just because you felt like it." Mom laughs as though she's being playful, but there's nothing amiable about what she's just said.

I pluck one of the yearbooks from the shelf. The pages are well worn and yellowed. I skim the book for Dad's name and find him under the senior section. I study his smililng face framed by the long hair that was in fashion at the time. I carry it back to the table, hoping it'll serve as a diversion.

The plan fails because Ofelia is already barrelling on. "How can he neglect himself like this? The last time he was here, the doctors told him he had to stop. It was good he had come back, of course. I thought things would be different that time around. But then he left, and it looks like nothing's changed."

I pause with my glass halfway to my mouth. "Sorry, *Lola* Ofelia, but what exactly are you talking about?"

"Oh, didn't you know?" Ofelia shrugs and says, "Your father came here last year for rehab. He's come here a couple of times before, but his condition's only gotten worse."

"Mommy," Mom says with a note of warning in her voice.

"His liver's taken a beating, and it was in tatters when he came here last. The doctors told him he had to stop. If he doesn't…"

"Mommy, stop."

But Ofelia ignores Mom. "If he doesn't stop, he'll die."

I feel as though Ofelia has wrapped her cold, fleshy hands around my throat. I choke on the juice I just swallowed. I always knew Dad enjoyed his liquor – my name is a testament to that, after all – but it only ever seemed a part of his jovial nature.

"Perhaps I shouldn't have said anything. I'm surprised you didn't know, seeing as you're his daughter. But we can't blame the ignorance of one on the lack of communication of the other. What have you been doing for him lately, Maria?" Ofelia asks the question nonchalantly, but her eyes narrow as she says it. "Of course, he's killing himself slowly, and he's as stubborn as an ox. Sometimes I think he does it just to plague me."

Mom snorts. "You're giving yourself a lot of credit."

Ofelia looks at Mom, and, for a moment, I think she'll snap, but instead she just sighs and looks away. "Sometimes, I wonder how Eduardo would be, if only he had ended up with someone else."

"Well, that someone else left and, even if she stuck around, it would be no thanks to you."

Ofelia sighs again. "Only God can know how things would have been if everything had been done right. I'm sure it would have been better than this, though. But, alas, here you are."

"Here I am," Mom says, holding Ofelia's gaze.

The steady stare is only interrupted when Dad returns, and he's just as inclined to stay as the rest of us. "The driver called," he says. "He's fifteen minutes from here, so we may as well head out now."

We put aside our half-empty cups.

"Mommy, it was a pleasure as always," Dad says.

"Of course, Eduardo. Until next time." As he turns to go, Ofelia grasps his hand and squeezes it with surprising tenderness. "And there will be a next time, right? Come back anytime, Eduardo. Come home."

But Dad stopped listening long ago.

28.

WHEN WE FINALLY EMERGE FROM THE hospital, it's as though we've escaped a trap that was closing all its doors and threatening to suffocate us inside. I blink in the sunlight, after sitting so long in the dark, and become aware that I've carried a souvenir out with me. "Should we go back so I can return this?" I ask, holding Dad's senior yearbook up for him to see.

Dad looks at the yearbook, looks back at the hospital, and shakes his head. "We're not going back in there even if you somehow managed to take Mommy's scooter with you," he says, making Mom and I laugh.

The remainder of our journey to Boracay consists of a five-hour drive and a thirty-minute boat ride. The first hour is taken in silence. I study Dad's reflection in the rear view mirror and try to digest what I have learned about him in just a few minutes at my grandmother's. I wonder who the man before me is; the father who's here but is never really here.

At the one-hour mark, Dad asks Jerry to stop for a quick washroom break. Jerry pulls off the highway and stops at a McDonald's.

I hesitate only a moment after Dad exits the car. "How long did you know he had this problem?" I ask, turning to Mom.

"Probably as long as you," Mom says, resignation in her voice as she watches cars drive in and out of the parking lot. "Don't tell me you didn't know, Benni. You always did."

I think again of Dad at Christmastime – all the cigarettes and booze – and when he'd fight with Mom, banging cupboards in search of bottles in the house. "I didn't know it was a problem. I didn't know he was here for rehab."

"He *was*," Mom says, stressing the latter word.

"You knew and you never told me."

"What was there to tell, Benni? What could you do? What was the point of troubling you? You might be grown up, Benni, but I'm still your mother, and I can still protect you." When I don't say anything, she continues. "Your dad needs to go back to rehab, Benni. You heard your *Lola* Ofelia. He needs professional help. It's help neither you nor I can give him. Now that we're here, though, we can support him, and do what little we can do. We need to be present for him. Manila is the best place for him to be right now. As much as your *Lola* Ofelia and I have our differences, she can get him the best care he needs until he finds himself again."

I nod, for once agreeing with Mom. Right now, being in the Philippines seems like the best option. I can't shake the feeling that it's not only the best place for Dad, but for all of us.

29.

WHEN WE FINALLY REACH BORACAY, we take another ride by jeepney to our beachfront resort. Celeste reserved a room for us in a place called Verity. I catch glimpses of inland Boracay on our way there. It is littered with tin roofs and dirt paths poorer than any part of the Philippines I have yet seen. Even the clothes hanging out to dry on thin lines look as downtrodden as the people who watch our progress with expressionless faces. Soon enough, the packed earth roads give way to wider, sandier ones, and tin roofs turn to roofs of clay shingles. We pull into a sandstone clearing, where we can hear the waves and catch glimpses of the sea between stuccoed resorts.

The setting sun decorates the sky in large swaths of orange, yellow, and pink that blend like watercolours into the sea. The sunset backlights the palm trees, creating dark paper cut outs silhouetted against the sky. It looks too beautiful to be real.

"My God," I say as I emerge from the jeepney's carriage. I am unable to finish the thought, so it sounds like a prayer.

"Benni, pass the camera and turn for a photo," Mom says.

I toss the camera to Mom, but say, "No. No pictures this time. I'm going swimming."

Dad and I share a grin before we start running. We don't need to say where we're going. We're both there, meeting the water at a sprint; it is warm and molten orange in the sun.

Dad and I stay in the water for an hour, silent except for

random bursts of laughter. We face the sun, drinking its last rays into our skin. When the upper rim of it touches the horizon and the reds and yellows have faded to blue, Mom joins us in her one-piece bathing suit, her bottom covered with an attached bathing-suit skirt.

"How could you two run into the water like that?" Mom asks. "Didn't you want to take time to change?" She eyes our soaking clothes.

"It was too good to miss, Maria," Dad says, voicing my thoughts exactly.

I wake up the next morning to an empty penthouse suite and the sound of the ocean outside my window. The two-bedroom suite has two king-sized beds and a lounge area with a large flat-screen TV. I exit onto the balcony in my pajamas to find an unobstructed view of the sea. My eyes follow the sound of Dad's raucous laughter to find him and Mom in bathing suits on the patio below.

"Hey, you're both changed," I call out. "Did you swim already? How long ago did you two get up? Why didn't you wake me?" I'm bothered by the idea of missing time. I tell myself it's because I don't want to miss out on the oasis that is Boracay, but perhaps I just don't want to miss out on time with my parents.

"Don't worry, Princess," Dad says. "We won't go anywhere without you."

I don my bathing suit and join them for breakfast. The resort offers freshly-cooked *longaniza* sausage with eggs, fried rice, fruit, and toast, accompanied by jugs of freshly-squeezed pineapple and mango juice.

"What do you want to do while we're in Boracay, Princess?" Dad asks. We received word that the Consuelos won't be joining us until later this evening, so Mom, Dad, and I have some time alone. "Everything in Boracay's on me. This is my turf."

I laugh. "How so, Dad?"

"You haven't heard?" he asks in mock shock. He looks at Mom. "You haven't told her?" Mom shakes her head. "Well, then, it may come as a surprise to you to hear that your very own, very humble father is the King of Boracay. I know all the good places to go, and I'm friends with all the important people like businessmen and cops, if need be." He winks.

"Is that so?" I ask. "And how did you attain this status, Your Grace?"

"I used to own a bar here. A small place of no matter, really."

"Used to? And then what happened?"

Dad shrugs. "I sold it. It's more fun visiting a bar than owning one. But I still get free drinks, and I still have all my connections – the two things that really matter. I'll bring you there sometime. I have a fun time planned for you today though. If you're with the King of Boracay, you need to experience Boracay as a Princess."

Dad rents a boat in the afternoon to take us out onto the ocean. The Diversa is unlike any boat I've seen before, despite the many drifting along Lake Simcoe during the hazy summer months in Georgina. Two large extensions made of bamboo poles reach out from both sides of the boat, coming to rest just above the water. "The bamboo keeps us steady," Dad explains. "The waves get bad here during typhoon season."

Today, under the scorching sun and without a cloud in sight, the Diversa has a makeshift roof made of two spotted bedsheets strung along its centre pole, pulled taut and tied to its bamboo extensions.

Mom, Dad, and I spread out along the boat, which can fit at least ten people. Dad and I perch on a box in the back, catching sea spray as we speed out to open water. "Have you ever been snorkelling before, Princess?" Dad yells over the wind.

"Never," I say.

"Well, you'll snorkel today."

When we're far enough out that the beach has become a

mere smudge above the water, the driver stops and distributes life jackets and snorkels.

"This is awesome, Dad," I say, before jumping in.

And it is.

The aqua water is warm; it feels like stepping into a bath. I duck my head underwater and see a whole other world beneath us, a world of coral and schools of brightly coloured fish darting about. It's completely different from the murky brown water of Lake Simcoe, where you're just as likely to find a boot as a fish.

Tom and I camped once before, and I vowed never to do it again. "I'm just not an outdoorsy person," I remember declaring after experiencing the mosquitoes, deer flies, and the way the mud oozed between my toes when I went for a dip in the lake.

But I'm an outdoorsy person now. Everything is awash in beauty.

Even Mom, whose definition of a well-spent sunny day is one inside, is enjoying herself. She grabs the bamboo extension on one side of the boat and leans back, closing her eyes. "Oh, Ned, *ang galing nito*," she says.

I don't know how long I spend with my head below water. Water fills my ears and I'm surrounded by silence. For the first time in a long time, I am away from the world and able to breathe. I study the fish passing just out of reach. They are shocks of colour against a wash of blue.

I startle when I feel my big toe being yanked. I turn and rise, sputtering through a mouthful of salt water, to find Dad laughing. "I've been trying to get your attention for the last five minutes," he says.

"I couldn't hear you."

"I figured that much."

"I'm having a great time."

"Are you?" His face lights up with a large smile. "I'm glad you are."

"Of course I am. Can I move here yet or what?"

"Princess, you're a first-world kind of gal, just as I raised you to be. There's no life for you here."

"You're here."

"I'm here," Dad concedes, "but only for now. And you're here for now, too. So buck up. We're heading out."

"Where are we going?"

"To grab some grub. Aren't you hungry?"

As soon as he says it, I feel my stomach grumble. "I am. I guess I lost track of time. But when can we come back?"

"Next time," he says.

We clamber back onto the boat but, instead of turning toward the beach, we head in a different direction. "Where are we going?" I yell to Dad.

"Why do you always ask? Haven't you learned to enjoy the ride yet? It's a surprise."

The driver brings us further out to sea before heading back to land but instead of sand, we pass a series of jutting rocks studded with scraggly trees. We turn towards a large outcropping of mottled grey and green. The rocks grow larger the further in we get until we approach the geography of a different island.

The sound of Tagalog reggae music reaches our ears before we round another rock to find a small, sandy oasis cleared of trees. Three white plastic garden chairs surround a blue linen-covered table. The cloth waves in the breeze as though flagging us home. A wooden sign nailed onto a palm tree reads, "WELCOME TO MARIA BENEDICTINE BEACH."

"Eduardo, what is this?" Mom asks.

"Surprise," Dad says, beaming. "Remember the fish farm I told you about? Well, this is a remnant of it."

"You called it 'Maria Benedictine Beach'?" Mom asks.

"What's the fun of owning an island if you can't call it what you want? And I only ever think of you and yours, my dear."

The driver hops off the boat when we reach shore and guides us to land.

Dad climbs off the boat to give Mom and I a hand. "Hello, hello, hello!" he bellows once we're finally on solid ground.

A man appears from a dusty path at Dad's call. "*Hoy Señor* Ned! Welcome!" he says, wiping his hands on a dishcloth. "I'll bring everything out for you now." He disappears up the sandy path and behind the trees just as quickly as he came.

"Have a seat, Princess. Sit down, Maria," Dad says, pulling two of the plastic chairs out for Mom and I.

"I'm lost. What is this place?" I ask. "And where is that music coming from?"

"It's our own little island. I purchased it for the fish farm. The farm hasn't been too successful, but it's a hell of a place to get away to, isn't it? I wired speakers around the island. The closest ones are in the trees over there." I follow Dad's finger to see where he's pointing. Two speakers rest like blackened coconuts in a palm tree. "I thought it would improve worker morale. It did, I suppose, but it didn't do much for the fish."

"Can we see the rest of the island?" I ask.

"There's not much else to see. I didn't clear the rest of it. It's uninhabitable and unmanned, except for a hut just around the corner. That's where the workers stay when they're here. Anyways, dinner is served."

Sure enough, the man from before returns with platters laden with steaming white rice and fried fish.

"It's a simple meal, Princess, but a home-grown one," Dad says.

Either I'm starving from snorkelling or the fish is exceptionally good here because I devour my meal within minutes even though I'm not a big seafood fan. While Mom takes her time with her food, I stand to explore. Night is falling, and I wander up the sandy path from where Dad's help came.

Just as Dad mentioned, a small hut is nestled far back in the woods. Smoke rises from a hidden smokestack, and the smell of frying fish fills the air. There is nothing beyond the hut but the blackness of crowded trees. I wander to the entrance, drawn by the sound of voices from inside. Light streams through a crack in the door, which has been left ajar. I pause to listen, hearing the voice of the man who served us earlier. He pauses, and the voice of a child picks up where he left off. I nudge the door open and peek inside. The man sits by a portable stove, cooking fish in a frying pan. He speaks in Tagalog, pointing out the cooked parts of the fish to a young boy who can only be his son – so alike do they look. The boy crouches before the stove with a bowl in his hands and gestures to an uncooked part of the fish. "*Hindi pa luto ito?*" he asks.

"*Hindi pa,*" the man says. "That part is not done. Wait for it to cook." The two watch the fish for just a few seconds, then the man hands the boy a spatula. "*Gusto mo bang i-*flip *ito?*" I lean forward to watch the boy flip the fish – he holds the spatula with a look of great concentration – but my bag knocks the door open and the two look up.

The man stands up. "*Kamusta, po,*" he starts, but I'm already backing away, regretting my imposition. I want to explain that I was touched by his gentle instruction to his son, but I know the language barrier would prevent any understanding.

"Princess?" I hear Dad calling. "Are you looking for ghosts?"

I back away, pulling the door shut as I go, and head back to the table. The door opens and the man emerges after me, holding a platter of just-sliced mango and watermelon. He places the dish on the table with an apologetic smile that seems to suggest he thinks the fruit is what I had come looking for. I mumble my thanks before turning my attention to Dad. "Why would you start a fish farm in the first place, Dad?" I ask.

Dad shrugs. "I wanted to try something new. The science of fish farming is quite simple. You just create ecosystems for your fish to thrive in, like pools or ponds. This island has about eight or nine pools now but unless you're ready to do it in earnest, you get pennies in return. It's a nice place though, isn't it?"

"It has a nice name," Mom says, smiling at Dad.

I pick up a watermelon slice and take a bite. "It's an odd thing to invest in."

"That's exactly what I said," Mom says.

"Why not just put some money into the hospital?"

"And answer to your *Lola* Ofelia?" Dad asks.

Mom wrinkles her nose. "I wouldn't recommend the hospital as an option either. The more we deal with your mom, the more I have to hear about Sarah."

"Sarah?" Dad asks with surprise. "Where'd that come from?"

"Where do you think?" Mom asks. "Why is Sarah still visiting your mother? That was an unpleasant surprise. To top it off, when you went outside the other day, she continued talking about Sarah while we were alone with her."

"Who *is* Sarah?" I ask. "I didn't hear *Lola* Ofelia mention Sarah yesterday when Dad wasn't there."

"And no one should mention Sarah now, especially during this nice dinner," Dad says.

"Well, you can't leave her unexplained," I say.

Mom stares at Dad as though to say, "This one's yours."

"Sarah's nobody. She was just a girl I used to date," Dad says.

"A girl he was once married to," Mom adds.

"What?" I turn to look at Dad. "You were married before Mom? Who the hell are you?"

"Your mom is being O.A.," he says, using the Filipino term for overreacting. He turns to Mom. "Why dig up the past, Maria?"

"I don't know. Ask your mother," Mom says.

"Sarah and I were hardly married."

"You two said your vows."

"We were young."

"So were we when we got married," Mom counters.

"But Sarah and I were younger. And drunk."

"Stop," I interrupt them, "and start from the beginning."

"Your mother's making it sound like more than it was," Dad says.

"No, your refusal to share the story makes it sound like more than it was," I say, exasperated.

"What's up with you and your mother ganging up on me?" Dad asks, raising his hands in surrender. "Fine, fine. I'll share the story. Sarah was a girl I dated in high school. We were young and silly. *Kuya* Miguel and I were out partying one day, had a bit too much to drink, and decided to get hitched to our girls. It was a civil ceremony."

"You two eloped? Together? That's a little beyond the bounds of a bad bender, no? A little permanent. It's like waking up with a bad tattoo."

"You're one to talk; you have one. Anyway, my marriage, if that's what you want to call it, wasn't so permanent in the end. Sarah and I divorced without a problem."

"Her parents made her do it," Mom says.

"So, why is *Lola* Ofelia still going on about it? Sounds like you dodged a bullet on that one, Dad."

"Mommy liked Sarah. She was my first serious girlfriend. She helped me settle down to a certain extent."

"His mother wishes he did things right. She wishes he ended up with the woman he loved, and clearly I stopped that from happening. 'He hasn't been the same since.'" Mom says in a spot-on imitation of Ofelia. I suspect she's imitated Ofelia more than a few times before.

"That's harsh," I say.

"Tell me about it," Mom says.

"It's terrible because it's untrue. I did end up with the woman I loved, and still love." Dad smiles at Mom and squeezes her hand.

"What happened to *Tito* Miguel's girlfriend? When did they split?"

"Never," Dad says, gazing out at the shoreline. "You don't always grow out of your first love." The silence draws on, and I wonder if Dad ever grew out of his first love after all. I clear my throat to bring Dad back to the present. Dad shakes his head. "Anyways, Sarah was completely forgotten as soon as I met your mother."

"Lies! You were a heartbroken little puppy when we met," Mom says.

"Maybe I was when we met, but then you changed all of that," Dad says.

"Wait, didn't you and Mom meet after university? And didn't you and Sarah marry and divorce after high school? That's a long time to be hung up on a girl."

Dad shrugs. "I was a bit heartbroken still, I guess."

"A bit is an understatement. Your dad was very heartbroken, but we started off as friends, so that was fine with me."

"And then we fell in love. The end," Dad says.

"No, not the end. Your dad was heartbroken, in addition to being his usual rebellious self."

"And your mother was a goody two-shoes – squeaky-clean and fresh out of Assumption College."

"That sounds like a match made in heaven. How did you two end up together anyways?" I ask.

"Your dad and I met at work and became good friends. He had a playboy personality, but I could tell it was all a ruse. He told me all about Sarah. Did you know that he left the Philippines because of her?"

"Oh, come on, Maria, I left because I needed a change."

"No, we both know that you left because you wanted to find her," Mom says. She turns to me. "Her parents sent her to the States shortly after the divorce," she explains.

"So, how did Dad end up in Canada?"

"Canada's immigration laws were far more relaxed. Your dad thought he could visit the United States after he moved though."

"All this Sarah stuff is made up. I wanted a change of scenery and a better life, and it's a good thing I made the move. It's the reason why your mom and I talked so often in the first place. Your mom was chasing me for a visa."

"*Sige*. Keep talking, Mr. Hotshot," Mom mutters. "You and I both know that I chased no one. I could have had any man I wanted without having to ask." She addresses me. "Lucky for your dad, I wanted to hear more about Canada, and we stayed in touch on that pretence. Then we started dating while he was abroad."

"You learn a lot about a person through their letters," Dad says. "For example, I learned how madly in love your mother was with me."

"Yeah, right!" Mom says, smacking Dad's shoulder.

"Did I say that? I meant how madly in love I was with your mother."

"That's more like it."

"I came back to the Philippines a few times, and one time I brought your mom back to Canada with me."

"For good," Mom says, patting Dad's hand.

"For good," Dad agrees. "And that's how your mom and I ended up together."

"Because of Sarah," Mom says.

"Oh, please. Because I knew what kind of woman I wanted to spend the rest of my life with, and I grabbed her as soon as I found her."

"A bit of that, but mainly because your dad was pining for Sarah, which led him to Canada, which somehow led him to me."

Dad sighs. "I can never win."

"Well, you won out in the end, didn't you?" Mom asks, gazing past Dad at the welcome sign. "It all worked out in the end, didn't it, Eduardo?"

"It did, my love," he says.

30.

IT'S DARK BY THE TIME WE RETURN to mainland Boracay. After speeding through the blackness of sky and ocean on the Diversa, it's disorienting to enter the main lobby of our building. The foyer light, which is usually warm and inviting, seems too bright in comparison to the moon and stars we've just left. It takes a while for my eyes to adjust before I spot Jerry sitting on one of the tribal-patterned chaises by the front desk. He sits with a casual air that makes it impossible to tell if he's been waiting there for a minute or an hour. "*Señor* Ned, Mrs. Manlapaz," he says, standing when Mom and Dad finally spot him. "The Consuelos have arrived."

"Where are they?" Mom asks. Her cheeks are rosy pink and she has a big smile after tonight's excursion.

"They are staying on the opposite side of Verity, *po*. It's a ten-minute walk from here, crossing through the beach. *Inday* Rose asked me to escort you if you are up for a visit."

"Of course," Mom says, just as Dad says, "I think I'm okay." Mom's smile falls, and she glances at Dad.

"You go ahead, darling. You and Rose should have some time alone together."

"But…"

As though divining the reason for her hesitation, Dad interrupts. "Not to worry, dear. I'm staying in tonight."

"If you're sure," Mom says, sounding unconvinced.

"I'm sure," Dad says, and reaches out to give her a kiss.

Mom looks as surprised as I am by his unexpected display of affection. "Don't worry so much about me. You have a life, too," Dad says.

With so much persuasion, Mom, Jerry, and I depart. At this time of night, the beach looks like a vast expanse of grey in our very own black-and-white film. I breathe in the salty tang of the surf, which fills me with all the openness of the sea.

Within minutes, the world comes to life in colour again, with pinpricks of light standing out against the darkness. From this vantage point, Verity looks like a small metropolitan city built up amidst the sand. White stuccoed buildings stand in clusters along sandstone walkways that are lined by street lamps. Glass and metal balconies dot the buildings, and the tops of palm trees peek out from what must be gorgeous rooftop patios.

Jerry brings us to the second block of buildings and rings the doorbell. A dark-skinned woman, clad in a typical uniform, opens the door. We are led into a soaring, two-storey space with an open-concept living and dining area.

"Jerry, is that you?" Rose's voice calls from the second floor. "Did you bring Maria?"

"I'm here, *Ate* Rosie," Mom replies.

Rose emerges from a room above. Lisa comes out from another. "Maria, where's Eduardo?" Rose asks.

"He's staying in tonight," Mom says.

"Staying in, huh?"

Mom colours. "He's tired."

Rose doesn't dwell on it. "Well, it's good you can come and keep me company then. We'll have a fun night together. Come on in. Isn't this place fabulous?"

"It's beautiful," I say. "How was your flight?" I ask as Rose and Lisa come downstairs.

"It was fine," Rose says.

"It's such a relief to be here," Lisa says. "It's been getting pretty hairy at home."

"*Ay nako*. Don't even talk about it, Lisa. It's all so silly," Rose

says, before disregarding her own advice and addressing Mom
with all the relish fresh gossip brings the Dychingco sisters.
"It's ridiculous, Maria. There are reporters at our house non-
stop. It's gotten worse since Sam Paolo released a statement.
Can you believe it? The man is actually *bakla*. He could have
had the decency to tell Ariel. Now the heat's back on him.
Reporters think this confirms their suspicions."

"It's crazy. We had to leave in the middle of the night to
avoid the press. It's so nice to be where the news can't reach
us," Lisa says, picking up a newspaper titled *Boracay Daily*
from the coffee table. She flips it open at random, her eyes
skimming the page. "We can count on weather and the latest
parasailing ads..." Lisa pales midsentence.

Rose, who's pointing out the free snacks in the mini-fridge to
Mom, notices Lisa's abrupt stop and comes over to investigate.
"Lisa, what is it?" she asks.

Lisa doesn't reply. She's still but for her eyes racing across
the page.

"Lisa? Lisa, answer me." Rose snatches the paper from Lisa's
hands to read it herself. After a minute, Rose throws the paper
to the ground. "*Puñeta*. This is ridiculous. Take that away,"
she tells the help.

The paper is picked up and hidden.

"Think nothing of it, Lisa. Journalists these days just want
to sensationalize everything."

"'Ariel's wannabe, less-than-average step-daughter steals
away under the cover of night'?" Lisa intones.

"It's nothing. I can't believe they're reporting this here. What
has the world come to, that this makes news now?"

"'The step-daughter, who thinks she can act, thinks she is
actually of enough importance to take leave'?"

"Nothing nice in the paper, I'm guessing?" Mom asks.

Rose shakes her head, warning Mom not to continue.

"This is ridiculous," Lisa says, standing up.

"It's nothing, *apo*. Think nothing of it."

Lisa's colour returns. "I know. It's fine."

"It is fine," Rose says, as though repeating it will make it true.

"There's nothing to worry about. We're here, after all," Lisa says.

"Exactly," Rose says. "That's the spirit."

"Exactly. Anyways, *Ate* Benni and I are going out."

"Yes, you and Benni are…" Now it's Rose's turn to stop mid-sentence as she realizes what Lisa's just said. "Wait, you are?"

"We are?" I ask.

"Yes, we are," Lisa says with a bright smile.

"There's no way the two of you are going out in Boracay alone, Lisa. Especially with your name and face all over the papers. It won't be safe."

"Not to worry, *Lola* Rosie, we'll stay in Verity. We'll just hit up the pool. It's like hanging out at the Manila Golf and Country Club. You can't expect Benni and I not to go out at all, can you?"

Rose looks skeptical but doesn't protest. "Okay. Just make sure you bring Jerry with you."

"Bring Jerry with us? In Verity? *Lola*, don't be crazy."

Rose studies Lisa's flushed face. For a moment I think she'll refuse, but she finally nods. "Well, as long as you stay in Verity. I want your cellphone on you at all times."

"Of course," Lisa says.

"You watch out for each other, okay, Benni?" Rose says, looking at me.

"Of course, *Tita* Rosie," I reply.

"C'mon, *Ate* Benni," Lisa calls, already at the door.

"Now? Do I need to change?"

"Yes, now. And no, there's no need to change. We're not going anywhere special, after all." This last comment is addressed more to Rose than to me before Lisa heads out the door.

31.

"**H**EY, LISA, WAIT UP," I SAY, following her outside. "Sorry," Lisa says, turning around when she reaches the end of the walkway. "I just needed to go out." Her voice sounds strangled. "I'm sorry," she says again, "but it would be nice to go *somewhere*. You know, to party or something."

Her words remind me of how I felt after Tom and I broke up and the rash decision I made to travel somewhere if only to alleviate the pain. "Sure," I say, shrugging. "Lead the way."

"There's always a party happening in Boracay," Lisa says as we continue walking. I can tell she's trying to make polite conversation, but she ends up talking in fits and starts about the weather instead.

"Calm down, Lisa," I say when she pauses to take a breath. "We're okay. We'll have a nice night out." I smile and squeeze her hand.

She squeezes mine back. We fall silent as we walk. After a few minutes, the sound of chattering voices and heavy bass reaches us. We round the corner to find a raised infinity pool overlooking the ocean. A bridge runs from the edge of the pool to a bar at its centre. A DJ spins music and people crowd the area, chatting and dancing. The place is packed, despite it being a weekday.

"Bingo," Lisa says. "Let's grab a drink." Lisa pushes her way through the crowd to the bar, and a bartender approaches right away. "Two liquid cocaines," she yells over the music.

"Liquid cocaines?" I ask, wrinkling my nose. "I see we're not easing into this."

"I never do," Lisa says, flashing me a smile.

Energy pulses through my body as the reverberating boom of bass-heavy trance music shakes the floor. The drinks arrive just as I hear a voice near my ear say, "Fancy seeing you here."

I turn to meet the smirking gaze of a fair-skinned, spiky-haired man in a pressed dress shirt and khaki shorts. His aftershave tickles my nose. He looks familiar. "Do I know…"

"Abe," Lisa says, interrupting. She sticks out a hand, and he shakes it. "Lisa and…"

"Benni. I remember," Abe says with a crooked smile.

It's his cocky air, not his name, that reminds me of who he is. "Ah, Abe Razon," I say.

Abe's smile widens. "I see you remember me, too."

"Of course she does," Lisa says before I can reply. We watch her shoot the first, then the second, liquid cocaine.

"Hey, I thought one of those were mine."

"Don't you worry," Lisa says to me. "Look, Abe, do you have anything?"

Abe raises an eyebrow.

"Lisa, what are you…"

Lisa shoots me another bright smile and laughs. "Not to worry, *Ate* Benni. Everyone who's anyone in the Philippines always has something good. Isn't that right, Abe?"

Abe glances at me with a raised eyebrow before shrugging and pulling a small mint case out of his pocket. He shakes it open to reveal three blue diamond-like candies. And then it dawns on me – it's ecstasy. "Is she always like this?" Abe asks me when Lisa turns to order another round of shots.

"It's been a rough night," I say. Abe nods. "What are you doing in Boracay?" I ask as Lisa downs two more shots.

"I came with friends. It was a last minute thing." He nods over at two men sitting poolside. "I wasn't sure if it was a good idea for me to come or not since there's always something or other to do for the business, but I'm glad I came." He smiles, and a small part of me flutters at the thought that a man worth seven-and-a-half billion dollars is happy to see me.

Lisa rejoins the conversation. "What are we waiting for?" she asks with sparkling eyes.

"You," Abe says.

"Well, I'm here," she says.

"Lisa, we need to go back to *Tita* Rosie at the end of the night."

"I know, and *Lola* Rosie will probably be sleeping already and will be none the wiser. Are you always so reluctant to live a little, *Ate* Benni?" Lisa says this lightly, and I know she's being playful, but the comment gets to me nonetheless.

I took E once before with Tom in the early days of our relationship. We had gone to a party in downtown Toronto. It was a formal but terribly boring affair. His friend had E – a blue diamond like this one. We had taken it to spice things up, but the night ended in tears when Tom left me to go home and attend to a petty request from his mother. On the one hand, I had felt selfish picking a fight when his mother wanted him. On the other hand, he had left me alone, high, in his friend's apartment – a man I hardly knew. The next morning, as an apology, Tom had brought me breakfast and two dozen roses and all was forgotten. I should have seen the red flags.

Remembering Tom decides the matter for me even more than Lisa's comment. I'm ready to experience life on my own terms. "When in Rome," I say, shrugging.

Abe smiles. "All right then. Open up," he says.

Lisa opens her mouth, and he drops a diamond on her tongue. Abe looks at me. I'm about to ask why I can't put the thing in my mouth myself but I shrug again and open wide. Abe's fingers graze my lips just before I feel the small candy fall onto the centre of my tongue. I accept the bottle of water he offers and down it in a few gulps.

The wait begins.

32

THE FEELING STARTS AN HOUR LATER in the pit of my belly and the tips of my fingers. Lisa, Abe, and I join his friends sitting on a set of leather sofas that surround a glass-top table. Maybe E really is a thing in the Philippines, because Abe's friends are already high when we join them.

The feeling builds with the bass of the trance music, which now seems to drill into the inside of my skull. This building high feels nothing like what I experienced with Tom, and I wonder if it's because this pill is stronger or because this music is better. And then I catch my train of thought like a third party observer and put a stop to it. *Don't think, Benni*, this spectator in my mind tells me. *You're in the Philippines now.* I comply with my interior self and lick my lips, marvelling at their smoothness on my tongue. I catch Abe's eye across the table.

He studies the movement of my tongue and smiles. "You're feeling it now, aren't you?" he asks.

I nod.

"You're feeling it now?" Lisa yells from beside me. "So am I, *Ate* Benni." She lets out a *whoop* and throws her arms up in the air. Lisa has been downing shot after shot since dropping her pill – a heady concoction of Head Shocks, Fuzzy Worms, and absinthe. Abe and I had both advised against it, but she shrugged off our warnings. The better I feel though, the less worried I am, and I grin at her now as she yells at no one in particular, "I'm so happy. So, so happy." Lisa's arm brushes against mine, and I shiver. "Feels good, huh?" she asks. "Rub your hands together."

I do as she says and am mesmerized by how good the simplest of actions feel. "So smooth," I murmur.

Lisa laughs and gives another *whoop*. "I'm so glad you're here and you're doing this with me," she says, giving me a hug and a fierce kiss on the lips. She pulls back, her eyes dreamy. "Amazing, huh?"

I nod. "I'm sleepy though," I say as I feel my eyes closing.

"Oh no, you're not. Not tonight. Get up, *Ate*. Let's dance." Though all I feel like doing right now is curling into a warm, happy ball, I am pulled up by Lisa. Abe and his friends stand and follow us into the crush of the crowd. I feel a moment of intense paranoia at all the people around us before I feel cool, smooth hands on my face.

"Relax, *Ate* Benni," Lisa says like she's reading my mind. "We're only here in Verity like *Lola* Rosie said we should be. We're completely safe."

I gaze into her deep, chocolate brown eyes and feel like I can look into them forever with her palms on my cheeks.

She studies me before breaking into a smile and planting another kiss on my forehead. "Let's dance," she says again.

Abe and his friends secure a spot against the corner of the DJ's booth and clear a small space for us to move. Lisa sways to the beat, looking like she belongs in a music video. I raise a hand, bury my fingers in my hair, and sway my head from side to side. I feel sexy and vibrant. My cheeks are warm, my back is sleek with sweat, and the perspiring bottle of water serves as a cool contrast against my skin.

I see Abe waving his hands to call our attention. I lean close to hear what he's saying. "Wait for it," he yells, his finger pointing up in the air. I study his face, trying to figure out what we're waiting for, and see his head is cocked to the side, bobbing to the beat of the music. I study his movements and suddenly feel what he feels – the anticipation in the beats leading up to the song's climax. And then... "Now," he yells. We hit euphoria at the height of the song.

I don't know how long we dance for. But every song seems to fit so well, one after another, while my heart swells with the build and fall of the beat. I've never appreciated music like this before. At one point in the night, my eyes are closed and my head is swaying when I feel solid hands on my face that are firmer and rougher than Lisa's touch. I open my eyes to see Abe. He puts his lips to my ear.

"You're clenching," he says, massaging my jaw. "You're grinding your teeth." He hands me an orange lollipop. "Suck on this," he says, and I am filled with a deep sense of gratitude that he's looking out for me.

The night goes on. The music pounds. I gaze up and see a million tiny stars blinking just beyond the pool lights. They look so close, I'm sure I can touch them if I tried. But I don't need to; it's enough to know they're there. I dance with my face to the sky, turning in slow circles until a new thought suddenly seizes me: *This feeling will go away, escaping from every part of me, from the tips of my fingers to the strands of my hair as if I'm in a rinse cycle, and the night sky is the drain.*

I stop abruptly, frozen by the overwhelming dread of never feeling this good or this happy again.

Lisa sees me and grabs my hand. "Are you okay?" she asks.

"No. I'm freaking out." Just like that, and with those words, I feel the world closing in on me. I can't breathe. My heart is pumping too fast. Surely, I'm going to die.

Abe hears me and ushers Lisa and I back to our chairs. "What's wrong?" he asks.

"She's peaking." Lisa's huge smile seems ill-suited to this moment. "*Ate* Benni, this is the best part." She leans in to hug me, but I shrug away from her, panicked at the thought of even more contact, even more confinement.

"Stop. Don't touch me," I say.

"Okay. It's okay," Abe says. "Benni, close your eyes and we'll breathe together."

I shake my head.

"Trust me," he says. And, since I feel like there's no way out, I close my eyes and follow along as he says, "Breathe in. Breathe out." He and Lisa breathe along deeply beside me. With my eyes closed and the sound of my breath in my ears, I feel my heart open up with each inhale. An intense sense of peace floods me. I open my eyes and gaze into Abe's. "Better?" he asks.

"Yes," I say, and then giggle. I can't keep him straight in my line of vision.

"You have the eye wiggles," he says.

"This is the best part," Lisa says again.

And it is.

We return to the dance floor and spend years there. The longer the music plays, the higher I get, and the better I feel. I never want to leave this sense of well-being and warmth. I never want to escape this high. I refuse to step into the real world that will only steal this feeling from me – this feeling that I long to hoard along with all the stars in the sky.

By the time Lisa starts vomiting, I've already reached nirvana.

33.

"LISA, LISTEN TO ME. ARE YOU OKAY? At least nod if you're okay, or tell us if you need anything." My instructions are useless. Vomit dribbles out of the side of Lisa's mouth and onto her already spoiled clothes. Her head flops to the side. She lolls in Abe's arms, her arm hooked around his neck.

"She shouldn't have had so much to drink while popping," Abe says for the fifteenth time. I study his face as the impersonal third-party Benni and regret to note that his high is over. Thankfully, I'm still buzzing, and while I know Lisa is in bad shape, third-party Benni reassures me that all will be okay. This is only an amplified version of my panic attack, and I got through it fine with Abe's assistance. We're in a safe place.

Verity's four-storey condos twinkle into view. "We're almost there," I say. Lisa groans and flops to her other side. Her new position makes it more difficult for Abe to carry her, but I take her movement as an encouraging sign that she's starting to come to. "It's crazy, but I can still see the strobe lights. Do you see that flashing?" I ask Abe.

"Actually, I do," he says, looking around perplexed. He stiffens and curses under his breath. "Hey, you. Who are you?" he yells.

Lisa groans at the sound of his raised voice.

I turn, surprised by his combative tone, and see the bulb of a camera flash from behind a bush.

Abe takes a step forward, Lisa still in his arms, his hands curling into fists beneath her, as though getting ready to fight. Having been spotted, the photographer emerges from his hiding spot accompanied by two more also armed with cameras. Abe curses and stumbles as quickly as possible to the Consuelos' condo with Lisa in tow.

By the time we reach the front door, the photographers and reporters are all around us. Questions fly through the air.

"Mr. Razon, how do you know Lisa Consuelo?"

"What's wrong with her?"

"Would you say Ms. Consuelo has a problem with alcohol?"

"Is this because her father is gay?"

Abe must be familiar with this treatment. While all I want to do right now is hide, Abe greets the barrage of questions with stony silence and plods on. I wonder why everyone is asking questions, and no one is offering to help when I hear, "Lisa Consuelo, do you know what time it is?"

I freeze. The voice, raised in anger, sounds much like my mother's.

I look up to find Rose instead. Her hands, clenched to her hips, bunch her housedress into folds. Her eyes glint in the lamplight, landing first on me, and then past me at the limp form of Lisa in Abe's arms. I hear her sharp intake of breath as she rushes past me. "What happened?" she asks. "What's wrong with her? Jerry, come and help!"

Lisa opens her mouth as though to speak, but she ends up vomiting at Rose's feet, scattering the reporters around her. The sound of bile hitting sandstone is deafening in the night.

Abe surrenders Lisa to Jerry with apparent relief. "Go. Go on in," he says to me, seeing us to the door before shouldering himself through the small crowd of reporters. The majority of the photographers stick around though I see a couple dog him before the door closes.

I try to look useful, hovering around as Lisa is dragged into the washroom.

"Benni, you're staying here tonight," Rose says before closing the bathroom door.

I'm wide awake but go to the living room and lie on the couch, relieved I don't have to hold up the pretence of usefulness anymore. My high is fading, and I stare at the ceiling two stories above with a sense of loss now that everything is becoming normal again. And the normal world sucks. I hear Rose murmuring and Lisa sobbing behind the closed bathroom door. She's woken up then. Third-party Benni, who is slowly fading into oblivion, notes that this is a good thing.

The door opens and closes. I hear Rose's slippered feet climb the stairs to her bedroom. As I listen to the sound of my breath and the occasional heave from Lisa in the washroom, I watch the clock beneath the TV change from one hour to the next. At four a.m. on the dot, Rose returns to the bathroom, checking on Lisa without a word before returning to bed. This happens again at five and at six. Finally, by seven a.m., as the rising sun brings definition to the room, I feel nearly back to normal enough to sleep, but too thirsty to commit. I decide to grab a drink of water when I hear Rose return to the bathroom once more. I wait for her to go back to her room, but she doesn't return. After half an hour passes, I get up.

I freeze at the sound of voices behind the bathroom door. Rose forgot to close the door this time, and I can see her sitting on a stool by the toilet, stroking Lisa's head as Lisa rests her cheek on the seat. Rose's shoulders shake. I hear tears in her voice. "I don't know what to do, *apo*," she says over and over again. "I don't know what to do."

From here I can see Lisa's tears, running tracks through the filth and makeup on her face as she whispers, "I'm sorry," each time in response.

34

I WAKE UP ON THE COUCH TO SILENCE. The clock reads two p.m. I feel groggy and sore from dancing but otherwise okay. I check to see if Lisa's still in the washroom but find it empty and sparkling clean.

I tiptoe upstairs to her bedroom and peek in to find her slumbering frame beneath the blanket. I approach and lay a hand on her forehead. Her eyes flutter, but she doesn't wake. She looks pale but intact.

I turn to find Rose leaning against the door frame. My apprehension passes when I see her smile. "She's just resting," Rose says as I follow her out the door. "She loves to party and sometimes forgets her limits. It happens to us all, I suppose, but it's harder on Lisa, considering her condition."

"Her condition?"

"Her eating condition, remember?"

"Oh, yes."

Lisa mumbles something from inside, giving us pause.

Rose closes the door. "Poor girl. I want to give her as much rest as possible and all the help she needs."

"Of course."

"It's too bad the reporters were there. How long were they following you?"

"They were only there at the end of the night."

Rose shakes her head. "They're going to have a field day with this. We've requested for the papers not to be delivered.

It'd be better if we just try to forget about it. Lisa doesn't need to see any of the coverage from last night."

I nod.

"You had an okay night though? Nothing crazy happened otherwise?"

"Other than Lisa getting sick, no," I say, trying to figure out how much Rose knows. "Lisa just drank too much, I guess." Rose's look of unease lessens. "Okay, good. Sorry again that you had to see that."

"*Tita* Rosie, no apologies needed." The sense of well-being from last night resurfaces. "We're family."

The Consuelos stay in for the next couple of days to allow Lisa to recover, giving Dad, Mom, and I plenty of time together. Dad takes us jet skiing, fly-fishing, and banana boating; he also orders massages and mango slushies for Mom and I on the beach.

The next evening, I join my parents during their visit to Rose's and sneak up to Lisa's room to see how she's doing. I open her door to the sound of sobbing.

I enter to find Lisa leaning against the foot of her king-sized bed, the garish print of a magazine in hand and crumpled tissues surrounding her like fallen petals on the floor. "Lisa, what are you doing?" I ask.

Lisa tucks the magazine away before turning her head to look at me.

"Why are you hiding that? What is it?" I sit beside her on the floor and she pushes the magazine to me with disgust. "How did you even get this?" I ask.

"Just because *Lola* Rosie cut off the papers, doesn't mean I can't get the truth."

"This isn't necessarily the truth, Lisa, just because it's printed," I say. I study the front cover – it sports a full-page photo of Lisa in Abe's arms from the night before. The camera must have been a good one; the picture clearly shows the vomit glistening on her chin and clothes. I flip the magazine open to the main story and skim its content. "Hey, at least Abe Razon didn't comment," I say. I note with admiration the fact that he neither confirmed nor denied any relationship with Lisa, and he refused to comment on what the media referred to as "a drunken hot mess." His failure to do so resulted in further speculation about his social life, a hassle that he could likely have avoided if only he were a less honourable man.

"And much good that did," Lisa says. "I love reading about how I'm not worth Abe Razon's shoe buckle."

"Well, look on the bright side, Lisa. You've finally hit the front page." My wry humour is a long shot, but Lisa takes it.

She laughs in a blubbery way. "I said I wanted to be in print media but not like this."

I flip through the magazine. "Hey, at least you're not this chick," I say, showing her a "Hot or Not" photo of a woman, unfortunately large, dressed in tighter-than-skin-tight clothing, who has been placed in the "Not" category.

Lisa laughs, and I take it as encouragement.

I spend the rest of the evening going through the magazine with her, looking for the bizarre and ugly. I make her laugh until she takes the magazine, rips the cover off, and hands it to me.

"Take that and frame it, *Ate* Benni. It was an epic night," she says.

"It was," I say.

Before I can say anything else, she squeezes me in a hug. "Thank you for everything," she says.

"Don't thank me," I say. "This is what family's for, right?"

35.

O N OUR FIFTH DAY IN BORACAY, Dad calls me to the beach as the sun lowers for a final excursion. "I hope you aren't scared of heights," he says.

"Heights? Why?" I've been scared of heights my whole life and am annoyed Dad doesn't know that, but I bite back the urge to dampen his mood. He seems so excited, he's glowing.

"Because I've arranged a little treat for you," he says.

"Dad, you've treated us a lot already."

"And here's one more," he says as a boat passes by. "It'll be the best treat of all."

"A boat ride?"

"Only for a bit, and then we go up in that," Dad says, pointing upwards.

I gasp. "Wow, that's high." We watch what can only be parasailers soaring above the ocean. They're too small to be seen from here, and their parasail looks like nothing more than a speck.

"Of course. What kind of view would you have if you were any lower?"

"Aren't there regulations about how high you can go on those things?"

"Maybe in Canada, but we're in a lawless country, and lawlessness has its advantages. Are you ready?"

On board the boat, the driver's assistant straps us into life-jackets and harnesses us together onto one large parasail. The driver guides the boat far from the coast and looks to Dad for direction while taking us in large, lazy circles. We're soaked with sea water on the stern of the boat – a relief from the heat – but after ten minutes I call out: "Dad, what're we waiting for?"

"You'll see," Dad calls back with a smile. "Trust me for once."

Dad nods at the assistant after another ten minutes. The parasail is unfurled on Dad's signal. The fabric billows out behind us into a huge blue-and-yellow dome with a Superman logo on it. The faster the boat goes, the higher the parasail rises, and the more it tugs us from the boat's stern. The harness pulls taut once the parasail is far enough from us, lifting us completely. Dad and I sit for a time with our toes grazing the ocean before we soar even higher. "Isn't this amazing?" Dad yells.

"Oh, jeez," I say, closing my eyes, tightening my grip, and feeling the strap of the harness bite into my palms. I'm trying to still my overwhelming urge to vomit.

"Are you okay, Princess?"

"I'm a little scared of heights," I cry. "I'll be okay if we don't go too high."

"I don't know if you'll be okay then. We're only going higher. Check it out."

"That's all right," I gasp, squeezing my eyes shut even tighter. "I'm good like this."

"But you're missing out." Dad lets out a *whoop* and I feel him swinging about in his harness. "We're flying," he yells.

With my eyes closed, it does indeed feel like we're soaring of our own accord, and I don't know if I like it. I open my eyes for a quick peek and see Dad in my peripheral vision with his arms spread wide. The people on the beach have shrunk. The village behind the resort sprouts into view, and tin roofs glint beneath us. I can even see over the island to the other side of Boracay, where we went fly-fishing and banana boating the other day. I close my eyes again.

Higher and higher we go, beyond North American parasailing regulations for sure, and a second peek reveals that only the tallest trees on the untouched center of the island are now distinct.

I close my eyes and focus on my breathing: deep breath in through my nose, long breath out through my mouth. I'm not sure how long I'm doing this until I hear Dad yell, "Benni, open your eyes." He jabs me in the side.

"Don't poke me, Dad," I scream, trying to swallow back my growing hysteria.

"If you don't open your eyes, I'm going to…." I feel Dad shift his weight and the harness jiggles.

"What was that?" I cry.

"I don't know. Maybe you should open your eyes. Open your eyes. Open your eyes." Dad bounces in his harness with each word.

I panic, thinking of the stress Dad's two-hundred-and-eighty pounds is placing on the parasail. My eyes fly open, and I finally see what Dad sees, what he knew we would see and had waited to show me.

"My God," I breathe. "It's beautiful."

The sun sets over the island, reaching out with fingers of red and yellow and diffusing around us in an orange haze. Whereas the ocean looked like molten lava when we first arrived, today it looks like pure gold. The island spreads out below us in miniature. If I could, I would take it in hand and keep it for myself. Looking out at the sea and island beneath me, with Dad at my side, I am suddenly unafraid. I've gained invincibility with height and feel like we own the Superman logo stretched taut on the sail behind us.

The gold lingers for twenty minutes before the sun sets far enough to cast a muted pink that fades into light blue. The sky's blue is now almost the same as the blue sky that preceded the sunset, making it seem as though the world might, at any moment, erupt into deep orange hues again. We're not brought down until every last bit of the sunset fades from the sky.

I open my arms as we approach the sea to embrace the world in this one perfect moment and my superhuman experience of it all.

"You really are the king," I say, hugging Dad when we reach land.

36

MOM AND I SIT SIDE BY SIDE in front of the mirror in Zu-elueta – the salon Celeste had said has excellent service and amazing stylists.

"The salon is so good that I purchased packages for the two of you," Celeste had said over the speakerphone during her daily check-in on Lisa and Gia. "It's already paid for, so you two can't refuse."

I'm glad to have this quiet time after the past few days of activity. Celeste wasn't kidding either when she said Zuelueta offered the best in service and luxury. Mom and I are in the process of receiving foot and hand massages as our hair is styled.

"What do you want to do today, honey?" my stylist, a flamboyant man with flowing hair dyed in five different shades of red and blonde, asks.

"Why don't you get your hair coloured?" Mom asks.

I study my heavy black hair hanging in curtains by my cheeks. "Sure, why not? How about a cut and colour?"

"Excellent. Trim, cut, or chop?" the stylist asks, wiggling his eyebrows when he says the latter.

I pause only for a second before saying, "Chop."

"What?" Mom asks, turning to me and upsetting her stylist's careful attention to her grey hair.

"It's time for a change. Cut it off. Make it short. Dye it blonde. I don't care, as long as it's nice."

"Of course. Don't fear. Magic happens with these hands," my

stylist says, whipping his hair over his shoulder before pulling a comb and scissors from his back pocket.

His confidence is a nice change from Mom's co-worker in Canada, who cuts my hair in her unfinished basement and cries when I ask her to cut it short. I send up a silent prayer that my hair won't look like my stylist's and give myself over to his art.

The cut takes forty-five minutes. The majority of my hair is chopped off in five, leaving my neck cold and bare. I can't help but laugh at Mom, who is watching me with candid resignation. "You're crazy," she says.

I shrug and two hands descend on my head. "Don't move. It's time for the surgery." The stylist's snips become quicker and more precise. I can barely see what he's cutting as he squints at my head and darts a hand out here or there to trim a stray strand.

"So, are you enjoying yourself so far?" Mom asks as our stylists work away.

"Of course. Everything is so different here. It makes me wonder though.... What does *Tita* Rosie do all day?" Rose lacks any productive hobbies like Mom, and she doesn't have any of the little household chores Mom takes on in Canada since she has help to do it all for her. She has an unlimited amount of time with seemingly nothing to fill it up.

Mom laughs. "She doesn't do anything. I told you that when we first arrived. That's what I like about Canada: the variety. I lived my whole life with my family and in Assumption. When I met your dad, it was different. He was different. He was the complete opposite of what my family wanted for me. But he was so exciting."

"But what about all the riches here?"

"What is wealth without freedom?" Mom replies. "I always felt so stifled here, like there was nowhere for me to go. You're surrounded by people all the time."

I'm surprised by Mom's comment. I would've thought she'd love having a household like the Consuelo household, which is packed at any given moment with help or family. At home, in Canada, I feel like I can't leave the house for fear or guilt of leaving her behind alone. And yet, here she is, talking about freedom. "Mom, I'm serious. I want to stay here," I say. I can't tell if Mom hears me because, just as I say it, my stylist drops his scissors on the tray beside him. "All done?" I ask.

"Not even close. Off to the sink with you."

"Why?"

"No questions, remember?" he says.

I rest my head in the sink while his assistant gives my scalp a soothing rinse and a head massage. When I return to my seat, the stylist has set up a tray of foil and dye. I don't ask questions as instructed, and it's not until the foil is removed and he begins drying my hair that I see he's given me a jagged pixie cut with strawberry-blonde highlights. I can hardly recognize myself, but I like the weight off my shoulders.

"Interesting," Mom says. "You look good."

"Thanks. I feel good."

"You certainly aren't going back to Canada the same."

"No, I'm certainly not."

37

M Y NEW HAIR MAKES A SENSATION when we return to the resort. Lisa debates cutting her hair short, while Rose gives me a dramatic, congratulatory hug. "You definitely don't look even a little bit Filipina anymore, Benni," she says. I am struck by her comment, acutely aware now that, in the Philippines, it is more desirable to look *mestiza* or Spanish rather than Filipino. Mom was right. My fair skin is prized here.

As Rose and Mom go off to further experiment with Mom's new hair, Lisa and I go to her room. "*Ta-da,*" I say, pulling out another magazine that I picked up on the way back. Rose is still banning news from their unit, but I thought Lisa could do with another tabloid fix.

Lisa laughs. "An acidic gossip rag just for me? *Ate* Benni, you shouldn't have." Lisa's sarcastic response is just the one I'm looking for. I'm glad to see she's feeling better.

We spend time going through the magazine, giggling over ludicrous pictures like teenage girls, and trying to discern which story is real or fake. Sam Paolo has a new boyfriend? *Real.* His boyfriend is actually a woman tricking him into believing she's a man? *Fake.*

Lisa's embarrassment from the other night has been relegated to a small blurb in a larger piece about Abe Razon's business acquisition of a publishing house. Her exposure on the front cover is limited to a small photo with the caption, "Is she after his new biz?" While the photo and caption are less than flattering, its sidebar placement proves just how quickly news gets old.

Lisa and I are absorbed in our pastime until I hear a cough from the doorway. I turn around to find Dad. He smiles. "Your new haircut looks great, Princess. Way better than any of those goons in the magazine," he says, looking over our shoulder at the "Hot" page we're skimming over. "And you got it cut just in time for our night out on the town. We're visiting the Baracuda, Princess."

The Baracuda is the bar Dad used to own. After Lisa's incident the night before, she decides to stay in with Rose and Gia, and Mom decides to keep them company. "Are you sure you don't want to come with us?" I ask one more time before we leave. "We don't need to go to the bar. We can go somewhere else." The prospect of spending time with Dad in a bar is daunting after hearing about the consequences of his drinking from Ofelia.

"What do you mean? Of course we have to go to the bar," Dad says. "Don't you want to see the Baracuda? It's my handiwork, after all."

"Of course, but what about everyone else? We can just stay in together."

"Really, Princess? You're in Boracay and you want to stay in?"

It doesn't help that Rose's already turned the TV on to the newest Philippine reality show, *Little Sister*. The thought of staying in and watching yet another reality show, rather than going out and experiencing reality for myself, brings back all the mediocrity of our life in Canada. It's depressing to think of in the midst of this luxury.

"Go on," Mom says. "It's good for you and your dad to spend some time together. Just don't do anything I wouldn't do, and please be back by midnight."

"Act like you and be home by midnight?" Dad asks, feigning shock. "Then we wouldn't be doing anything at all." Mom narrows her eyes at him, but he eases his comment with a kiss. "Don't worry, darling. I'm just showing Benni the sights. I'll have her home in good time."

Inside the bar, hanging cloth lanterns tie-dyed pink, blue, and yellow offer dim lighting for the small space. The lanterns serve as the only other company besides the bartender. The bar's walls are panelled with chalkboards boasting the number of shots guests could down in a row. Dad points to his name on the wall. It's faded and dusty but still there for anyone to see. "It says I could do twenty-five here, but in truth I can do at least thirty. I was going easy that night," Dad says. He approaches the bar. "*Hoy,* Chris, two tequilas for my daughter and I, and a B&B each to chase it down."

"Dad, I'm fine. Just a Coke for me."

"A Coke?" Dad asks, surprised. "You're coming to my bar and only having a Coke?"

"Why not? You can have one too."

"Are you kidding me? This is our night out together, Princess." When I don't respond, he asks, "Have you ever even tried Bénédictine and brandy?"

"No. I can't stomach brandy," I say.

Dad lets out a hearty laugh. He hands me a glass filled with ice and topped up with a rich amber liquid. "Take just one sip," he says.

"I'd really rather not. How often are we out together, Dad? It'd be a shame to get drunk."

"Drunk? Whoa, Princess, who said anything about getting drunk? One celebratory shot and a glass of B&B will not get us drunk. We can leave right after."

Dad's words are so earnest and his look so genuinely eager that I think, *What harm can one drink do?* I cheers Dad and we down the tequila followed by the B&B, both of which burn my throat and numb my tongue, but the B&B leaves a rich taste behind that lingers on the roof of my mouth. Dad laughs as I cough. "Dad," I say, "that's the foulest chaser ever."

"We can get you a sweeter one."

"No. No more shots and no more chasers. Let's go and see the sights."

"What's the rush, princess? The night is young. Besides, I want to chat with Chris for a quick second, okay?"

I sit by as Dad asks after the well-being of old friends and business connections. I sip my B&B, growing accustomed to the taste. As he and Dad talk, Chris keeps Dad's glass full. I can't keep track of how many top-ups Dad's had, and Dad brushes off my entreaties to go until my hearing has grown increasingly dull. I realize with a start that I am beyond tipsy from my far-from-watered-down drink. I get up, surprised to find I can hardly stand. Friends in Canada used to tease that I was a cheap drunk, but I used to boast that it saved me money. Now I regret having taken even one sip of B&B. "Dad, we should go," I say.

"Go?" Dad looks at his watch. "Princess, it's only ten-thirty." Despite the number of refills Dad's had, he still looks as sober as ever, albeit with slightly more rosy cheeks. "How often do we get a night out together like this?" Dad asks for the fifth time tonight. In that moment, I hate myself for not paying enough attention and even more for wanting to leave. The statement is so true that I want to cry.

I take a deep breath, nod, and sit down, determined to cut myself off and monitor Dad. As soon as I sit, though, Chris refills my glass, and Dad holds his just filled glass up for a toast.

"To being here. I'm glad you're here, Princess. I'm glad we're all here together."

"For sure. We haven't done this in a long time. We hardly ever see each other anymore."

My statement subdues Dad. The sides of his mouth tip down and a look of dissatisfaction crosses his face. "Aren't you going to drink?" Dad asks. "It's bad luck not to drink after a toast."

I take a small sip and, not wanting to ruin the night, change the topic from booze and Dad's absence. "It's nice being here, Dad. I'm learning a lot. I never knew about Sarah, for example. Talk about an oversight."

"An oversight?" Dad laughs. "What do you mean? Why would I tell you about a girl I used to date?"

"You always talk about girls you used to date. You just told us about that chick you crashed your motorcycle with."

"Oh, but she was nothing."

"Unlike Sarah."

"Maybe," Dad says. "Yes, unlike Sarah. For a long time, Sarah was everything. I really did love her. I didn't feel right for a long time after we split up. Heartbroken, you know. The word's not a cliché for nothing." Dad shakes his head and looks at me. "Are you seeing anyone, Benni? Anyone I need to carry my shotgun for?"

"Dad, you know the answer to this already. I was seeing Tom."

"You guys split up ages ago. You're not seeing anyone new?"

"We split up three weeks ago, Dad."

"Tom was nothing though. You dated for all of two months, didn't you?"

"I wish. We dated for three years. I only thought we were going to get married. I'm only a bit heartbroken." I laugh, trying not to sound self-pitying, and take a gulp of B&B so I don't have to talk more.

Dad snorts. "That guy? You never seemed to like him much."

I choke on my drink. "Are you kidding me? Tom was great. He was a lot like me, and he made me feel like I belonged."

"Princess, you have no problem fitting in. You don't need someone to help you belong. Let's be honest here; what's really bugging you?"

I stare at Dad with glazed eyes, trying to focus. Something that he's said has stood out for me. It's one of those moments when you want to pull out a pen and put an asterisk beside it. I'm trying to puzzle it out long after Dad's lost interest in the conversation and ordered us a second round of shots.

I study my father's face, taking note of the grey peppering his hair that I hadn't noticed the last time I saw him, which was a long time ago. I don't have the heart to say that I finally realize I've been trying to fill the gaps he left – the sense of not belonging, of never being enough for him to stick around.

I catch myself lolling on the bar, my chin in my hand and my head drooping to the side. Dad is still talking to Chris. I catch sight of the clock on the wall. "Dad," I say, tugging at his arm. "Dad, listen to me."

"Hmm?" Dad turns to me.

"It's one o'clock."

"And?"

"Mom asked us to be back by twelve."

Dad straightens up. "Benni," he says in all seriousness, "you need to go."

"What? Why do I need to go? Come back with me."

"I can't," Dad says, "I need to beat my personal best."

"Your personal what?"

Dad gestures at the chalkboard behind us. "My personal best," he says again.

I look at the wall, trying to keep the writing straight in my line of vision.

"Benni, hurry. You need to go back to your mother."

I think of Mom and her request. Something is nagging at me.

"She's waiting for you. It will be so much worse if we both don't go back," Dad says.

"Yes, you're right," I say, shaking my head. "I'm not sure what I was thinking. I love you, Dad," I say and give him a kiss on the cheek.

I stumble out onto the sand, blinking. It's as though all the millions of faraway stars are too bright for my eyes. I don't turn to say bye when I go. Drunk as I am, I don't want to see Dad sitting there with his sandy toes clutching tight to the weathered bar stool, his heavy arm and moistened palms nursing a sweating beer bottle, his eyes open but seeing nothing.

At that moment, I prefer to see nothing too.

The sea is only a few strides away but remains unseen beyond the light of the bar's front door. I stumble toward our suite. Occasionally, I veer too far to the left or the right. On one far detour left, I feel water on my feet. The sea lies before me in an unseen sheet of blackness.

I wade out into the darkness, seeing nothing and feeling only the clothes on my skin and the wet sand under my feet. I keep wading. The water doesn't reach any higher than my calves. At one point the land dips and I wade in beyond my knees, but soon it levels out, and I remain ankle-deep.

I spot a white blur in the water and approach it, drunk and without fear. It's a white buoy, which during the day is just a dot on the horizon.

I gaze around me. "The tide's gone out," I say to no one in particular. "I'm standing in the middle of the ocean." I look around again before lying down on the sand. "I'm lying in the middle of the ocean!" I yell, my words sounding slurred, even to myself.

The stars are infinite from this position, studding the sky as far as I can see. The water is still warm from the day's sun, washing around and into my ears, while the waves cradle my neck and fans my hair out beneath me. I imagine this spot in the day, hundreds of metres below the crushing waves. I'm usually scared of the ocean, and I shiver, imagining the water returning to bury me the way Moses buried the Egyptians as they crossed the Red Sea.

But here Dad and I soared well above the tallest tree on the island, and now I lie on the ocean floor.

Here, I am invincible.

38.

I RETURN TO THE RESORT WELL PAST TWO A.M., still tipsy and dripping wet from my rest in the ocean. Our resort's section of the island is populated with older tourists who sleep rather than party at night. The effect is one of eerie silence, as though Boracay has become my own personal island. To amplify the feeling of seclusion, our building is the only one lit along the surf and it stands out now amongst a sea of shadowy black, beckoning me home. As the light washes over me, I watch my white shirt, green skirt, and pale limbs come into being from the shadowy, far-flung world.

"Home, sweet home," I mumble. "It was a good night." I think of Dad sitting alone at the bar, shake my head, and say again, "It was a good night."

"If you've had a good night, you can't let it end yet," a man's voice says.

I look up to find five men. They're locals, judging from their dark skin and dusty clothes. It's as if they, too, have just materialized, though I realize they must have been part of a larger group on the resort's patio that I failed to notice. The light that's beckoned me forward hasn't been for me, but for them, where they gather. I offer up a polite smile. I don't know what they want, but the beach has been friendly all night. My beach.

"Hello, beautiful," the closest man says. His words are slurred, his gait uneven. The other men are similarly glassy-eyed, stumbling through a reek of alcohol. I haven't seen these men at our resort before but I notice one of them is clad in the tropical uniform used by resort staff. "What are you doing tonight?" he asks.

Despite my alcoholic haze, I realize that I'm only one woman among many men. "I'm on my way back to meet some friends. I'm expected now," I say.

"Is that so? Your friends are lucky to be here with such a beautiful woman. You should join us instead. We promise we'll be nice. Especially to a woman with those legs, those lips, and that..." His voice trails off for just a moment as he stares at my chest, then slurs, "...dress."

I see now how ridiculously exposed and unprotected I am. I'm wearing a nearly-transparent shirt, clingy skirt, and am standing on a dark, empty beach where foreigners keep their windows closed and shuttered. My beach? *Ha.* Their beach.

I cross my arms over my chest.

"What are you doing? Why are you covering yourself? You're so beautiful, you could be a real *artista*. The only question is: can you perform like one?" He winks. "How about we set up a camera and see. Your very first role in a movie can be with me."

The men around him share a jeering laugh.

He steps forward with a decisive look just as someone yells, "Stop!"

Dad strides past me and plants himself between us.

"What do you think you're doing?" he asks.

The man pauses, confusion and resentment on his face.

"Do you know who this girl is?"

The other men start backing away.

"Do you know who I am?" Dad yells. "Benni, go upstairs," he says to me.

Though he's outnumbered, I know he'll be okay. His tone commands authority. The men hear it too, and the leading man's resentment gives way to worry. I slip unmolested toward the resort, though I have to pass the men on the patio to go upstairs.

Dad singles out the resort's staff in the crowd. "Your boss is going to hear about this," he says, pointing at the man, whose brow beads with sweat upon realizing we are customers at his resort. "That's right. If you come back, I'll have my men on you. Scram! Don't mess with the King of Boracay!"

39

"AND THEN HE SAID, 'DON'T MESS with the King of Boracay!' and the men ran away," I say as Dad sits proudly beside me.

Mom was asleep by the time we got back, and since she didn't comment on our late return, I assumed she was in bed before our midnight curfew. When she asked how our evening had been, both Dad and I omitted our lengthy stay at the bar. Instead, we focused on the eventful end to our evening, failing to mention it occurred well past twelve. It became an unspoken secret between Dad and I, and though a part of me feels guilty about failing my watch on Dad, the night's events now seem like nothing more than a dream in the sun and heat. It was a break in our day-to-day events – a shade of real life – and beautiful in its own way.

"Dad, you're my hero," I say, pretending to swoon.

"The King of Boracay?" Mom asks. "What if those men had pulled out knives?"

"But they didn't," Dad says. "No need to worry, Mother Superior."

"Or what if someone had a gun?"

"But no one did."

"Or what if they come back?"

"But they won't. Relax, Maria, it's our final full day in Boracay"

"It's comforting that you're so confident, your grace, but why was Benni alone in the first place? A young woman, foreign to the Philippines, who has no understanding of the language and has never been to the island before. Why was she alone in your kingdom, way past the time I asked you to be back, when she was supposed to be out for a night with the king?"

"I…"

"You what? Do you think I'm stupid? I would love to hear your answer."

"I was…"

"You were what?" When Dad doesn't reply, Mom stands up. "You're lucky those men were probably just as drunk as you were," she mutters as she leaves.

40

THAT AFTERNOON WE SWITCH TO A smaller unit on the bottom floor of our building. It's the only one left in the resort. The single room has only one queen-sized bed and lacks the luxurious balcony, seating area, and big-screen TV that equipped our penthouse suite.

"Is it really necessary for us to move?" I ask, surveying the room. I shudder when I find a cockroach in the corner. Since the room lacks even a sofa for me to sleep on, this means I'm sleeping with Mom and Dad in the bed rather than in the sleeping bag they had procured for me. God knows what else is on the floor.

"Thanks to someone," Mom says, staring at Dad, "this is the best we could get on such short notice. The worker from last night was fired, but he might have seen you entering our room, and I don't want him coming back."

"Why don't we just crash with *Tita* Rosie? Her living room is bigger than this whole suite."

"You can sleep on their couch, Benni, but I need a bed at my age, and they didn't factor in the fact that they'd need to take in extra guests due to the recklessness of a certain someone before they came here."

We spend the rest of the day on the beach, just as I would've liked to spend my last day in Boracay, but, that evening, Mom makes it clear that she wants all three of us to stay in for the night.

"Are you kidding me? We're in Boracay, Mom. It's beautiful here. It would be ridiculous not to go out."

"Can you not spend one night still?" Mom snaps. "You were out with Lisa doing God knows what, and then you were out with your father. Can you not just spend one night in with me?"

"Just one night? How about every single night in Canada?"

Instead of answering, Mom turns away under the pretence of looking out the window, but when she turns back her eyes are red. "It's not all that bad, is it, Benni? We can make our night in fun." She says this with the tone she used to use when trying to make cleaning or napping sound fun for me as a kid. The approach brings home anew how old my mother is and how far we've come from the days when I needed her. The moment strikes me with all the sadness of what feels like, finally, a mutual realization between her and I – a realization that my childhood has long since passed and yet my mother, who never adapted to her life in Canada beyond her role as a parent, seems unable to let go of without relinquishing her identity. "We can order in food, watch a good show, and spend time with the air conditioner," she says.

"The room is a bit small to stay in for dinner, don't you think?" I don't want to shoot Mom down again but, in our old suite, with its separate lounge area and big-screen TV, a night in could have been an appealing suggestion. Now, with our cramped quarters and television set from the eighties, it isn't.

Mom looks at Dad as though to say, "Say something. This is your fault."

"I know where to find the best pizza on the island," Dad offers. "Once you're eating it, it doesn't matter where you are." After a week of rice and meat, pizza actually sounds good. "I can pick up a couple of pizzas for us," Dad says, since I don't oppose the idea.

"Can I come with you?" I ask.

In the end, Mom, Dad, and I make the trip to Boracay's night market together. The market is packed, and we hold hands to weave single file through the crowd. The pizza place is in a generic three-by-three metre stall with room enough for the oven, chefs, and a few stools. It is one of a hundred stalls set up next to each other to form a makeshift shopping centre. Mom and I share the only stool available as we watch our pizza being tossed. I'm surprised it isn't fully baked before it enters the oven as the market is that hot. There are too many bodies and cookeries in such a tiny space.

After venturing into the night market, I'm grateful to return to our air-conditioned room where we don our loose pajamas. The pizza is even more flavourful than my favourite Canadian pizza from Pizza Hut. Mom turns the TV on to the season finale of *Worldwide Star*. Considering today is the *Worldwide Star* finale, I begin to question whether Mom wanted us to stay in for safety, or for TV company.

Just before the winner is announced, we hear a knock on our door. Dad and Mom exchange a look, and I wonder if, like Mom warned, the man from last night would actually return.

Dad stands to open the door, though Mom is closest.

I can't see who the visitor is; I can only hear, "Room Service," announced in a singsong voice.

"What are you doing here?" Mom exclaims.

I peek around the door to find Rose and Lisa with mango slushies for everyone in hand. "It's our last night here. What do you mean what are we doing here? Of course we wanted to spend it with you," Rose says. "Not to mention it's the *Star* finale tonight." She pushes her way past Dad and squishes herself onto the bed next to Mom.

Although I don't watch *Worldwide Star*, I'm entranced when Dani McGregor is announced the winner, and she takes the microphone with tears in her eyes. The moment is so emotional that even the hardened judges are crying. Dad holds a respectful silence while Mom sheds empathetic tears. "She's the deserving winner," Mom says, leaving tomato sauce on her cheek as she wipes her eyes. "She's beautiful."

"You can say that again, sister," Rose says, looking like a mirror image of Mom as she cries, too.

Lisa and I share smiles over our pizza slices. Dani McGregor sings her victory song through tears of her own.

"The mark of a really good singer is if she can sing well despite her emotion," Dad says with suitable solemnity.

I can't help but smile as I watch my family's reception of the winner's song.

I watch my parents and my heart swells with gratitude that I am here now, in my pajamas, watching TV with my troublesome father, stern mother, diva aunt, and friend cousin. Though the Consuelos have introduced us to extravagance, the real extravagance is being together here and now. I wonder if, in Canada, I would have ever been patient enough, at this age, to bear my parents' small and big squabbles, or to walk in public holding their hands, and then pile into a queen-sized bed to endure a night of snoring.

I realize that, before now, I never really had the chance to do any of this in Canada. I am blissfully happy that this is my present and remember all over again my promise to make this my future, too.

41.

"**E**DUARDO, YOU KNOW HOW I FEEL about smoking inside." Mom fans Dad's cigarette smoke away as she refolds clothes into her carry-on bag.

"Sincere apologies, my darling wife. I'll get out of your way. Are you done packing too, Princess?" I nod and join Dad outside.

Dad and I take one last tour of the shops around our resort, taking pictures of each other as we don silly glasses and souvenir hats. After we exhaust the shops by the beach, we wander to find the sandstone clearing for pickups and drop-offs, which is where we will depart with the Consuelos for our charter flight back to Manila.

"I'm surprised no one else is here for pickup," I say. "There were quite a few people arriving the same day as us."

"Of course, there were lots of people coming," Dad says. "But who would ever want to go?"

"True. I don't want to leave either."

"And yet you and the King of Boracay are going so soon."

We turn to find a gaunt, darkly-tanned man in the dusty clothes of a local. I don't recognize him until I study his cagey look. He's one of the drunks from the night before.

Dad has a harder time identifying him. "*Kamusta, compadre*," he says, no doubt assuming this man is one of his many island friends.

The man laughs. "You don't remember me, do you? The king must have trouble remembering all his subjects."

Uncertainty passes over Dad's face. The man utters the word, "king" with undisguised venom, making it clear that he is mocking him.

"You got me fired." The man spits at Dad; it falls between them like something diseased and ugly.

I shouldn't be so afraid. We're in broad daylight with only one man before us instead of ten. But Mom's words now ring in my mind: What if those men pulled out knives? What if someone had a gun?

"You deserved to be fired," Dad says, recognizing the man.

"I have a wife. I have kids. I needed that job."

"And this is my daughter, who your friends were harassing. What of that?"

"I don't care," the man yells.

Dad waits for the man's breathing to slow before asking, "So, what do you want now? My watch? It's fake. My phone? It's six years old." He holds each up as he speaks. "My wallet? There's nothing in it. I bought it at a *tiangge* two weeks ago. What exactly are you looking for? Gold? Silver? Another job? Not on me, *compadre*. And yet I am still a better man than you, because I chose to protect a young woman, my daughter, whereas you stood by and waited to see what other men would do to her instead."

The man's face crumples. "You're not a better man. You call yourself a 'king,' but you're an old drunken fool. An idiot, *tanga at hangal*. We could've killed you, fat man, but your life is worthless." The man spits these last words and walks away.

I don't know how to react after he leaves, so I do the first thing that comes to mind. "What a low life, eh, Dad?" I laugh and look at him, hoping he will dispel the tension.

"No, Benni," Dad says, looking pained. "There are some people in life to whom things come easy, and there are some to whom things come hard. Whether they make it hard or it just is, I don't know.... I suppose sometimes life just gets you down, and instead of being sad, or even angry, you become resigned or defeated instead. And I think that's the saddest thing, is it not? I think that type of difficulty deserves sympathy, whether it was brought on yourself or not. Right, Benni? Doesn't it?" He looks at me with eyes so beseeching that I'm at a loss for words. It seems all he wants is affirmation.

"They are just words," I want to say. "All those things that man said to you are just words."

But I don't.

They are just words of a defeated man, but as Dad and I stand alone in the clearing, I can't tell who is the more defeated, and there is no humour or excitement to be found in the other man's retreat this time.

42.

AS SOON AS WE EXIT THE SHUTTLE BUS to Boracay Airport, we find ourselves in the throes of a crowd of locals who wait around on the off chance tourists will come through. We push forward single file to the airport doors without making eye contact with the impoverished around us. Jerry leads us with hawkish attentiveness. Seeing Jerry with his gun exposed deters most, but two stragglers still manage to follow us on our way to the doors.

"Please, help my son," the first man calls out to Mom.

Mom doesn't even glance his way.

"Please," he says to Dad. "Can't you see he needs help?" He gestures to the young man beside him who waves the little that remains of his arms.

Dad shakes his head.

"Please. Don't you see he's not good for anything himself?" he says to me. He gestures for the amputee to come closer.

I clutch my bag close to my body. I'm disconcerted, not just by the two beggars, but by the crushing, chaotic crowd that scrambles my senses so I can barely understand anything but the feel of my clothes on my sweaty skin.

"Please," he says again.

Perhaps he senses my confusion or foreignness. Perhaps, here, confusion and foreignness are one and the same thing.

"Please. Look at his arms. Can't you see he's only good for begging?"

I refuse to look.

Finally, the maimed man himself comes forward and raises the stumps of his arms to my face. "Please," he croaks. His voice is hoarse, almost as though it, too, has been mutilated.

I shake my head, imitating Dad, and stare forward, imitating Mom, but I'm not like Mom or Dad. I can see myself through the eyes of a poor, native Filipino: I'm wearing Guess sunglasses, carrying a Kenneth Cole bag and, most of all, I am uncomfortable – unused to the heat, climate, and land.

"Please," he says again, and reaches for me. His stump brushes against my arm and it's surprisingly smooth and soft, as intimate as a lover's caress.

I jerk away as though touched by a hot iron. "Get the hell away from me!" I yell.

I sense all eyes turn on us and a hush falls. The transformation is instantaneous. The poor adolescent boy and beseeching father become cold, furious men who follow us doggedly toward the airport doors. They stop at the entrance, where armed guards stand. As we enter, I look back to see the older man gesticulating, no doubt cursing in a dialect I can't understand. The other stares at us with a hardened face before he thumps the windows with the stumps of his arms.

"It's freaking crazy here," I mutter. It's the first time I miss Canada, where strangers, by law, can't just touch you and breach your personal space. In Canada, there are rules in place to protect you from such violation. Here, it's just you and the poor. Though I've always made it a point to help out around my neighbourhood, whether by donating to local charities or volunteering around the holidays at city shelters, I can't seem to muster that compassion here. Placed in such close contact with the impoverished, I am surprised and ashamed to discover that I don't feel empathy or compassion toward the needy – only repulsion and fear.

"Shhh, Benni," Mom says in a pacifying tone.

"Did you see that? He touched me." I tug my bug-eyed

Guess shades over my eyes, cross my arms, and burrow in the terminal seat. "Crazy," I say again.

"You should have thrown a peso at him or something," Dad says, "and watched him try to catch it with those hands of his." He winks at me, a smile on his lips, and nudges me when I don't react. "Eh, Princess?"

We are quiet until Lisa attempts to stifle a sudden giggle.

I think of what Dad's said. "That's awful," I say. But the more I think of it, the more humorous it seems – a terrible joke that nevertheless manages to relieve the tension, much as I suspect Dad hoped it would. And then we all burst out laughing.

In the back of my mind, I realize that I am becoming further ingrained in the Philippine way of life, where poverty is simply a fact of existence. That small part of me feels ashamed again, and yet I hold my sides, bend over in laughter, and gasp with release along with the rest – an ending to yet another adventure where we've remained safe and sound.

43.

LISA AND I SPEND THE HOUR-LONG FLIGHT flipping through gossip rags. She's nowhere to be found in any of the magazines.

"The media really does have a short memory, eh?" I ask, turning the last page of *Phil Star Biz* before flipping it over to see the front cover again. "Don't you miss seeing yourself in these?"

Lisa laughs. "Sure. I'm inclined to go out and do something stupid again, just so I can see my face on the front cover. I've got a taste of fame, and now I can't shake it."

"You should definitely do something. Who is this Vanessa Hernandez chick anyways?" I ask, pointing at a picture of the woman that I recognize from all the billboards. "Screw her. Her illicit affairs have nothing on Lisa Consuelo."

Lisa laughs again. "At least she looks a little more ladylike than I did when I was on the front cover."

"Hardly," I say. "She looks like a 'loose woman,' as my mother would say, or, at the very least, a poser. You can never trust someone who wears sunglasses at night." The front cover shows the bodacious woman, in a silk gold gown, as she exits a limo at night with her sunglasses on. The words "NEW LOVER?" are plastered across the picture.

"She's not a loose woman, *Ate* Benni. Did you not read the article? They think Ms. Hernandez has finally found love because she's never been so secretive about her other lovers before."

"Oh, I'm sorry. Stupid me. I was too busy looking at the photos to read the award-winning content. But *Phil Star Biz* has failed us. They haven't exhausted all possibilities yet. Perhaps Vanessa is actually a lesbian."

"Or her new lover is just ugly," Lisa says.

We subside into giggles until Rose shushes us. "The way you two carry on, you'd think you were thirteen-year-old girls," Rose says. "Have some reserve and act like ladies."

Lisa and I quiet down, but spend the rest of the flight folding down pages in the magazine for the other to read later.

We return to Forbes Park around noon, driving up to the Consuelos' house just in time to see Ariel emerging with keys to the Escalade in hand and bug-eyed sunglasses shading his eyes. "Welcome home, family!" he says, pausing on his way out. "Oh, Benni, your new hairstyle is absolutely drop-dead gorgeous, my dear. I'm so glad you're all back. Unfortunately, I'm on my way out. I'm off to meet Celeste on set, but did you have a good time?"

"We had a great time, Dad," Lisa says.

"Oh, Lisa, I saw all that stuff about you in the papers...." Ariel shakes his head. "Well, it's no matter. You all got away to avoid this and avoid it we have. Media has short memory. We've unsubscribed to the papers for now, though. It's made life much easier, which is all anyone could ever want, right?"

"Not to worry, *Kuya* Ariel," I say. "We checked the papers today. There's nothing in there about us now that Vanessa Hernandez is sleeping around."

"That's great, darling," Ariel says, then stops and pales. "Wait, what?"

"Vanessa Hernandez – that pop singer. Don't you know her, Ariel?" Rose asks.

"I ... barely," Ariel says. He looks perplexed but only for a second. With a shake of his head, he regains his smiling composure. "Anyways, I must be off. I'm looking forward to seeing you all again tonight. You need to tell me all your stories. We've got a fun day planned for you in the meantime though." Ariel raises his sunglasses and winks at me. "You'll enjoy this one, Benni. Mom's been hankering to go to SM Mall since you arrived. You can't leave the Philippines without going at least once. It's the largest mall in all of Asia. The shopping trip is just in time. There's an after-party for some benefit concert at the country club tomorrow night. Attendance is a must. Celeste and I agree that a positive public appearance is required, and what better way to show you Philippine extravagance than this, no? Anyways, would you look at the time? I really must get going though I loved the chat. Have fun, lovelies!" He says all this in a rush and moves to the Escalade with one last flying kiss.

"Ariel is right. We must be off," Rose says. "Forget going inside. We need to go."

"What's the rush?" I ask.

"The traffic's going to cut into our shopping time. It's better to leave for SM in the morning."

"Are you and Gia coming?" I ask Lisa.

"Not today," Lisa says. "We have enough party dresses."

"I'm bowing out of this one, too," Dad says. "I have one too many ball gowns in my closet already." He lowers his sunglasses, looks at me, and winks just as Ariel did. "Have fun, Princess," he says, with a mischievous smile.

I should've known then that I was in for an experience. Rose's frantic rush to reach the mall and the fact that Ariel told me it was the largest mall in all of Asia should have tipped me off. The trip begins with us sitting in traffic for two hours on the South Luzon Expressway. It continues for an eight-hour outing around the 407,000-square-metre monstrosity, during which Mom looks at everything, purchases nothing, and spends money only in Jollibee. Her dilly-dallying is painful, but there's consolation in the fact that Jollibee, and its Jolly Crispy Fries with spray-on cheese, is delicious. It reminds me of Taco Bell's Fries Supreme, and nothing says comfort food more than processed toppings.

I never did like shopping or large crowds. SM Mall of Asia has both. Yet I surprise even myself by enjoying the excursion. Rose takes us to all the upscale boutiques, and I purchase a new dress, shoes, and accessories to boot. The price of goods, though not much more affordable than in Canada, feels almost inconsequential. After my initial hesitation, I don't bother with the tricky math of conversion and make up my mind to spend whatever, if only to live as a well-off Filipina would. What else are my savings for, after all?

As the day progresses, the unpleasantness of this morning's airport scene recedes in the wake of the instant gratification spending power provides. By the eighth hour, however, I'm flagging and I can't hide it. "I'm sorry," I say when Rose suggests going to the unexplored entertainment mall – another full-sized mall attached to the main building. "I think I need a break."

"What do you mean?" Rose asks. "The mall is closing shortly."

"We can visit Jollibee and pick up some ice cream," Mom suggests.

"No. No more Jollibee. You guys go ahead without me. I'll sit in the food court and wait."

"Don't be silly, Benni," Mom says. "We can't leave you here alone. How will we ever find each other again? You don't have a cellphone." As soon as I see the disappointment register on her face that familiar sense of guilt I feel whenever I leave Mom settles over me.

Perhaps Jerry, who's followed us around and carried Rose's purchases without complaint, sees it too. "Don't worry, Mrs. Manlapaz. I can stay with Benni. I have my cellphone on me, so we can find each other easily."

Mom still looks hesitant, but Rose agrees. "Maria, let's go. They'll be fine. Jerry will be with her." I add to Rose's encouragement, and, soon enough, Rose and Mom are on their way, leaving Jerry and I with Rose's shopping bags to find a place to sit.

"Thanks," I say to Jerry once they're gone.

"No problem, Miss Manlapaz."

"Please, call me Benni."

Jerry smiles but doesn't say anything in response. I study the weathered face of the man who's been with us on this trip as much as the Consuelos themselves, and I realize this is the most I've said to him for this entire trip. Suddenly, the prospect of spending another hour with him is unnerving. Mom advised me to keep the help at a distance, but I can't pretend the man's not here for another hour.

"So," I say, "what would you like to do?"

Jerry stares at me.

"I mean, where would you like to go? Is there anything you need to pick up before we sit down?"

"No, Miss Benni." He's said my name as I've asked. I forfeit my battle against the title "Miss." Old habits die hard.

"Where's the food court?" I finally say. "Let's go and sit down."

Jerry brings me to the food court – one so large it may as well be a mall unto itself. We sit down at a table for two, and I'm left gazing at passersby, feeling like I would have been better off walking around the entertainment mall instead. Anything would be better than this awkward silence.

I begin sifting through my purchases for diversion and enjoy the unusual thrill at seeing all the new things I own. I've never been a shopper before and never understood those who like visiting the malls every day, but I can see the appeal now. I feel proud at being current and having pieces that will make me more attractive and stylish.

I knock over one of the bags by accident while sifting through my things. Jerry catches it before it hits the ground. I look up, feeling guilty, realizing I forgot Jerry was even there. "So, do you come here often?" I ask to make conversation.

"Only when *Inday* Rose needs me to, Miss Benni."

"Oh. Well, do you ever visit here in your spare time?"

Jerry looks at me and shrugs.

I think of our vacation and realize I've never seen or heard of Jerry having any spare time. "So, how long have you been with the Consuelos?" I ask.

"Almost thirty years, Miss Benni."

"Thirty years? You don't look old enough to have been working for thirty years."

"I started working with *Inday* Rose when I was thirteen, Miss Benni."

"Thirteen! Why were you working at such a young age?"

"I didn't come from a well-off family, Miss Benni. I needed to work. I'm grateful *Inday* Rose took me in."

"Oh," I say, unsure of how to respond. "Do you have a family? A wife or kids?"

Jerry shakes his head. "No, *po*. I never really thought of it. I…" He stops.

"You what?"

"I don't think I could afford a family, Miss Benni. But I'm lucky to work with *Inday* Rose. I have a place to live and food to eat, always."

"How much is the average salary for…" I stumble on my words. I know the question is rude but curiosity overwhelms my propriety. Do I ask how much the salary is for a driver, a bodyguard, an all-purpose helper? All sound rude, so instead I switch midsentence and end up sounding even ruder. "How much is the average salary for you?"

"About five thousand pesos a month, Miss Benni."

"Five thousand pesos…. Wait, did you say 5,000 pesos *a month*?" I ask, failing to hide my shock. Quick math turns the figure into $150 Canadian.

"*Opo*."

"That's crazy!" I say, forgetting who I'm talking to. "Is that normal?"

"Better than normal, *po*. Regular staff are paid three thousand pesos a month."

"Three thousand?" I ask, doing the math in my head; that's $90 Canadian.

"*Opo*."

I crunch the figures. At that price, even I can live quite easily on my own here with a driver, cook, and maid. Jerry's silence reminds me to be careful not to voice my opinions to the wrong person though.

"Let's see where Mom and *Tita* Rosie are," I say, pushing away from the table and standing up.

I look at the stores around me, all this space that promises so much extravagant life, with a renewed interest.

44

THE CONSUELOS' PERSONAL HAIRSTYLIST and makeup artist arrive to prepare us for the gala. The formal will be held at the Manila Golf and Country Club. The guest list is limited to the Philippines' rich and famous. "It would be nice to go to a fancy event at least once, considering it's your last few days here," Rose says, not realizing this whole trip has been extravagant for us. I can't believe we're leaving in a couple of days.

Celeste, Ariel, and Rose dress first, seeing as they're the first to go. Celeste and Ariel plan on making an early appearance to lay to rest any rumours circulating before the evening begins. Rose goes with them like a worrisome hen, fretting about Ariel being exposed to the public's potentially hostile eye.

Mom and I see the stylists next. Lisa defers their attention to us. "This is the fiftieth event like this that I'll be attending this year," she says when we protest. "After a while, you won't even want to go anymore."

I can barely recognize myself by the time the stylist and makeup artist are done with me. My skin is luminous under layers of shimmer. My eyes look bigger and brighter due to the excessive mascara coating my long, fake lashes. My eyebrows are filled in to precise lines, accentuating the length of my nose, and my cheekbones are finely contoured with blush and bronzer.

Mom also looks like a different person, so unused to as I am to seeing her made up. Her eyes look like bruised shadows set deep in her face, and her hair is blown out and hardened with hairspray. She looks happy and excited. I can't remember the last time she's had to get this dressed up.

Though it feels odd to do ordinary tasks in my ballroom getup, I nab the computer in the corner of Mom and Dad's room while waiting for Dad to dress.

"Where's your dad?" Mom asks, re-entering the room after her third visit to the powder room to check her red lipstick.

"He's changing." I hear the words as a whisper close to my ear and feel breath on my neck.

I swing around and look at Mom. "What did you say?" I ask, already knowing that Mom couldn't have said it. Even if whispered words could carry from one end of the room to the other, breath can't.

"What? Why would I answer my own question? Didn't you say that?" Mom looks surprised. I know she heard the whisper too and felt the breath on her neck just like me.

If Mom didn't say anything and I didn't say anything, and we are the only ones in the room, it can mean only one thing. After all the stories I've heard and all the things I expected to see, I'm chilled at the thought of having a ghost's voice in my ear and a ghost's touch on my neck. It's the only explanation. "Holy crap," I say. I fear the touch of cold hands and whispering in my ears, so I cover as much of myself as possible. I hug my knees to my chest, press my back against the seat, and gather myself into a tight ball.

Mom looks around in confusion.

Dad emerges from the bathroom in a towel. "What's happening?" he asks, noticing my panic.

"We heard a voice," I say.

"A woman's?" Dad asks.

"How did you know?" My panic grows. "Did you hear it, too?"

"Your dad is just trying to scare you"

"No, really," Dad looks puzzled. "I heard a woman's voice, too. Quite close to me, actually. It gave me the spooks."

"What did you hear?" I ask.

"A woman's whisper by my ear, quiet but distinct. 'He's changing,'" Dad says.

I squeal and push myself further into the chair as shivers run up my arms.

"Benni, stop panicking," Mom says. "Ned, you're not helping. Look how terrified Benni is. It wasn't anything. I was the one who said it." Mom, usually so eager to share ghost stories, is adamant to disregard this one. "I thought I didn't say anything, but I must have. I asked the question, 'Where's your dad?' and then answered it without thinking. 'He's changing.'" She tries and fails to recreate the whisper. Her words are muffled and indistinct. It doesn't carry close to my ears. It doesn't reach behind doors.

A new set of chills wreak havoc on my spine. "I'm scared. I knew there'd be ghosts on this trip. There had to be. We're in the Philippines, after all. I wonder who it is. It's a woman's voice."

"Don't be crazy," Mom says. "There aren't ghosts in this house. It was built new."

"Unless..." Dad says, but Mom shoots him a look.

"Unless nothing. You're being silly, Benni. Don't mention this to *Ate* Rosie. She'll be a scaredy-cat, just like you. Hurry up and get dressed, Ned. We need to go."

45

THE DRIVEWAY TO THE COUNTRY CLUB is filled with stretch limos, Hummers, and black Escalades with tinted windows. I realize that I'm embarrassed arriving in the minivan; the Escalade was taken earlier by Ariel, Celeste, and Rose.

Jerry drives the minivan into the queue to reach the front door. We disembark into a crowd of long gowns and three-piece suits as light chatter and delicate laughter flutter about our ears. A live band is playing soft music. Dad offers Mom his arm, and she hangs onto it as we're pulled into the club on a sea of silk and velvet.

We walk into a whirlwind of action as soon as we step through the doors. One waiter offers to take my shawl. Another hands me a champagne-filled glass. Our attention is called with a shrill, "*Hoy*, Maria. Over here." We turn to find Rose. She looks garish in heavy blue eyeshadow and orange-red lipstick. She waves us over using her clutch purse as a beacon. Celeste and Ariel are linked arm in arm beside her. Mom pulls Dad with her before he can grab a drink. I follow behind. Before we can say hello, Rose grabs Mom's arm and pulls her close, tugging her away from Dad. "Maria," she mutters. "Carlo is here."

"Where is he?" Mom asks, looking around.

"Don't make it obvious that you're looking," Rose says, yanking Mom's arm to pull her gaze back. "I don't want him to know we've seen him."

"I don't know what you expected, Mother. We attend the club in his name, after all," Ariel says with annoyance.

"Maria, he's with that *bruha*," Rose says, ignoring Ariel. "Do I look okay? Help me, sister."

Mom looks Rose over, from her overblown hair down to her sparkly red shoes, and squeezes her hand. "You look beautiful, *Ate*," she says.

Rose sighs. "Okay, just stay close to me so I don't have to meet him alone."

"Sure. I'm not going anywhere. Do you hear that, Ned? Stay close." Mom looks around, but Dad's already gone to find a drink.

"Where's Lisa?" Celeste asks.

"Jerry's on his way home to pick her up now," I say. "She had her hair and makeup done after us. She said she'll follow when she's ready."

"I'm here." Lisa comes up from behind me, looking dazzling in a sequined dress.

"That was quick," Celeste says.

"You know me, Mom. I'm always eager to come to these things."

"Shush, baby," Celeste says. "Keep your sarcasm in check. We're making appearances tonight."

"Oh, yes, we are," Ariel says, sounding as excited as Lisa.

"Celeste!" The woman's shriek startles us as much as the ambushing flourish of her gown's blue and green feathers. "Celeste and Ariel Consuelo, it's so good to see you both."

"Vanessa, what a pleasure," Ariel says, reacting first. He's gone from sullen to charismatic in a matter of seconds. "I didn't think you were coming."

"And I didn't think you two darlings were coming either, considering the news." Vanessa winks. "Ariel, did you see Sam yet? He just arrived."

"No, I didn't. Celeste and I will be sure to say hello."

Vanessa laughs as though Ariel said the funniest thing. "Do,

Ariel, darling. Do."

"You surely don't believe the rumours, my dear," Celeste says.

"Of course not, but isn't it all such good fun? I'm being rude right now, though. Hello, there." Vanessa turns to Mom and I with a great sweep of her peacock-feathered skirt.

"*Tita* Maria, Benni, this is Vanessa Hernandez, one of our nation's most popular singers. Vanessa, this is my mother's sister, *Tita* Maria, and her daughter, Maria Benedictine," Ariel says.

"*Kamusta*. And it's so good to see you again, *Tita* Rosie and Lisa. Lisa, how's that acting career of yours going?"

"Still working on it, *po*," Lisa says.

"Well, work harder, baby. You need to do your parents proud." Vanessa whirls away at the sound of someone else calling her name.

Lisa grabs my arm. "Let's grab a drink," she says.

"Just one," Rose calls after us as we head off.

Lisa orders two shots of tequila at the bar, giving one to me. "To making appearances," she says by way of a toast before downing it. The tequila burns the back of my throat, and I cough. Lisa sighs as she turns to face the crowd. "I can't wait for tonight to be over. I hate these things."

I turn, trying to see what she sees, but see only glitz, glamour, and immeasurable wealth. "I don't know about you, but I wish I could live like this always," I say.

"We should switch," Lisa says.

"Really, Lisa, I think I'm going to move here. I haven't figured out the details because I have to go back to Canada first to sort it all out, but I'm going to come back after."

"Are you serious? Why would you want to leave Canada?"

"Canada's boring. There's so much more here. Look around."

Before Lisa can answer, someone taps my shoulder and says, "We have to stop meeting this way." I turn to find Abe in a three-piece suit, his mouth cocked in that familiar half-smile I learned to appreciate in Boracay. "How are you doing, Lisa?" Abe asks.

"Much better than when you last saw me, thank you very much. I owe you one, Abe, and I'll pay the favour back right now by going to see where my parents are. See you in a bit, *Ate* Benni. Have fun." Lisa leaves us alone without a backwards glance.

"That girl is a piece of work," I say, shaking my head.

"Hey, I don't mind," Abe says. "I'm glad I got to see you again."

"Yeah, about the other night.... Thanks for all your help."

"It was the least I could do."

"The least you could do for what?"

"For spending an evening with you," Abe says with a smile.

I know it's a line, but my stomach flips at receiving a billion dollar smile. "Do you come to these events often?" I ask, looking around at the dancing figures to hide my blush.

"Yes. They're terribly boring, are they not?"

"No, not terribly."

"You're right, actually," he says, catching my gaze. "Not terribly boring anymore."

46.

A BE AND I STAND ON THE COUNTRY CLUB'S balcony overlooking the pool. We're both laughing over something
mundane – a throwaway comment previously made. I'd been
drinking champagne to get rid of the tequila burn and am
pleasantly buzzed as a result.

"Can I ask you something, and can you answer me honestly?"
Abe asks, turning to face me, suddenly serious.

"Mmhmm?"

"Why did you blow me off when I first met you?"

"Blow you off?" I ask, feigning disbelief. "When? I never..."

"Oh, come on, Benni. You know you did. Why?"

I shrug. "I don't know. It's the way you approached us, all
haughty-like"

"Haughty-like!"

"Yes, haughty-like. You know. 'Why, hello there, ladies.
I'm Abe. Abe Razon.'" I break into a fit of giggles. I am enjoying this opportunity to chat. As different as it is from our
feel-good high earlier this week, the sense of contentment
and intimacy has carried over, and I feel like I'm talking to
a kindred spirit.

"I wasn't acting like that."

"You were." When it looks like he's about to deny it, I cut
him off. "A bit. Just a tad. Admit it."

Abe leans against the balcony railing with a *humph*. "Okay,
maybe a bit."

I study his crossed arms and small pout. "Don't tell me you're getting sensitive about this."

"I'm not," Abe says, but the contrary look doesn't leave his face.

I poke his side. "Snap out of it. What's bugging you anyways? I'm sure it works on ninety-nine percent of women."

"It does," Abe says, laughing and uncrossing his arms. "I don't know. I guess I never realized that I come across that way."

"The first step on the road to recovery is admitting it." Abe looks at me, puzzled, and I'm struck, not for the first time tonight, how different our social references are just because I was born in Canada and he in the Philippines.

"Every day I'm told I need to be a certain way because of where I come from," Abe says. "The person I'm supposed to be has already been dictated by my last name. There's no discovering or making myself. I just am." Abe's words hold such a note of confusion and near despair that the smile slips off my lips. This isn't just flirting on a balcony; this is a confession. "Growing up, all I wanted was a wife and kids – a family. I wanted to be like my *Lolo* and *Lola*, who were retired by the time I was born. I just wanted to be happy, in love, and surrounded by family like they were. Not like my dad, who had no time for his family because of work, and not like my mother, who had no time for her family because of friends. I thought the true mark of success would be if I had a happy family of my own by twenty-nine. But here I am, at thirty-one, and more like my dad and mom than my grandfather and grandmother. I'm a Lothario at the poolside."

"Well, Lothario's a bit harsh."

Abe laughs. "I'm sorry. I must sound crazy. I've just never met someone I could talk to so easily." He grasps my hand. I look down at it with my heart in my throat, avoiding his gaze. "I'm glad I met you, Benni. I wish you didn't have to go."

"I'm thinking of staying." My voice comes out as a whisper.

"Please, do," he says, gripping my hand tighter. "Benni,

you're beautiful. You're perfect, just right, and exactly what I need. You're everything I've been looking for."

I flush, hearing words of affirmation I never thought I'd find. Hearing Abe say them is like hearing someone say, "Here. This is where you belong." Finally.

"What do you want, Benni? I'll make it happen." Earlier tonight I had told Abe about my love for reading and my English Literature degree. I had even shamefacedly admitted to my lack of a real job and my current status as office secretary; in other words, nothing more than a regular Jane playing Cinderella on vacation. He seizes on this now. "I recently acquired a publishing company. I can make you the editor or an author. I can find you a great spot in our marketing department or accounting. Name it. What will make you stay?"

I think of what Abe is offering – a career, something to make something of myself, and a little love on the side. People leave third-world countries looking for the so-called American, or Canadian, dream. They look for chances to be bigger, to be better, and to be special. But those dreams are mediocrity in disguise. Those dreams are nothing more than work, work, and more work to end up only inches from where you started. Real dreams happen when you can actually live life. Real dreams happen here.

I feel him leaning closer and hold my breath until…

"Princess, there you are."

I whirl around to find Dad peeking out onto the balcony. "Dad," I say, snatching my hand back from Abe. "What are you doing here?"

"I can ask the same of you," Dad says, eyeing Abe.

"Dad, this is Abe. Abe, this is my Dad."

Abe steps forward and offers Dad his hand. "*Kamusta na po kayo*. It's a pleasure to meet you," he says.

"*Humph*," Dad says, ignoring Abe's hand and taking a sip from his drink instead. He gives Abe the once over, turning to me after he's done. "You're missing out on a party, Princess.

There's no need to be hiding out here on a balcony. Come back with me."

"Sure," I say, flushing. I feel like I'm thirteen again, the way he's treating Abe. "See you later, Abe," I say, turning to see him one more time.

"See you," I hear Abe say before the door closes.

Dad takes my arm. "Stay away from men like that, Princess," he mutters in my ear. "Ten-thousand-dollar suit, two-thousand-dollar shoes, and more product in his hair than a woman."

"Dad, Abe's a nice guy."

"A nice guy would speak to you inside at a party with your family and friends. He wouldn't take you out onto a balcony alone. Trust me on this one, Princess. I know."

I roll my eyes at Dad's overprotectiveness as he leads me out onto the dance floor.

We meet Rose, Mom, Lisa, Celeste, and Ariel. "Where have you been?" Mom asks, just as we hear someone clear their throat behind us.

I think for a second that it's Abe, come to join us, but see that it's a tall, pale, elderly Filipino man instead. His hair is dyed jet-black and slicked back to reveal his receding hairline. "Rosalynn, how are you?" he asks, bowing his head to Rose. A woman around my age clings to his arm. She's dressed in a slinky black low-cut dress. I wonder if she's his daughter.

"Carlo, fancy seeing you here," Rose says in a voice five octaves higher than usual.

Mom grips Rose's arm tighter before offering her hand to Carlo Consuelo. "Carlo, long time no see," she says.

Carlo is the picture of composure. He takes Mom's hand. "Maria, it's been a very long time. How have you been?"

"Fine, and you?" Mom asks. "What's new?" She looks at the young woman on Carlo's arm.

"Ah, yes. Maria, this is my wife Cheryl."

Rose speaks before the girl can. "How dare you introduce that *bruha* to my sister?"

Carlo ignores her. "Cheryl, this is my ex-wife's sister, Maria." He turns to Ariel. "Son, I hope you've been well."

"Son," Rose snorts. "You dare call him that after leaving us?"

"Celeste," Carlo says, nodding at Celeste. "Lisa," he says, turning to Lisa. "I hope things have been well. Particularly in your search for a…" Carlo pauses, "career."

"Can't you see what she's done to you, Carlo?" Rose asks, but Carlo simply nods and turns away with a, "*Magandang gabi*" in farewell.

"I'm going to grab another drink," Lisa says.

"I'm going with her," Ariel says, following her through the crowd.

Mom takes Rose's arm. "*Ate* Rosie, I'm sure this isn't the time or place to say these kinds of things to Carlo."

"Who are you to say that?" Rose asks, shaking Mom's hand away. "You weren't here when he left."

Mom takes a step back, opens her mouth, closes it, and shakes her head. "You're right, *Ate*. But I'm here now, and the night is still young. Don't let that *bruha* ruin it for you."

Rose takes a deep breath. "You're right, Maria." She musters a smile. "Where have you been all this time, sister? I sure could've used your help before." She pats Mom's hand in reconciliation.

"This party is pretty swanky," Dad says, by way of changing the subject.

"I'm glad you're enjoying yourself," Rose says.

Dad turns to Mom with a smile. "So, Maria, have you told Rose about the voice yet?"

Mom shakes her head at Dad, but Rose catches on. "What voice?"

"Ned's just being silly. But that reminds me that I meant to ask you… Whatever happened to *Tita* Pilar?"

"What do you mean?" Rose asks.

"Is she buried in Manila Memorial Park? Why didn't we visit her when we went to see Mommy and Daddy?"

Mom's questions about an unknown relative are unremarkable, but Rose's short response piques my curiosity. "Hmm?" she asks as she flags a waiter down for an appetizer.

"You didn't tell them, Mom?" Celeste asks Rose.

"Tell us what?" Mom asks.

"Maria, you didn't know?" Dad asks with a mischievous grin.

"Didn't know what?"

"I didn't think it was necessary," Rose says.

"Who is *Tita* Pilar?" I ask.

"She's our aunt," Rose says. "She was my benefactress of sorts. She lived with me after that *bruha* bewitched my husband and helped me financially through a lot of the divorce when I needed it. She was like my second mother. She died five years ago. I was devastated."

"Wait. Don't change the subject," Mom says. "What haven't you told me?"

"It's not important," Rose says.

"What is it?"

"It's the fact that *Tita* Pilar is in Rose's house, Maria," Dad says. "You can see her in the dining room, actually."

"In the dining room?" Mom squints her eyes as though seeing the dining room now. "What ever could you mean?"

"At the foot of the dining-room table," Dad says.

"Ah, you mean her portrait. Nice try, Ned. Though I must admit it is a very lifelike portrait of *Tita* Pilar," Mom says. I remember the portrait of the fierce elderly Filipina that I noticed the first evening here.

"I wasn't referring to the portrait. I was talking about her urn below it," Dad says.

"No!" Mom says, aghast.

"Yes," he nods.

"No!" She looks at Rose.

"Yes, Maria," Rose says. "I'm sorry. I didn't want to tell you I kept her ashes there because I thought you'd be scared."

"I opened it!" Mom says.

"Why would you open it?"

"Ned told me to."

Dad breaks into a full-out belly laugh when I say, "I opened it, too. Dad said I'd find something special inside."

"Why wasn't it sealed?" Mom asks.

"I didn't expect it to be opened," Rose says, "but it's okay. The ashes are in a box at the base of the urn. Still, that's a horrible joke to play, Eduardo. You should leave the dead alone."

Dad continues chortling into his drink. Even Celeste giggles. But I think of the woman's whisper near my ear from earlier tonight and, for once, don't see the humour in Dad's joke.

47

D AD STILL LOOKS AMUSED BY THE TIME the gala wraps up. We are wandering the halls of the country club, trying to find a washroom for Mom before we go.

"That's really awful, Eduardo," Mom says, looking at Dad's gleeful smile and discerning his thoughts. "There are certain pranks you shouldn't play, and I'm sure *Ate* Rosie doesn't appreciate us fussing with *Tita* Pilar's urn either."

"Lighten up, darling," Dad says, pulling Mom in for a hug as she struggles against him, trying to remain severe.

"This must be it, Mom," I say, pointing to a door with the familiar stencil of a stick woman.

"Great. I've had one too many flutes of champagne. I'll be only a second. Wait for me here," she says before she heads in.

Celeste stops at the end of the hall and calls to us, "Have either of you seen Ariel?" she asks.

"No, sorry, *Ate* Celeste."

"Not here," Dad says.

Celeste sighs. "I haven't been able to find that man since he left for a drink with Lisa. If you find him, tell him I'm looking for him."

We assure her that we will, and Dad sits on a couch in the hall. He checks to make sure Mom isn't coming before lighting a cigarette. "So, I sure got you, didn't I, Princess?" he says.

"It's not funny, Dad," I say, shivering at the memory of the whisper. "Mom and *Tita* Rosie are right. There are certain jokes you shouldn't play. You should leave the dead alone."

"Oh, come on. It's funny."

The way Dad brushes me off as he blows cigarette smoke into the air after taking a sip of his drink annoys me. He sits there, so self-assured, as though knowing I won't say anything while he breaks all of Mom's rules. "No, it's not funny, Dad," I say. "Not this time."

"Aw, is my widdle baby scared?" Dad asks.

Any other day, at any other time, his banter would have been okay. But today, after hearing the ghost and seeing him down shot after shot even with Mom telling him not to, I don't feel like taking it. "Yes, actually, I'm scared, and I'm stuck in that creepy room alone." I think of my windowless, rose-coloured bedroom and shiver.

Dad bursts out laughing. "Toughen up, buttercup. Ms. Hotshot here is afraid? Man up. I thought you were braver than that. Ms. Butch-haircut. Ms. Tattoo. Use your brain a little. You're smarter than to believe stories like that."

I know he's had a few drinks too many; I saw him drinking all night. But, for the first time, I resent the way he acts like we're chums – as though he can tease me like a pal rather than treat me like a daughter. "Smarter than to believe stories that *you* told me? All I ever hear are stories from you. Not just ghost stories, but stories about your goddamn fictitious life. Stupid strong-man stories that make you sound better than you are." My voice grows louder, but I can't help it. "What else can I do if not believe your bullshit stories? And by the way, do you want to know the real reason why I got a tattoo of my name of all things? Because I learned that I was completely alone. Ever since I was a kid, I knew I only had myself to depend on. I wanted the stupid thing since I was thirteen because God help me if I ever forgot for a moment that you weren't around to rely on. People get things like "Family" tattooed on them, but where is my family? My tattoo is meant to remind me that I only have one person that I can turn to or trust – myself.

Even now, I had to fly twenty-four hours just to see you again. There's never a halfway point for you, is there?" My breath comes in ragged gasps like I've been running a marathon to get here. I'm surprised I'm breathing at all.

Dad takes another puff of his cigarette, looks at me, and laughs. "You've got issues, Princess," he says, his voice light. "You should thank me if I'm the reason you're here. You've been going on all vacation about how amazing this place is after all. And, just for the record, none of my stories are bullshit."

I'm flabbergasted at his blatant disregard of everything I've just said. "Issues?" I explode. "I've got issues? No, you've got issues, Dad, and if I have any, it's because of you. Why won't you take ownership of that? It's not funny." I yell the last sentence and start to cry.

"Stop it," Dad says, getting up. "Enough! Don't you think I know that? Don't you think I'm aware that I've messed up? From the very beginning, it was all a mistake. I've only ever made mistakes. I know this already."

"What was a mistake?" I ask.

Dad doesn't speak for a long time. His face has lost all trace of jocularity. He looks into his glass as he takes another gulp, then studies his cigarette; he looks everywhere but at me. "You're not alone," he finally says. "Your mom's a good woman, and she's always around."

My voice is low when I ask, "Is she really? I feel like I'm always around, but who's around for me?" I study his face. "What was a mistake?" I ask again.

He doesn't reply.

"What is so wrong with what you have?" I ask. "What is wrong with us?" As I say it, I know I sound melodramatic and childish, and yet I realize I've been wondering this all along.

Dad stands and walks past me, leaving me alone in the hall with tears I don't care to learn the reason behind.

48.

THE SOUND OF CHATTER RETURNS TO ME in pieces over the pounding in my ears. I'm left alone in the hallway, waiting for Mom to finish in the washroom. I'm sick of hanging around for Mom, of always having to be the reliable one when Dad can't stick around.

I leave my post to wander the country club in search of a more isolated place. I walk to the back of the club in search of the pool. The further I go, the quieter it becomes, leaving me to pass door upon door of luxury with the lights turned off: a darkened restaurant, an abandoned billiards room, a shutdown bowling alley. I finally reach the glass doors leading to the pool area. Its blue glow lights up all the empty cabanas surrounding it. I push out of the country club, grateful for the fresh air. I expect to walk out into silence and solitude, but instead hear a feminine giggle being shushed. I pause. Another giggle emerges from my right, and a male voice joins in. I turn, trying to find the source of the noise, and see a couple in the half-darkness of the nearest cabana. The woman presses against the man, her lips to his ear as his face nuzzles into her neck.

I turn to go when a fresh wave of giggles seizes the woman, and the man, slightly louder this time, says, "Hush, my darling."

Something about the man's flourishing speech catches my attention. I strain my eyes for a second before finally realizing who it is. "Ariel?" I ask.

The man whirls around, his movement impeded by the fact

that his belt is undone and the buckle catches on the woman's feathered dress. Ariel pales at the sight of me. "Benni. My God. This is not what it looks like," he says.

"Oh, Benni, darling, this is exactly what it looks like," the woman drawls. I recognize her as Vanessa.

"I don't care what it looks like. Really," I say, backing away. My head's pounding. Tonight has been one drama too many. "I'm going to go."

"Benni, wait. Let me explain."

"Oh, Benni, no! Don't go!" Vanessa says in a mocking tone. "Ariel, it's much better for people to know you're sleeping with me rather than thinking you're gay."

"Shut up, bitch," Ariel snarls, turning on her.

Vanessa's reaction is instant, and the sound of her slap reverberates across the empty yard. "Watch what you say to me, Ariel Consuelo. Remember who's giving who favours. No one wants to sleep with a has-been, not even your wife." Vanessa blows by me without a backwards glance. It reminds me of Ariel brushing past me after fighting with Celeste a little over a week ago. Just like then, I'm not sure what to do. All I want to do is go to bed.

I turn to leave, but Ariel's voice stops me. "I loved her once, you know? Celeste. I really and truly loved her. I knew she didn't love me when I was getting into it, but I thought I could change that." Ariel sighs. "I should have known that you can't make someone love you. I know we must keep up appearances, but convenience can only take you so far."

"Some people may say love can only take you so far," I say, thinking of Celeste.

"After so many years, you need a bit of love, too. It's a hard combination to get right. Don't you agree? What do you think, Benni?" Ariel asks.

"I think that I'm the wrong person to ask," I say before leaving.

49

I WALK BACK TO THE CONSUELOS' HOUSE, relishing the feeling of not having to be escorted. One of the things I took for granted in Canada was being able to go wherever I wanted, whenever I wanted, all by myself. The last thing I want to do is go back to the family after fighting with Dad and catching Ariel, but I have nowhere else to go here.

The guards let me through the gates on sight, and I slip through the back entrance. I find Lisa lounging on the balcony with a cigarette in hand. The pool below is still; the air is humid and heavy with waiting.

She takes in my disheveled appearance and tear-stained face. "I think a storm is coming," she says. "I like to sit out here when it rains. It's nice to watch from under shelter."

"Mind if I join you?"

She gestures at the lounger beside her and I flop down. "Want a smoke?" she asks.

"Sure." I take the cigarette she offers with gratitude. It's the first smoke I've had in years. I take a long drag before blowing the smoke out, counting to ten as I go.

"Rough night?" Lisa asks.

"You can say that. I'm not sure how much more excitement I can handle. How about you?"

"Well, the night's been about the same as every other night for me. 'Oh, you're Celeste and Ariel's daughter? When will you be in a movie or on TV? When will you be wildly successful like your mother?'" Lisa laughs. "Actually, I've been meaning to talk to you about something."

I groan. "I can't handle any more heavy stuff right now, Lisa."

"I know there's a lot going on, but I'm running out of time." She hesitates for only a second. "You'll be leaving soon, and I'm planning on going with you, okay?"

I sit up. "Wait, what? Are you telling me, or are you asking me? Does your mom know?"

"Not exactly. I'm doing a bit of both right now though ... telling and asking you. *Ate* Benni, I've gotta get out of here. I'm done with the Philippines."

"But why? How can you just pick up and leave? I can't let you do that, Lisa, and I'm not taking you back as a runaway. You have a life here."

"And you have one in Canada, but you were planning on moving here anyways."

"That's different."

"How?"

"There's more in the Philippines, Lisa. There's more variety, more difference, more change. Not to mention that people do things for you here that allows you to take ownership of yourself. You have a cook, a cleaner, a driver.... In Canada, it's just day-to-day living. And in Canada, you live in a small box. It's all the same there. Everything is so blandly uniform." I think of how I'm labelled in Canada as a "chink," a "flip," another piece in the great quilt that is North America. But even as I say all this to Lisa, I wonder if I mean it. I think of the liberating feeling I had walking back here alone – that rare freedom of being nobody.

"Are you kidding me?" Lisa asks. "You're talking about living in a box? There's no smaller box than the one you're put in here, from the shade of your skin..."

"Everyone is stereotyped based on their skin," I say.

"...To the mother and father you have," she continues, "the house you live in, the school you go to, what your grandparents did fifty years ago.... People think they know you, know all about you, and often times they do. All anyone can do is ask me when I'm going to be famous like my mother. I like what I do, but..." Lisa trails off and tosses the butt of her cigarette away before immediately lighting a new one. "But I want to start new. What if I wanted to get up tomorrow and be something different?"

"Are you still talking about being an accountant?"

Lisa laughs but barrels on. "Who knows? Maybe. But whatever it is, that kind of change doesn't happen here in the Philippines. You can't start fresh whenever you want. You can't choose to be somebody, or anybody, or nobody. You just are."

"So, you want a fresh start."

"Yes, I want a fresh start."

"I hear you."

"Do you really? Do you even know what you have in Canada?"

"Sure I do." I pause and look at the smouldering end of my cigarette. "How about we make a deal? Ask your mom and see if you can come visit me sometime. Stay with me, and I'll show you around. You can make your decision then. We're not ruling the idea out, but we're just going about it a little more wisely."

Lisa nods. "Fair enough. I guess it would be too much trouble taking me back now anyways."

"If it were just a matter of taking you, I'd have no problem at all, but who knows what the fallout will be."

Lisa laughs. "Someone's getting tired of the family drama, I see."

"Ugh, don't talk to me about drama. This whole trip has been one drama after the other, and I just got into another ridiculous fight with my father. All of this is so embarrassing. We're your guests."

"No, you're our family. Seriously, *Ate* Benni, when will you realize that? Shit happens."

A moment passes. We smoke our cigarettes. I think of what the smell of cigarettes reminds me of most – Christmastime. Each year until I was thirteen, Dad followed Mom and I to church late so he could dip his shoes in ashes and leave footprints by the fireplace to make it seem like Santa visited. "It's weird being here with my dad," I say. "It brings up a lot that I hadn't thought of before. And staying with your family... It's nice the way you all stick together, regardless of what's happening."

"If there's anything I've learned, it's that your life is made up of stories, and you have to choose which stories are yours. There are no right versions, just versions we tell ourselves over and over again until we believe them." As Lisa speaks, she continues to stare at the pool and the still trees – the landscape that, like us, is waiting for the storm. "I hung out with the wrong crowd growing up. My friends came from wealthy families, and our partying was extravagant. It started with beers at house parties and progressed to whatever we could get our hands on. Pot, 'shrooms, K, E. Oh, club drugs are heavenly." Lisa leans her head back and closes her eyes. "I prefer MDMA, as you could probably tell. When you're on it, you just feel happy and in love with the world, and everything makes sense. My friends and I thought we were so clever. There are no known negative side effects to E. But have you seen people who are always on it? They grow thin, have dark bags, and their skin turns pasty." I study Lisa's dark bags and pale skin. "It's probably just from being out late all the time and not getting a lot of sleep," she says, shrugging. "I've known for a while that I have to cut back. It's hard, though, with it so accessible, and I always want to forget who I am or be somebody else. I've grown to think we're a society of people wanting to forget. It causes problems, you know? I'm pretty embarrassed you had to see me at my lowest point, though. I know better than to mix E and alcohol like that, but I was pretty upset from the gossip rags." Lisa shudders.

"I can hardly remember the evening after we popped, but I know enough to know I've disgraced the family. I think *Lola* Rosie just thought I was drunk in the beginning."

I remember Lisa's dead weight on our way back to Verity. I'd left that evening with a good feeling but now, with her retelling the story, I try to picture the evening through her eyes. It helps me understand the anguish in the voice of this young woman who somehow always feels less, somehow always finds herself falling short – despite of, or perhaps because of, all the money, family, and connections.

Lisa cracks a wry smile. "I remember, during one of *Lola* Rosie's hourly check-ins that night, that she just sat there, looked at me, and said, "I don't know what to do." It was the first time I'd ever heard my *Lola* admit uncertainty. That's when she started crying, and me too. Mind you, I was crying before out of self-pity and shame, but only then did I cry because I saw how much I hurt her – someone who loves me so much and who I love, too. Really, no matter who I've been with in the past or what I've been on, I've never felt that overwhelming sense of well-being that I do when I'm with my family. It's why I got my tattoo in the first place. In the end, after all the money and all the fame, all you're really left with is family." She turns to look at me. "With all that said and done though, I'm sorry you had to see me like that."

It reminds me of how I apologized to her just a couple of weeks ago when I hardly knew anything about this family of mine. "Shit happens. Don't worry about it," I say.

Lisa sticks her tongue out at me.

"Anyways, you may not remember the evening, but it was a good night until you started puking."

"Ah, that's right. Abe Razon was there. My *Lola* thought you two would make a good couple."

I laugh. "I doubt *Tita* Rosie would be as happy with him if she knew he was the one with the blue diamonds that night."

Lisa stares out at the waiting landscape in thoughtful silence before speaking again. "*Lola* Rosie, ever the diva, has been covering up for me from the beginning. She made up this excuse of an eating disorder to explain any irregularities. I've never had an eating disorder but, in a weird way, *Lola* Rosie loves me enough to tell everyone otherwise, because she thinks she's protecting me. It's more acceptable to have a sickness, perhaps, than an addiction. It's more talked about, at least. And *Lolo* Carlo wasn't bewitched by his mistress. He and *Lola* were on the rocks for a long time, and he was never faithful to her. I agree with the supposed curse though, because sometimes that's what she needs to hear. These are the stories we tell each other. Sometimes, they're all you have left to work with. Whether you're working with one story of events or another, what does it signify in the end?"

The storm breaks. We watch it in silence. We watch the dents it creates in the once-perfect glass of the pool, and the way it beats the leaves of the palm trees down only for them to spring back up again.

I think of my fight with Dad, of how he laughed and said, with such nonchalance, "None of my stories are bullshit." I think of the pieces of his life I'm finding – of the untold stories of his life here, and of his life of alcohol, and of his first love that came long before me. I think of Ariel and Celeste's stories for appearances and Rose's and Lisa's stories to protect those they love. All the stories in our lives that we tell and do not tell and of the stories I felt compelled to share with Tom before we no longer had a part to play in each other's life anymore. Because, in the end, perhaps that's how you know you really love someone; you build a story together after building one for yourself.

I close my eyes, listening to the patter of the rain and distant rumble of thunder. "I feel like being here is forcing me to see things I don't want to see," I say, "or deal with things I don't know how to deal with. It's not just the stories we tell ourselves, it's the fact that I don't know how these stories end." I open my eyes and look at Lisa. "How do you deal with a character like my father?"

Lisa shrugs. "I don't know. Maybe with a very strong supporting cast."

50.

I WAKE UP LATE THE NEXT MORNING. Rose invites me out for a final shopping trip, but I refuse. Lisa and I stayed up late talking, and I want to talk to Dad and apologize for the night before. If there's anything my conversation with Lisa reinforced for me, it's that family members need to stick together despite any shortcomings each may have. There's no one else to stick by you otherwise.

"If you need anything just let us know," Rose says. "Ariel, Celeste, and the kids are out, but you won't be alone. The help is always here, and your dad is staying behind, too."

"He said he's feeling ill again," Mom says, peeking over Rose's shoulder with a sour look. "If that's what he wants to call it."

I grunt and bury my head under the pink comforter. When I finally emerge from bed, the house is quiet.

That's when I hear it: a guttural gasping – a haunting, hallow noise. My first thought is that the ghost has returned. I bring my hands to my ears to block the sound. It reminds me of the time one of my Manlapaz cousins had scratched his nails along my bedroom door when we were kids, and I, convinced it was a ghost, had folded into a ball tight with fear. Five minutes later, he walked in to find me crouched by my desk, saying, "Stop. Please, stop." In my ten-year-old mind, I just had to be brave enough to ask the ghost to go away, and the ghost would have mercy and leave. I heard no end of teasing from my cousins over that. I learned the hard way that there was no bravery in whispering fearfully to myself like a child. Remembering this, I unfold myself, remove my hands from my ears, and determine to find the source of the noise. For all I know, it may be Dad, or some other relative returned early, trying to scare me. Already I hear the culprit tiring. The gasping grows weaker.

I enter the dining room to find Dad on the floor – one hand grips his chest, the other is clenched in pain. His wide eyes find and reach out to me.

I don't know how long I take to react. How long do I hesitate? Too long.

I press my lips on his too thin, too moist mouth and blow air into a void that makes a horrible gasping for more. But the gasps are just noise; Dad takes none of it.

Pushing against his chest, my arms feeling too weak for use, I remember days when he'd ask for a back massage and I would complain that it was like trying to rub feeling into wood – impossible.

Or perhaps I'm doing it wrong. Perhaps I'm not breathing long enough or pushing hard enough. I don't know what's happening. I don't know when I start screaming for help while Dad rejects all my requests for him to stay.

Realizing the futility of my actions, I run out of the room, trying to find my way to someone who can assist. But the house is a maze, and I'm scared I won't be able to find my way back. I return to the room and to Dad.

When I look up, I see a woman kneeling over Dad's body in the dining-room mirror. It's a woman with choppy hair laced with strawberry-blonde streaks. Her face looks old and her eyes brim with tears. It's a woman I don't recognize.

"He's dying. He's dying." I hear it as a whisper by my ear. Later, I'll reason that the voice was the ghost's, telling me the moment was predestined and that there was nothing I could do. But I'll never be certain if it was really a ghost, or if I was thinking it, or screaming it, instead.

Throughout the trip I was looking for ghosts around every corner – in the ancient rocker by the foot of my bed, on Melissa's street, at Assumption College, in Mom and Dad's room. The ghostly voice – the same voice I hear now during Dad's heart attack – is it imagined? If it isn't, is it kind? And if it is kind, then am I not doing enough to save him?

The next thing I am conscious of are hands shaking me. "Miss Benni!" Jerry yells. "Miss Benni, I'll take him to the hospital. We need to get help."

It takes me a minute to register who's talking to me. "Do not touch him," I yell. "We need an ambulance. Call an ambulance."

"Miss Benni, trust me. I can bring him," Jerry says again, but my Canadian sensibility revolts at the idea.

"I want a professional. Get an ambulance. What are you waiting for?" I'm screaming now. "He's dying."

Jerry gathers a few of the nearby help to help carry Dad out. I rush forward, opening doors, trying to do anything at all to be useful.

I emerge to shouts and the sound of camera shutters clicking and flashing. "What can you tell us about Ariel and Vanessa?" one reporter yells from behind the gate. "How long have they been having an affair?" another asks. "Does Celeste know?"

"Who are you? Get away," I cry. In another second, Dad emerges, his limp form dragged along by Jerry and three other men.

Someone behind the gate gasps, then the shouting and yelling escalates. The sound of sirens adds its wail to the noise.

"Get out of the way," I yell. "Leave us alone."

But my yelling is to no avail, and Dad doesn't move behind me.

51.

WE RIDE TO THE HOSPITAL IN AN AMBULANCE, Dad and I, but we may as well have walked. Traffic is slow. The rest of the family make it there first. They were closer to the hospital than us.

If I thought having my lips on my dying father was bad, it wasn't. It's bad when I see Mom at the hospital, and we can't look at each other. Everyone cries when they see Dad covered in a white sheet as though we didn't know this was going to happen.

But we did.

And if I thought having my dying father's spasmodic hand in mine was bad, it wasn't. It's bad when we're brought into a dim room and the nurses remove the sheet from Dad's head. They remove the sheet gently, as though to cushion the inevitable plummet.

But they don't.

And if I thought having my dying father's last breath in my mouth was bad, it wasn't. It's bad when we see that the nurses failed to relax Dad's face, and I can't tell if we cry from fear or sadness anymore.

It's both.

52.

I SIT WITH MOM AND ROSE LESS THAN twenty-four hours after yelling my last words at my father. "We need to make some tough decisions," Rose says. "First and foremost, Maria, are you extending your stay?"

"Is there a point?" Mom asks.

"That depends on another decision you have to make. Will you have a funeral here?"

"Is there a point?" Mom asks again.

"Maria, focus. I know this is hard, but where do you want the body to rest?" I hate *Tita* Rosie at that moment for speaking about Dad as a body rather than a person.

"I have that spot in the mausoleum back home. Why not use it?" Mom asks.

"So, you're bringing him back to Canada?"

"If I bring him back, there would be no need to extend the trip, and Ofelia already said she wouldn't come to see Ned if there wasn't going to be a funeral. She said she doesn't want to remember him that way." She laughs. "I wonder how she wants to remember him. Does she want to keep the memory of the last time she saw him? It wasn't that great, let me tell you."

"Be nice, Maria. I know you've just lost your husband, but *Tita* Ofelia has also just lost a son."

"Don't you think I know that?" Mom snaps. "I just find it funny the little embellishments we tell ourselves to make things easier. Isn't that right, *Ate* Rosie?"

"If you're making some allusion to embellishments I make, just say it."

"Someone's getting a little defensive, eh? But don't worry, I wasn't even thinking of your bewitched husband." Mom puts a malicious twist on the word, "bewitched."

Rose sighs. "Maria, we're old, and we're sad, and we're lonely women. We don't need to fight. I know just as well as you that my husband simply decided to leave me. Is that what you need to hear right now? That is neither here nor there. Your mother-in-law, me, you … we are all trying to find comfort where there is none. You can snap at me all you want. I'll be here to take it."

Mom rubs her eyes. "I'm sorry, *Ate*. You are only here for me, when I was never there for you."

"Think nothing of it. You're here now. Twenty-six years overdue, mind you, but that's in the past. Let's discuss the matter at hand."

Mom cracks a wry smile. "If I bring Ned back, I'll finally get to see him more often." She laughs.

"Is that what you want, Maria? A rushed flight back to Canada with your husband's ashes on hand? There's no need to decide it all now, sister. You can stay here with me."

"What life is here for me?" Mom asks. "I have my house to go back to, my work…."

But Mom's arbitrary mention of her job – this construct of usefulness that she's seemed to wrap around herself – sets something off in me. "Mom," I say, standing up. "What life is there for you in Canada?" Up until this point, I've sat here quietly, following the flow of conversation. I leave the table. There are too many threads to keep track of and no room in my heart to hold them all.

I enter Mom and Dad's room and look at the mess of Dad's belongings. Never one to be organized, throughout the trip Dad simply wore his clothes and discarded them where he stood, leaving them strewn over the bed, desk, and chair, in contrast to Mom's neatly-packed luggage. How unnatural it seems for a person to be here one day and gone the next. It feels like Dad is only gone for a little while and will reappear after his next big adventure.

I pick through his things – a T-shirt thrown here, a pack of cigarettes thrown there. I find a copy of *Phil Star Biz* lying on the bed and am about to throw it away before the front page catches my attention.

I pick up the magazine and study it in disbelief. A blown-up photo of me takes up the cover page. My makeup is running, my hair is a mess, and Dad is slumped behind me on the Consuelos' front steps. It's a photo taken through the bars of the gate yesterday afternoon. The title reads, "Tragedy Strikes the Consuelos."

I skim the article inside.

Tragedy struck the Consuelos yesterday after allegations were dispelled that Ariel Consuelo was gay with a plot-twist that no one was expecting. It was discovered yesterday that the old *Dance, Dance Pinoy* star has actually been having an affair with pop singer Vanessa Hernandez. *Phil Star Biz* reporters visited the Consuelos' residence yesterday for more information, only to witness first-hand the tragic death of Eduardo Manlapaz.

I read on and am shocked to find a picture of Abe and I on the balcony from the night before.

Though Maria Benedictine Manlapaz's history is unknown, it is suspected she is the latest woman hot on the trail of billionaire playboy Abe Razon. Considering her cousin, Lisa Consuelo, recently had a terrible evening with him, it's surprising any woman from the family is still on the prowl. When asked about this latest development, Abe Razon said, "I know Benni and Mr. Manlapaz very well.

I knew their family was having trouble because Benni practically begged me for a job the other night, and Mr. Manlapaz – may his soul rest in peace – was almost too inebriated to stand. That being so, it is still sad to hear of Mr. Manlapaz's passing. It's a hard day for the Razons. The tragedy reminds me of a novel our publishing house will soon be releasing titled *Shadow*. It will be in stores later this week."

I throw the magazine away in disgust, but I take small consolation that my heart is too filled with pain to allow in more.

Beneath the magazine, I catch sight of the Saint John's Academy yearbook I'd brought back from Ofelia's place. I flip through the book, finding photos of a much skinnier, much younger Dad with shoulder-length hair and a handlebar moustache. In one picture, he sits over the ledge of a thirty-foot high bridge, his expression inscrutable as he stares off into the distance, a cigarette dangling from his lips. In another, he stands with his arm draped around a petite girl with a short bob. He is looking down at her with a large smile. He looks happy.

I study the two for a second before flipping to the graduate photos. A thirsty curiosity has taken hold of me, and I study the names and faces of each young woman until I find her: Sarah Abogadie, Arts Council Chairman, Cheering Squad, Glee Club, Plaid Tones Sports Reporter. The quote beside Sarah's smiling face is, "The miserable have no other medicine, but only hope." She's styled her straight hair so that it curls around her face, creating the appearance of a shiny helmet. Her eyes are heavily outlined and the trace of a smile seems to hover over her lips. Sarah seems like a well-rounded girl. I remember Dad's comment from our first evening here – "There are girls for marrying," he had said – and I wonder anew what the big mistake he was referring to was, the last time we talked. Perhaps he regretted letting go of his first love, marrying Mom, having me. "Don't you think I'm aware that

I've messed up?" he had said. "From the very beginning, it was all a mistake."

As I bring the book closer to study the photo, Sarah's business card falls from its pages. I'd forgotten I tucked it away there after our quick getaway from the hospital. I read her card. Sarah works as a head recruiter at an HR firm in Makati. I stash the card in my pocket as Mom opens the door and peeks in.

"What are you doing?" she asks.

"Just looking at old pictures of Dad," I say, closing the yearbook.

"How are you?" she asks.

I don't know how to answer her question, so instead I ask, "How are you?"

"Fine," Mom says, picking up one of Dad's discarded shirts and folding it into his suitcase.

"Really?"

"Yes, I'm fine," Mom says, picking up another shirt and putting it away, too.

"*Fine?*" I ask, spitting the word. "You're *fine?* Dad dies, and you stand there and say you're *fine?* What kind of sick joke is that?"

"Now, now, Benni," Mom says, as though talking down a petulant child.

"The stories we tell each other in this family are complete bullshit. You and Dad spouted these goddamn lies all the time – lies like everything is *fine.* It's sickening."

"Benni," Mom says, more sharply now.

"No, it's not fine. Just like Dad and his stupid lies were not fine. None of it was fine."

"Benni, enough. Your dad never told lies."

"Another story! Thanks, Mom. Dad told lies left, right, and centre. Lies to us, lies to himself, lies about his whole pointless life."

"Enough, Benni," Mom says, folding and refolding the same shirt over and over again. "Your dad deserved help, understanding, and maybe even pity, but in no way did he deserve this attitude from you."

Something in the way Mom says this reminds me of Dad on our last day in Boracay and the way he spoke with such resignation after our confrontation with the man from the resort. What was it that he'd said? "That type of difficulty deserves sympathy." When he said it, he'd looked to me for sympathy, and I had none to give him. I couldn't tell him that I understood; I didn't then, and I still don't now. I push the thought away. "What difference does it make? He's dead. And what difference will that make to us? He was never around, and he never followed through anyways." Even now, as I rage against my father, I am struck by the fact that he's not here to hear me yell at him. In all my ineffectual anger, his absence infuriates me even more. "And you, too. You knew he had a problem."

"And so did you, Benni," Mom says, finally placing the shirt down. "There was nothing we could do."

Mom's not fighting me, but I'm not ready to stop being angry yet. "Well, I'm sick and tired of all these useless, pointless stories that we tell ourselves. We may as well be upfront with each other, and tell it like it is."

Mom walks to the door without looking at me. Before she exits, she pauses and says with complete composure, as though telling me not to forget the lights, "Your *Lola* Ofelia sent a letter for you. It's on the table there."

I'm left staring at a gently closed door and feel like screaming at the unfairness of it all. I stride to the door, throw it open with a bang, and rush past Mom towards the foyer.

"Benni, where are you going?"

"Out," I call over my shoulder.

I push through the mahogany doors into the humid outside air, breathing in that heady mix of sweat and trash that has grown somewhat familiar over the past two weeks. I'm hardly thinking when I try to open the doors to the minivan and the Escalade. In my anger, I forget that, here, I don't have the freedom of going for a drive like I used to back home when I needed to clear my head. Both are locked. I head to the front gate on foot. I try to open the wrought-iron gates myself, but they, too, are locked.

"*Hoy, anong ginagawa mo?*" A guard dressed in camouflaged fatigues emerges from behind the gate.

I shake the gate again. "Can you open this?" I ask.

"*Hoy,* miss, *anong ginagawa mo?*"

"I don't understand what you're saying. Can you open this? Let me out."

"*Saan ka pupunta? Hindi ka pwede lumabas.*"

"What are you even saying? What is this – a prison? Let me out of here."

"*Hindi ka pwede lumabas.*"

"Let me out of here!" I yell, shaking the gates, feeling as though the heat and humidity are beginning to suffocate me.

A horn honks behind me. "Miss Benni, do you need a ride?"

I turn to find Jerry idling the minivan behind me. I haven't seen him since he helped carry Dad out yesterday. I hesitate for only a second before climbing into the passenger seat beside him.

"Where to, Miss Benni?"

"Anywhere. And stop calling me 'Miss.'"

He doesn't ask questions. He signals for the guard to open the gate, and they let him through. We glide through the quiet Forbes Park streets before merging onto the South Luzon Expressway.

53

I STUDY THE BILLBOARDS FEATURING Vanessa Hernandez, the passing buses, cars, and jeepneys, and the trees towering just beyond the highway's reach. For a time, we drive within sight of the airport, and then we pass it on a route that feels familiar. "Please don't tell me we're going to the mall," I groan.

"Trust me, I won't take you to SM Mall," Jerry says, laughing. The way he says, "Trust me," reminds me of the way he asked me to trust him when Dad was on the floor, and I didn't.

The expressway climbs over a bridge covered in advertisements. Once over, Jerry turns off the highway and wends the minivan through a series of residential streets. The houses we pass become smaller and more downtrodden the further in we go. "Where are we?" I ask.

"Barangay 177."

"What's that?"

"The name of this town."

"That sounds awfully impersonal. Why are we here?"

"This is where I grew up. You said you wanted to go anywhere. The first place I could think of was home." Jerry smiles.

"How long can you stay out?" I ask.

"As long as you need."

"No one knows where I am."

"I'll text *Inday* Rose so she doesn't worry." Jerry brings me further into the subdivision. The houses here are even smaller than the ones before. They are mere shacks. We are in the slums. "This is where I used to live," Jerry finally says.

I study the slick and muddy streets. No concrete jungle has encroached on this land. Whole houses are made of sheets of tin soldered together and patched over and over again where there are holes. Garbage piles in corners and along house fronts. Some houses have only bedsheets as walls. Children crouch in corners, barefoot and forgotten, blending into mud and dirt. One house is lined with flat and slashed tires – a sad attempt at a flower bed, perhaps, where no flowers seem to grow and colour washes away into dull brown.

"This is my family home," Jerry smiles as we stop before one of the tin shacks. He turns off the minivan and climbs out. "Come in," he says.

He pushes through the rusted front door. The house consists of one square room, but further observation is prevented by the shrill voices of multiple children yelling, "*Tito* Jerry!" all at once. A swarm of six children attack Jerry, jumping on his back, leaping into his arms, and pulling at his legs. Jerry yells and wrestles the kids, tossing each one by one onto the couch. The movement clears a way for me to see what is left of the room. A stove sits in the back, a small metal breakfast table sits before it, and one sofa sits to the side, where Jerry tosses each child.

"*Hoy, anong ginagawa mo?*" An elderly lady calls from beside the stove. She wears a flowing house dress and brandishes a wooden spoon at Jerry to call his attention. "*Hoy,* Jerry, *makinig ka sa akin!*"

"Ma, we have a visitor," Jerry says.

"A visitor?" the lady switches to English. She spots me for the first time. "*Ay, kamusta, po,*" she says. "Excuse my bad manners. I didn't see you there. *Hindi ka marunong magsalita ng tagalog?*"

The question is familiar to me, and I shake my head no.

"Ah, okay, English it is. Kids," she brandishes the spoon again. "We're speaking English, okay?"

"Okay, Mama," the kids say in unison – balls of energy and sunburnt brown limbs.

I remove my shoes and move to the side of the house. The kids, in all their raucous laughter and playful fighting, take up most of the space. The lady sees my hesitation and brandishes her spoon again. "Kids, get out of here. Go play outside."

"Oh, no, you don't have to do that," I say.

"Do what?" the lady asks, amidst chimes of "Okay, Mama," and a scramble for flip-flops as they run to the back door. "I just asked the kids to go outside." She smiles at me.

"Ma, this is Miss...," Jerry looks at me and stops. "This is Benni." He smiles at me. "Benni, this is my mother."

"You can call me Thelma, *po*," the lady says.

"Nice to meet you, *Tita* Thelma," I say. "Please, don't call me '*po*.'"

"If you bother with '*Tita*,' I can bother with '*po*,'" she says. "I was so sorry to hear about your father, *po,*" she says. "God bless his soul."

"Thanks," I say, shrugging. I left the house because I didn't want to think about my father.

Perhaps Thelma senses my discomfort because she changes the subject. "Have a seat, please," she says. "I was just about to start dinner if you'd like to wait around."

"No, thank you, *Tita* Thelma. I probably shouldn't stick around too long."

"Well, you can at least have a seat," Thelma says, "and a drink. Come, talk to me."

I sit at the small kitchen table and scramble to find something to say while Thelma grabs me a drink. "You have lots of children, *Tita* Thelma," I say.

Thelma laughs. "I do, and I don't," she says. "I have seven children of my own, but they're all adults now. Except for this one here, who never seems to grow up."

"Are you singing my praises again, Ma?" Jerry asks, sitting down beside me.

Thelma ignores him. "The kids here are my children's children. I look after them while their parents are at work."

"That's nice," I say. "You must have a full house."

"Tell me about it," she says. "Ah, well, such is a mother's burdens." She smiles. "And I do have some help, I suppose. This one's not such a waste of space as he seems."

"Aw, thanks, Ma," Jerry says.

"In all seriousness, though, Jerry is such a great help, and we are so indebted to *Inday* Rose for all she has done for our family."

"Is that so?" I ask, raising an eyebrow.

"You don't know the story?" Thelma asks.

"There's a story?"

"Of course there's a story," Thelma says. "There's a story for everything." She settles further into her hardbacked, white garden chair and sets her wooden spoon down. "My husband passed away a little over thirty years ago, God bless his soul, and I was left alone with seven kids. I was working twelve-hour days at a nearby cigar factory but I still didn't make enough to support the children. I tried to keep the kids in school but I could only afford schoolbooks and uniforms for one child at a time. Jerry finished the fifth grade, but at the rate we were going, he would have been sixteen by the time he could go back for the sixth. We needed another breadwinner so Jerry, as the oldest, went looking for work. He took odd jobs here or there but couldn't find anything steady. We would've had to revert to begging if Jerry hadn't run into one of the Consuelos's help. *Inday* Rose took pity on the boy and took him in. She gave him a roof over his head and food to eat. She gave him honest work and sent home the clothes she didn't need. My children had shirts on their back because of her, and they were able to finish school because she paid for it all."

"I didn't know all that," I say.

"Well, now you do," Thelma says.

Jerry stands in the silence that follows. "Ma, we need to go. I can't keep Benni away too long."

"Jerry's right, *Tita*," I stand up too. "Thanks so much for the drink." I hug her.

"Thank you for coming, *po*," she says. "God bless."

We leave the house and climb into the minivan in silence. I study the small house's tin roof and thin walls sparkling in the afternoon sun. It's a small home, but it's a home nonetheless, and a happy one at that. I think of our house back in Georgina and of all the times I complained about living in a dump. I wonder what would have happened to Jerry's family if he hadn't met Rose. Life in the Philippines suddenly strikes me in all its cruelty. In many ways, it's a country of pure chance, where nuns can only shake their heads and say, "Such is the way of the world," when faced with the nation's poverty and lack of social support. We sit there for some time with the engine idling until Jerry finally asks, "Back to Forbes?"

"No," I say.

Jerry begins driving. He brings me further into the slums. He doesn't speak, giving me time to think.

"*Tita* Rosie thinks of you as family," I finally say. "She trusts you."

"I know."

I think again of how Jerry offered to drive Dad in his hour of need, the way he shook me to make me move, of all the help he tried to give me, and of how I refused because I didn't understand how things were done here. I think of the way Rose asked, "Why didn't you get Jerry to drive you?" when she saw me get out of the ambulance with a sheet over Dad's head.

Minutes pass. It feels like hours. The slums seem to stretch on forever.

The memory of Dad's death replays in my head for the millionth time; if only I hadn't hesitated for those seconds or minutes, if only I had known how to perform CPR properly, or even just let Jerry drive. I am convinced that Dad is dead because of my lack of knowledge and skill. Because I was the one there and no one else.

Just when I feel like I'm about to scream out with the pain of self-conviction, Jerry says, "That's not true."

"What?"

"*Señor* Ned didn't die because you were the one there."

"Did I say that out loud?"

Jerry smiles at me. "I'm not sure how it is in Canada, but here we have to depend on each other. We have our fights – everyone does – but you can't go it alone here. *Inday* Rose – she's my second mother. We fight like mother and son sometimes, but we love each other in the end. If there's anything I learned growing up, it's that it all works out in the end."

"I feel so responsible," I whisper. My tongue feels thick with the weight of the words. "I knew he had a problem." I think of our night in Baracuda and wish I'd pushed harder to leave. "Why didn't I do more?" I ask, knowing I'm asking a question with no answer.

"Everybody knew he had a problem. There's only so much you can do alone."

I feel Sarah's business card in my pocket. I pull it out and read the address. "Is this far?" I ask, showing Jerry the card.

"Not too far."

"Can you take me there?"

Jerry doesn't ask questions. He turns the minivan around and brings me to the heart of Makati City.

54

SARAH WORKS IN ONE OF THE TOWERING skyscrapers in the Makati development aptly named, Luxury Centre. Jerry drops me off in front of her building and assures me that he'll wait outside. I pass through a promenade of manicured palms and flowering fountains. The lobby boasts ceilings that are three stories high and walls complete with trickling waterfalls to support verdant greenery.

"*Kamusta, po.* How may I help you?" the powdered receptionist at the front desk asks.

"Hi, I'm here to see Sarah Abogadie. She works at HR Link on the seventy-sixth floor, unit 7601."

"Certainly. Is she expecting you?"

"Not exactly."

The receptionist gives me a once-over before picking up the phone. "I'll contact her receptionist now. Who should I say is coming to see her?" she asks.

"Benni Manlapaz."

The lady waits as the phone rings. I half-expect her to hang up and tell me Sarah isn't there or perhaps sense that I'm here on a whim and tell me to leave.

"*Kamusta.* There is a visitor here to see Ms. Abogadie – a Ms. Benni Manlapaz. Shall I send her up?" The lady listens for a second then looks at me and mouths, "She's checking." After a second, she says, "Yes, I said 'Manlapaz'. Ms. Benni Manlapaz." She holds her hand over the receiver. "She wants to know why you are here," she says to me.

"May you please let her know that I am Eduardo Manlapaz's daughter? He was her classmate from Saint John's Academy. My father," I hesitate, finding it odd to say, "passed away. I know she was close to him. I just wanted to let her know."

The receptionist relays the information and pauses for a second before she nods and says, "I'll send her right up." After she hangs up, she looks at me with pitying eyes – a look I am quickly growing to hate since Dad died. "Take the elevators to the left, sweetie."

I try to smile but can't hide my distaste for her sugary-sweet nickname. I take the elevator as she instructs and am on the seventy-sixth floor in no time. I turn left and am faced with HR Link's unit number. Only now do I hesitate. What do I want to accomplish? Why do I want to see Sarah? What possessed me to visit my father's ex-wife in the first place – the person who seemed to be his one true love?

The unit number is printed on a mirror and, looking at it, I see myself: a woman with a blank look on her face, confronted with all her father's mysteries and unsure of how, or if, she should solve them. *You're grieving*, I tell myself. *But there's no need to be irrational.*

I turn to go, but the door to Unit 7601 opens and Sarah steps out.

"Please, come in. I'm sorry to startle you. I was so curious to see…" She trails off. "I was waiting for you at the door, looking through the peephole, and I saw you hesitate. But don't leave. Come in." She holds the door open for me.

I enter Sarah's office to find a breathtaking view of the city. One entire side of the office is a floor-to-ceiling, wall-to-wall window with the cityscape spread out below. The hardwood is espresso brown, the tiles marble, and the furniture all sleek leather and chrome. A desk is positioned to the side and is manned by another powdered receptionist.

"Please, give us some time," Sarah says.

The lady gets up and leaves the two of us alone.

"This place is beautiful," I say.

"Thank you, darling."

I study Sarah. She is the complete opposite of Mom, shorter and slighter in figure. Her hair is blown into a stylish bob. She wears a smart, three-piece dress suit, and multiple gold diamond rings on her fingers, which doesn't help me determine if she's married or not.

"I'm glad I came into the office today," she says. "I wasn't expecting anyone. Certainly not Eddie's daughter."

"I'm sorry to drop in like this. I don't want to take too much of your time, especially if you have the chance to go home early."

"I have no one to go home to, darling. My children are all grown up, and my husband and I divorced long before he passed away. I can't complain. I enjoy my work, and it's brought me back here to the Philippines, after all."

"I see." I wonder how Dad would have felt had he known Sarah was single. Did Ofelia ever get a chance to mention it to him? "So, you're a recruiter?" I ask, not knowing what else to say.

"Yes. I work mainly for marketing and PR companies. How come? Are you interested?" Sarah flashes me a smile – a well-worn, often-used business smile.

I shake my head. This is not the time or place, and I no longer want this kind of help.

The silence between us stretches on. I wonder again why I am here when Sarah says, "You mentioned your dad had…" Sarah struggles with the word, and I'm surprised to see tears in her eyes.

"My dad passed away yesterday. He had a heart attack." I'm amazed at how I can say it with a level voice. It doesn't feel real yet.

"I'm so sorry to hear that. Your dad and I were very good … friends."

"I learned about your relationship with my dad recently. He spoke very fondly of you."

"Is that so? What, if you don't mind my asking, did he say?"

"He told me that you never really forget your first love."

"How true," Sarah says, looking past me.

I take her short response as license to continue. "Yes. Is it not true that he went to Canada to find you? You were sent to the States after your divorce, and he went all the way to North America just for you. That's real love, if I've ever heard it. Actually," I pause, wondering how much I should say. And then I recollect that Dad is dead, and so what does it matter? "I believe you're his one true love."

Sarah's eyes settle on me. "Oh, my dear, how wrong you are. Where did you hear that?" She shakes her head. "Well, it's no matter. I can set you straight on that account. Eddie never knew where I went after we divorced. He went to Canada on his own, and I found him after the fact."

"What?" I ask. "That can't be right." I try to recall all the stories Dad told me.

"I assure you it is. I found out through mutual friends that he'd moved to Toronto. I was living in New York at the time and made the ten-hour drive to see him." She laughs. "Love makes you do crazy things. I don't know what I expected.... To rekindle an old flame after six or seven years? To find him there pining for me, the same way I had been pining for him? Regardless, it was an embarrassing experience. I try to forget it, but at my age, what is there to hide? If you don't share the story with anyone, after a while, you're left wondering if it ever happened." She shakes her head again. "I truly loved Eddie and would have married him again. I wanted us to start our lives together as mature adults. I promised I'd never let my parents force a divorce on me again, but he told me he had fallen in love with another and that he was returning to the Philippines to marry her."

"My mother?"

"Your mother. That was the last time I ever truly spoke to him." Her eyes well up. "I suppose now that's the last time I will ever speak to him again."

55.

I RETURN TO FORBES PARK AND SNEAK BACK into Mom and Dad's room. Mom is nowhere in sight. I pick up the envelope from Ofelia. Ofelia's sharp, spidery writing marks the thin airmail paper. It's addressed to Maria Benedictine Manlapaz.

I open the letter and two things fall out: another envelope and my university graduation photo. I read Ofelia's letter first:

Maria Benedictine,
  I am sending this letter with a couple of your father's personal effects.
  Eduardo kept this picture of you constantly by his bedside whenever staying in Iloilo. When friends visited, he would show them the photograph of his beautiful daughter. He was very proud of you.
  The second is a letter I received just a short while ago addressed to your father. I meant to send it to him but, after hearing of his passing, decided to send it to you. The writer mentions you, so you will probably understand it better than I.
  Love and prayers,
  Lola Ofelia

I study the picture, remembering how angry I was that Dad didn't return to see me graduate, especially after how hard he and Mom had pushed me to attend that particular university.

It was "one of the best in North America," Dad would often say. I never told him how angry I was, though, and had sent the picture without a message after he asked for it. Taken a few years ago, it is probably the most recent one Dad had of me; I hadn't sent him any since. On the back, he scribbled the date of my graduation and the words, "Princess graduates with distinction."

The second envelope is already open.

To Mr. Manlapaz,

Thank you for sending the walker. It is of great service to me. I told your daughter that my chair was as good as anything, but must admit now that the walker is better.

It was a pleasure meeting you and your family at Assumption.

Many thanks, and may the Lord bless you,
Sister Esmeralda

I refold the letters and place everything back into the envelope. I sit on the bed, and the words Ofelia wrote come to mind: "He was very proud of you." I wonder if Dad knew that I was proud of him, too. And for the first time since Dad passed away, I begin to cry.

56.

────────────

WHEN I WAKE UP, MOM IS LYING BESIDE ME holding my hand. "Why did you keep waiting around for him?" I whisper.

"Because I loved him," Mom says, stroking my hair the way she used to when I was a little girl. When I don't reply, she says, "Because he loved us."

"How did you know he loved us?"

"I just knew. You may not think I know a lot, but I do know when to have faith. Your father and I married in an unconventional, un-Filipino way. I know your father so well though. It was true love until the end."

"But it didn't work out in the end."

"I don't know, Benni. When is it the end?"

We don't speak for a long time. Mom is the one who breaks the silence. "I've been thinking, Benni," she says. "I'm going to move back here."

I sit up and look at her. "Why on earth would you do that?"

Mom cracks a wry smile. "Weren't you the one who kept asking why I left?"

"Yes, but what's changed your mind?"

Mom shrugs. "I've gone through life without question, Benni. I left the Philippines because it seemed like the next logical thing to do, and I lived under the assumption for years that I'd made the right choice without thinking twice about it. It made sense for a long while, while you were growing up, but

I grew up here, and your father lived and died here, and my sister is here, and we can use each other's company. And you – you're a grown woman, Benni, and you have to make your own choices. You don't have to live with me just because, or live without question, and I admire that you don't. We can move here together like you mentioned when we first arrived."

I think about Mom's offer, and about her life lived without question, about moving from one event to another without much thought or deliberation. I think of how she said that I don't do that, but is that really true? I think of my conversation with Lisa the night before and how badly she wants to escape, if only to live an anonymous life that is truly her own – a life only possible in Canada. I think of the cruelty of fate in the Philippines – of being born to be one thing and one thing only – of being born in a box. If there's anything I've learned from Lisa, from Abe's false offers, it's that there's no easy way out. There's not even the small opportunity to take a long drive alone to clear your head or the bigger one to choose to be either a star or an accountant. And the Philippines might hold memories of Dad's life for Mom, but for me, now, the biggest memory it holds is of Dad's death.

When I answer, I answer slowly, as though pulling the answer from deep within. "I'm happy for you, Mom, and I'm happy you've made this decision. But I think I'm going to go back home and make something different of myself this time around."

I squeeze her hand, filled with the lightness of knowing I've made the right decision. It's time to make a change; it's time to make a move. It's time for me to step out of the shade.

ACKNOWLEDGEMENTS

Thank you to everyone who helped make this book a reality. Thanks to Diaspora Dialogues and their amazing team for the opportunity to participate in their mentorship programs and for championing my novel afterwards. Thanks to Sandra Birdsell, my mentor from the Humber College School for Writers, and David Layton, my mentor from the Diaspora Dialogues long-form mentorship program, for providing edits, advice and, most of all, encouragement for me to continue this manuscript. Thanks to the team at Inanna Publications and to editor Luciana Ricciutelli for believing in this story and for helping me make it a finished product.

Most of all, thank you to my family. Thank you, Mom and Dad, for accepting my writerly tendencies. My love for storytelling grew because you never thought I was too young for ghost stories, always encouraged my imagination, and indulgently read everything I wrote as though it were gold, whether it was a short story or even just copy for wallpaper samples or greeting cards. You were my first readers. Thanks as well to my siblings for keeping my feet on the ground while my head was often in the clouds. And thank you to my husband, Mathew, and son, William. I love you guys.

Photo: Jennifer Pinuela

Mia Herrera's short stories, feature articles, and reviews have appeared in various online and print publications including CG *Monthly, Live in Limbo, Side Street Review, Hart House Review,* and TOK: *Writing the New Toronto, Book 7.* She is a recipient of the Youth Scholarship Award from the Tatamagouche Centre and Writers' Trust Fund Scholarship. She graduated from the University of Toronto with an Honours Bachelor of Arts degree in English Literature, Book and Media Studies, and Cinema Studies in 2009, and in 2011, she obtained a Certificate in Creative Writing from Humber College. She lives in Bradford, Ontario. *Shade* is her debut novel.